There must be
more to love
than death

There must be more to love than death

Three short novels
by Charles Newman

Swallow Press · Chicago

Copyright 1976 © by Charles Newman
Printed in the United States of America

First edition
First printing 1976

Published by
The Swallow Press, Incorporated
811 West Junior Terrace
Chicago, Illinois 60613

ISBN: 0-8040-0748-9

Library of Congress Catalog Card Number LC 76-17743

Portions of this work previously appeared
in a somewhat different form in
The Antioch Review and *TriQuarterly*.

for Tula

There must be more to love than death

Some bodies, words and objects

I looked for the war,
but the war it didn't find me.
—Paul Verlaine

Enclosure A

Garbage and Wastes
a) edible
b) non-edible (see AFM-103)

AFM-103 *Latrine*
a) Fixed
b) Field (see 142-023)

142-023 *Field-Type*
a) straddle-trench type
b) deep-pit type (see 92-372)

92-372 *Deep-pit*
a) Location: 100 yards from water supply.
75 yards from eating area. 33 yards from sleeping
quarters.
b) Size: May be any length but must accommodate 8% of command at any one time.
c) Depth: Dig two feet for 1st week, 1 ft. deeper
for each additional week of use for duration.
d) Containment: Begin with rocks or similar
approx. the size of coconuts on bottom, ending
with rocks approx. the size of walnuts on top.
e) Maintenance: Spray twice a week with
Calcium Hypochlorate or residual fly spray.
Avoid spillage on uniforms or vegetation.

Rules of usage
1) Every man is responsible for the location,
disposition and decontamination of his own
waste.
2) The latrine is not a break area. Loitering or
conversation will not be tolerated.
3) Keep clean. Internally initiated disease has
historically killed more soldiers than
hostile forces.

Enclosure B: Transcript from testimony

PROSECUTION: You knew the accused well enough to call him by his nickname?

WITNESS: I guess his father's name was George too, anyway, Patek was at home called Gee. It stuck. But there was this other Patek in the 91st Air Evacuation Squadron, so Gee's nameplate was supposed to read *G. Patek* so he wouldn't be confused with the other just regular Patek. It was easy enough to tell who was who, but that new nameplate came out wrong, *Gpatek,* probably because it was wrong this way on the new computer roster, without a period, see, and Gee interrupted Sergeant Whitehead twice in ranks for always squinting at the roster a minute and then calling him "Gap-tech;" that's why he got that double shift of latrine duty. You should've seen how fast he dug that mother. He was really strong. We all admired him for that. I didn't really know him too much, though. He wasn't unfriendly or anything, but he just didn't have much to say for himself. . . .

DEFENSE: Objection.

Enclosure C: Classified, Eyes only

George F. Patek, Sr., is Sterling Professor of Remedial Reading Science at Wieboldt State Teacher's College serving the greater Indianapolis area. Airman Patek, Jr., can read 2,000 words per minute with 94% comprehension, but dropped out of Wieboldt the second semester of his first year for no apparent reason and was called by the draft. (No contestation.) One informant attributed his forfeiting of formal education to the fact he did not wish to become a teacher, while another was of the opinion he was "afraid of competing with the old man." In any case, before his induction, the accused had solicited and had been offered an electrician's apprenticeship which pays nearly the same as what his father's current salary is, as well as providing deferment under Section 4 of the National Security Act. No informant volunteered an explanation of his rejection of this employment. Furthermore, there is no evidence of prior experience or other disadvantageous circumstances which would logically connect the accused with either the Gonzales incident, or the alleged attack on Commander Pompillo. His neighbors assert without exception that he demonstrated a normal and active interest in girls, "going steady" at least twice in high school, and that the friends and hours he kept were within the norms of the community. Despite an adenoidal condition, eczema, and mild if chronic obesity, he earned varsity letters in football and wrestling, and held offices in several school clubs. Except for one instance of pushing in line at mess, and a reprimand for minor insubordination in ranks, his service conduct record is otherwise trouble-free. Psychological profile recommended.

4

Enclosure D: Excerpted Interview from This Week
in Indianapolis

"On my last birthday, Gee painted my initials in Trooper Roman Bold on the station
wagon so if it was a little newer it would have looked just like a suburban estate car. I drove
him to the train in it. If the government hadn't been too cheap to pay for a private
compartment or at least a sleeper, maybe none of this might have happened. I know you
can't buy every soldier a sleeper, but we would have paid the extra if necessary, particularly
since this was his first time away from home. I'm not going to judge that mess, Gonzales,
but somebody like that would naturally take to somebody as big and decent looking as Gee.
He was always patient with weaklings, probably from having helped to bring up his brother
Harold, who before he died was sickly, only two years younger than Gee but almost
100 pounds lighter. Gee's the sort of person that people on trains and planes would
immediately start talking to, even if they're going to get off in half an hour. That's what
always got him in trouble. He was just too nice. And he's not the kind to attack his own
commander. When I took him to the train that day all I told him was not to worry and write.
He said it was too bad Dad couldn't be here for once at a time like this, but as usual he
had to be at school. He was always just an average student, not like his father. I remember
once in the fifth grade, when he had gotten two Fs and an incomplete, I picked him up at
school and we went for a short drive in the park. When I demanded an explanation, he said
he was bored and I said that was the one excuse he couldn't use and hit him twice in the
face, a good paper cut across the nose with the report card. Parents don't do that any more,
I know, but he knew it was for his own good, and he never got a single F again.
   " 'You can get right out,' I said, 'You've a chance to go to hell but you have no right to
be bored.' That's what I told him. This time, at the train, I just told him to lose a little
weight and asked him if he was afraid. He said not any more than anybody else. I told him
to remember that his Dad and I were always behind him, no matter what, and you can bet
we still are. . . ."

THEIR TRAIN THEN: column of filth in the bright morning, the
soot of Gary given way to a thunderstorm at midnight, and
now the encumbrage wore the yellow badge, rivet-deep dust
of the Ozark fault. They'd missed St. Louis, the river, nigger-
town, mudflats, all in the sharp angled rain.

"Think we'll be shipped right out?" Gee offered.

"Who wants to stay in Texas anyway," Airman Gonzales
said.

"Yeah. Who does."

In Arkansas they bought two cheese sandwiches but were
turned down for beer.

"Texas looks pretty good to me. You got people there?"

5

"Everybody in Chicago. Mother and sisters. My father was from Texas. He got killed in the war."

The cheese was old or dry and stuck to the roof of Gee's mouth. The water cooler was empty. Somebody had hawked a lunger in the drain.

"He was a bombardier," Airman Gonzales went on as Gee licked chapped lips, "B-29s." His large rabbit-type teeth were glowing. No beard at all but a funny sparse moustache.

"No shit."

Gee felt his belt, which usually cut him like a cord, ease. He looked down to find the polished brass buckle disappearing beneath a fold of his stomach, somewhere in which, like an oriental eye, lay his navel.

"Jesus," Gee sputtered, mouth full, "don't you know you could get out on that?"

"What?"

"Your old man gone like that."

"Don't make any difference."

"Bullshit it don't."

"You coulda got out too. Right?"

"Maybe."

They both feigned naps.

"Jesus, lookit, there's *hills* in Texas!"

The indigo savannah grass had crept like a lagoon to the tracks. Gee's eyes were sour as his mouth.

"Must be north Texas," Gonzales murmured without opening his eyes.

"My old man wasn't anywhere near the shooting," Gee rambled. "He was just gone all the time, giving tests to jerk-offs in quonset huts on some island. Don't ever talk about it, though. I'll give him that."

An air policeman came by, checked their I.D.'s and told them to get into pressed uniforms before they got to San Antonio. Buff those boots too.

6

"My eyes no good enough to fly," Gonzales said. "That's why they make me medic. I also have heart problem," he smiled proudly. He showed Gee his arsenic pills with a pharmacy label in genuine Spanish.

"They let you in with a bad ticker?"

"They don't know. You think they give you electrocardiogram? Shit, they take a hunchback if you not turn around."

"Don't know why they made me one. Aptitude the guy said. Aptitude for what I said. Pushpills you fuckoff he said. Well, maybe we're lucky, maybe we won't get our asses blown off for nothing then."

"Your ass, my ass," was all Gonzales said.

The base had its own railway spur onto which the cars with military personnel were shunted. The mesquite was chartreuse, rough trunks cork-screwing the ground, a divining thrust, topmost branches locked in a thirsty frenzy. Bars of visible heat boggled like a phantom split rail fence on the horizon. Derelicts of past victories were randomly interspersed among the flat white cementblock buildings. Amphibious tanks and topheavy howitzers, barrels soldered shut. Queasy fighters squatting knockkneed upon raised pedestals, cockpits milky with age. A *Flying Fortress* and a *Liberator,* ankle deep in concrete at the end of the parade ground. Radar on the horizon, bonewhite spheres twice as big as the stationary sun, bearing a crescent patchwork of girders nodding wisely in all directions at once. A clever underground sprinkler system perpetually marinates the dust with inverted bells of amber spray. The lawns are cropped closer than even those of Indianapolis. At five in the morning, the sky lies six feet off the ground. And in that stripe of air, Gee can make out the long files of new recruits, still in their colorful civilian clothes, like premium fruit and vegetables individually wrapped in cellophane and displayed in a white enamelled cooler. For this, the vets call them "rainbows."

7

They were put in a four-man room with Boyce, a college grad washout from officers' training (nerves) who bunked below Gee and shook the frame all night in self-induced reverie; Monastatos, a Negro who hadn't made it through Special Forces (no nerve) who each morning, when the recording of reveille triggered the loud speakers of the compound, coiled into a ball and kicked up through Gonzales' mattress, sending the kid spiraling to the ceiling. Somehow he always landed on his splayed feet. Mono did this because the very first day Gonzales told him in the shower that he, Gonzales, was a Communist with a small c; whatever that was.

"You're a goddam spic," Mono yelled at him.

"I'm American too," Gonzales insisted.

"You're just a spic. We all came from somewhere," Mono insisted. "I'm mainly African. Boyce is Irish or something. Patek . . . Patek I don't know what, but it isn't American. And you're a spic!"

"Get off his back," Gee said. "We're lucky to get a private room. Now we got to get along."

"He's a Mexican-American," Boyce corrected Mono calmly, "or more precisely, an American of Mexican extraction. Actually, I think the term you're using applies more to the Caribbean. . . ."

"Yeah," Gee confirmed.

"I'm American," Gonzales said, suddenly without a trace of accent. Gee thought of the little pissed off bandit in a sombrero riding a poor burro through fields of corn chips. The Mexican who wasn't a spic. The Communist with a little c.

"We don't call you nothing, Mono," Gonzales said, "so shut up."

"He's a fuckin' fairy!" Mono screamed. "An' Boyce is a dumb jagoff—and Patek—you a, you a—you're just a fat asshole!"

"I'm a fuckin' American," Gonzales said angrily, jerking his socks over the blades of his dark flat feet. "I never even been to Mexico."

8

Just like a goddamn movie, Gee was awed. Here we are and when one of us gets killed, Boyce first probably, after proving he's really the bravest of us all and all his education is just coverup for a basic shyness, and Mono gets a terrible wound but still carries faint Gonzales through the jungle then we all start to pull together to save ourselves and we wave to the rescue planes as they come over to bomb shit out of the enemy who had surrounded us by then, and when we get home we all trade addresses and promise to get together again so it will be the same at home as it was in the jungle but none of us never see each other again and because I'm the quiet one with no personality I'm the guy who gets to tell the story.

They drilled three weeks but no orders came. Gee met another medic clipping the grass with surgical scissors outside the 121st Air Dispensary who told him without leaving his knees, that he'd been waiting six months for orders. Gee couldn't understand it since the main hospital, which looked exactly like the Indianapolis Holiday Inn, had its full complement of wounded. The surgical staff was particularly noted for treatment of wounds in the stomach or groin, and soldiers were sometimes flown right across the ocean into Texas for their operation, with aeromedics like Gee and Gonzales keeping them on morphine or just out of shock en route. Once a man with a whole live mortar shell in his stomach was flown straight to Texas where it was successfully removed in a special quonset away from the other buildings on the runway. Gee asked Boyce why they weren't being *used* for anything, and Boyce explained that they were a mobile unit, had to be ready to move the whole dispensary on twenty-four hours' notice, and if it was being used, they couldn't move it in time.

A week later, nevertheless, they were given a refresher course in dispensary medicine. Gonzales set a squadron record for typing and confided to Gee that he wanted to be a secretary when he got out. Gee was given an advanced field surgery course, how to fold intestines back in stomach cavity so

9

that the soldier could be transported, and also how to perform a tracheotomy with a penknife and the bladder of a fountain pen. It was the first time Gee had ever seen a fountain pen, and discarding the mandatory issue of black plastic ball points, carried an old fashioned gold-tipped bone mottled German model from that day on, even though in ranks inspection he was twice given demerits for its bulge.

Mono was best at playing wounded during field maneuvers. Unable to master any career field (no aptitude for available slots) he was appointed leader of the tactical unit whose job it was to run into the woods and hide. The doctors would tape rubber or plaster mockups *(moulages)* of various wounds upon their bodies, paint them with piratical lacerations, powder shock, daub gangrene, or sometimes just hang a sign around a willing neck: "Sucking Chest Wound. How should I be carried?" Then Mono and his rangers would take off into the boondocks, running like crazy, holding on to their wounds so they wouldn't drop off, and secrete themselves in the brush within a 250-yard radius of the skeleton of a movie set burned-out aircraft. Fifteen minutes later, a kerosene fire was ignited in the aircraft, its bowels aflame for perhaps the 1,000th time, and a doctor would cry out, "Crash, crash, crash! There can't be many left from that one." A siren yawped, signaling Gee and his crew to take off and find the victims, diagnose their calculated infirmities for the doctors who followed safari-style in a jeep, then figure the best way to transport them back to base camp.

"What's wrong with him, boy! No time to dawdle."

"Shock, Sir. Third degree burns. Simple fracture of the left arm. Lung possibly punctured. He's abreathin' funny. I keep him warm and raise his feet. Keep him on his back. No morphine."

"Carry on, Airman."

Mono almost always managed to be the last one found,

hung up in a tree, dug into a trench and completely covered with sand, only his sluglike nose visible, the very earth moving with his stifled laughter, face sweat-streaked with just a vestige of powder to indicate prior shock, *moulages* tied about his musculature with shopping twine, a shattered thigh bone now about his ankle, a compound fracture in his stomach, the once Frankensteinian lacerations faded to the sort of bruises that one finds on young girls' necks.

"Make me com*fort*able, you mothafuckers," he yelled, "Here be the only survivor!"

They usually got him back to Base Ops on a four-man stretcher, grinning like a potentate. Gee was the only one strong enough to get him back in a one-man sling carry.

"Next time you pull that," Gee hissed at his burden when he dropped him at the finish line, brandishing a disposable syringe of pure air in Mono's grin, "I'll shoot a bubble right through your whole fuckin' system."

Boyce was of course given a managerial role in the dispensary, responsible for the requisite sterility, keeping the dope locked up and the records in order.

"Always let the phone ring three times," he admonished the sergeants he oversaw. "You answer it one ring later, they'll think we're screwing off, sooner than three, they'll think we're not busy enough."

And so they practiced on each other, binding and splinting their camouflaged limbs, injecting hypos of saline solution to get the technique down, mouth-to-mouth resuscitation on the lawn outside the dispensary, Mono blowing his fetid breath into Gee until he thought his lungs would burst. Gonzales in turn hunching over him on all fours to shield them from the supervisor, inhaling and exhaling like a little engine that could, but faking contact with Gee's lip like some Tijuana whore. In the west, a poor copy of an El Greco thunderhead pustulates with sheet lightning.

Dearest Gee,

I haven't had a minute to write what with Dad not being able to sleep and the usual school functions. I sometimes wonder what we'll do with ourselves when Dad retires! Both Dad and I feel that since you had to do it anyway, this will be a maturing experience and you'll maybe be able to get more out of school when you get back. Of course, Dad was older than you when he went off, so he didn't need the maturing as much and he certainly wouldn't have ended up in this dumpy college if he hadn't lost those five years. And you probably don't remember, but compared to a lot of people, we got along pretty well, you and me, even when we were alone in that filthy apartment on Manketo Boulevard and we didn't know if Dad was ever coming back. Sometimes I feel guilty that I couldn't give Harold as much attention as you got, and maybe that's why he's always been the weaker one!

We all miss you, Chipper too, who still sleeps on your bed just as he used to. Part of Dad's problem of sleeping has been Harold who has been very difficult since you left. He has probably gotten into the wrong crowd at high school since he can't make any of the teams, but mostly I think he just misses you being around. But when you can write, don't mention any of this because it will just make matters worse. Maybe the whole thing is that he's just always been jealous. And if he and I had been alone together when he was young as much as we two were, maybe he might have turned out more like you. Tell us what you're doing unless it's secret, naturally, and if you made any new friends. I've got to run now. Lord bless,

Your loving Mom

P.S. Had dinner in the Patio Room last night, and enjoyed dancing to an excellent combo, but the evening passed much too quickly. It would have been so much fun if you were here. But that camera! The film slipped off the reel so we used up the flashbulbs for nothing. I did want a few informal snaps but now I have none. I am trying to convince myself I didn't want the pictures anyway, but that's hard to do.

When the reassignment to California came through, Mono wasn't excited at all.

"Just one jump closer," he said.

"Look at it this way," said Gee. "We're still two jumps away."

Gonzales didn't care as long as they didn't have to take the train. Boyce said we ought to trade the whole fuckin' south to Russia for Sakhalin Island.

The plane was a deactivated air refueler, afterthoughts of jet assistance slung under her thickened wings, defunct refueling spout hanging like a dildo beneath the tail assembly. It reminded Gee of some statue he saw once; a goddess with no eyes and nine tits. They entered her at the gills, to find an empty cavernous two-deck fuselage and themselves the only passengers in what was merely a reserve training flight. Gee recalled his spotter's manual, the black knockwurst profile, remembering that it was all-purpose aircraft, capable of carrying fuel for six fighters, or 100 infantrymen in full battle pack, or four tanks, two jeeps and a small howitzer, or a life support system and 160 passengers, or 85 lying-in patients and a paramedical crew, but on this trip it would carry only the four of them, and a crew of the same number. They were moving the unit out by speciality, one by one, and not as a dispensary team after all.

Gee wondered sometimes why American planes had always been fatter than the enemies'. The Hellcat fatter than the Zero, the B25 fatter than the Mitsubitsi, the Liberator fatter than the Stukas, the P51 fatter than the Focke-Wolfe, and then after the B29, they got so big there was nothing left to compare them to in fatness or anything, except now it was funny it was the Russians who were fatter, the MIG fatter than the F-111, the Ilyushins and Tupelovs fatter than the Boeings. Even their rockets and rifles were fatter. American planes had always been the ugliest and had always won. Now they were the handsomest. But they had been told in a Texas briefing that there was a new plane on the drawing boards right now, long as a football field and nearly a third as fat, that could carry a whole regimental command with full equipment and armor anywhere in the world in one jump. Fatness was again within the winning tradition.

A Loadmaster installed a row of tubular canvas seats for them. Then he carried on two sets of golf clubs, a tuxedo in a polyethylene bag, and a case of beer, trailing the wires from his headset like a leashed chimp. As the starboard engines coughed, a fork lift delivered a large sectional chintz sofa strapped in a cargo net through the rear hatch.

After taking off, Gee and Gonzales decided to sit on the couch, and it was there that Gonzales told him about his "problem"; that he wished he were a woman. He whispered this even though the engines deafened everything.

The pressurization system didn't seem to be working very well. Gee held his nose and blew out through his ears until it seemed that he was blowing the winds from his brain into the cabin. The Mexican Communist with a little c wants to be a woman now.

Gee was actually pretty used to people talking to him about their "problems," and when he took a good look at Gonzales for the first time, noting the delicate features, the soft hairless face except for the faint traces of a moustache, the perfectly round brown eyes, he could see that as a matter of fact Gon-

14

zales could be quite a pretty chick. If you like the Spanish type.

"Is that why you want to be a secretary?"

"You think I crazy, don't you? Did you ever watch 'em just walk around? You know, pull their skirts across their legs? You think I crazy, don't you? Shit."

"Nope," Gee said peremptorily as he had been taught. "But maybe you mean you just want to be *treated* like a woman, more than you really want to *be* one. I mean, look, girls aren't even treated like women any more."

"Look at one next time," Gonzales said. "Don't think about how you'd like to make her, think of how she's feelin' when you're looking at her that way. You try that, OK? Shit."

Then Gonzales told him matter-of-factly about his collection of dresses and wigs, which he kept padlocked in his Air Force duffel bag at the foot of his bed at home, and how he really didn't care about *going out* at all, but how he liked to sleep in a nightgown with no blankets but two genuine feather pillows pressed on top of him, how some salesgirls would give him the eye, suspicious when he tried to buy girls' underthings but didn't know the right size to ask for, and then have to bring them back wrinkled later to exchange when he couldn't get into them at home. He told this with such candor and charm, with such fine gestures, gestures neither feminine nor southern, which Gee had never seen, that it was a relief for a change not having to *pretend* to be tolerant. And that lying in bed business, your whole body alive and warm and filling the room and the lightness of pillows surrounding you sure seemed better than just holding your cock in the cold, watching the room tighten and close. But then Gonzales smiled in self-mockery, and pulling up his trouser leg, demonstrated how he had shaved himself clean to the kneecaps, and that was the only thing that made Gee a little uncomfortable.

"You know," Gee said, tracing one of the flowers in the chintz with a forefinger, "you can get out of this mess. If you went to see the base psychiatrist, I'll bet anything he could get you out on just a medical. You wouldn't even get your job record loused up then."

Gonzales looked at him wide-eyed. Disbelief.

"I'm not afraid, if that's what you mean, man. I can cut it. Besides, I *like* to fly."

He threw his arms wide as if to praise the windowless interior, the wires and pipelines of the hydraulic systems exposed like entrails all about them.

"OK," said Gee. "But don't tell nobody else about this."

Five hours out, Gee walked up to the cockpit. The outer port engine had been stuttering for most of the trip and he wanted to see what was up. They had forgotten to put a honeybucket on board, and somebody, Mono probably, had taken a crap between the steel runners of the loading ramp. He looked out the porthole in the loading door, the only window in the fuselage, and saw they were only about 6,000 feet up, the chocolate and butterscotch canyons of the southwest a frozen ocean below them. The crew wasn't regular, a commercial airlines bunch doing their weekend reserve duty, keeping their hand in. They complained about the instrumentation and the fuel injection system, winking at each other. Gee wasn't fooled. But when they crossed the Rockies, they made him go aft and strap himself in. Once the Loadmaster had gone on forward, Gee unbuckled himself and stood before the single porthole again, watching Death Valley's defiles white and ribbed like a bum's gum slip away to Mount Whitney, the biggest frozen polyp in the West. Cruising the heavy air of California, Gee saw the sea for the first time, then after a sharp bank they were past the blinding whiteness of Frisco, approaching from the ocean and cleaving two golden eroded female foothills, the light like that of a kerosene lamp in a fir forest after Texas' high fluorescence.

16

The base was ringed by hills, sheep and pig farms beyond a security perimeter of prefab housing, bars and gas stations. Everything temporary but nothing new. They hit hard twice acrosswind; Gee had tied himself with a cargo strap to the ratlines so he could stand and sway before the single porthole. As they reversed engines, he could make out a strike force of round-the-world supersonic *Peacemakers*, wings drooping, tips just off the ground like a dozen falcons slicked down with cylinder oil for a carnival, wingtip to wingtip on their own runway which for some reason was colored rose. What looked like an ice truck was scurrying between them now, blue light revolving in the dusk like the tropical fish in his old man's aquarium; the bubble of expelled oxygen rises and explodes into the real air where it's home but nothing.

A blue school bus drove directly across the runway to pick them up. The crew threw their golf gear desultorily into the bus, leaving the plane before it was chocked, calmed, checked out. The chintz sofa was removed from her maw and taken away protruding from the back of an ambulance. The troops were taken to open transit barracks where Gee got the lower in the corner, Gonzales grabbing the upper over Gee, producing in place of a duffel, bright red matching leatherette luggage with his initials, including an over-the-shoulder overnight case. Boyce in a rush got the last lower so Mono could only kick air here.

One Sergeant Hatchette woke them at five:

"When you get married," he drawled at inspection, "it's *she* who says he's too *big*, right? Well, after a while, it's *he* who says *she's* too big. Right? Well, that's where we are now. I don't know why we ain't been called yet, but it can't gonna be much longer. So you better get it up or you ain't gonna have any left. 'Cause that snatch out there, she's a gettin' bigger all the time. We gonna have to be some big men to make her ooh. That's the story."

He said that quite softly, graciously, necklessly, though not with as fine gestures as Gonzales. A career man, Korea at 18, busted down from Master Sergeant maybe three times. He'll take his pension after twenty and hit old Mexico where a man can live on nothin' and lay anything that moves 'cept armadillos.

"I won't fuck you over if you don't fuck me over. That's the story."

A southern mountain man, sandy cowlick like a plume sprouting from behind his flight cap. Eyes washed blue, mica geist in the bottom of a mountain stream. Issue of men who have been drained because too much has been written about them.

"This man here's mah right guide!"

Hatchette grabbed the man nearest to him and shoved a stanchion with a pennant in his hand.

"This Joe will set the pace. He will get the cadence from me. If he don't, there'll be another."

They moved off, column of fours, towards the mess a mile away with Hatchette singing the cadence, driving his left heel into the mud like an adze.

Ten Hut, listen up.
Going to tear
Your playhouse down.
Going to knock
That dickstring loose.

Strut strut strut
Heel heel heel
Number 6 forward
Number 3 back.

I'm a happy man
And got a place
For you.
Black, White, Jew
Strut, strut, strut.

Stand tall
Stretch it out
Ankles stiff, knees loose
Easy does it

Hands cupped
Chest out
Now you got it
Easy does it

Got you one
Crate o' eggs
On your back

Got you one
Glass o' water
On your head

Stretch it out
Stomach's bone
Don't spill a drop!
Don't break an egg!

Hole it
Hole it
Eyes . . . right!

By the time they reached the mess hall, their fatigues were black with sweat. All Gee had for breakfast was four glasses of grapeade. He had been strangely exhilarated by the march. Slouching as he was, his paunch nevertheless remained behind his belt. He struck himself in the gut, then started as Gonzales grabbed his wrist.

"Didja see how beautiful his eyes were?"

Gee's first duty had been with an Evacuation Unit whose emblem was the numeral three severed by a bolt of lightning, as only three of its pilots had survived the first days of Korea; his second, the Mobile Dispensary Unit in Texas; now they were assigned a Terminal Unit which didn't even have a slot for a medic. The closer he got to the action the less they were using his training. At this rate, he'd never get to work on one real wounded. He felt his fountain pen in his breast pocket as Hatchette marched them by the hospital, its miniature golf course crowded with pajamaed putters in the warm morning, then out along the runway and into the main warehouse.

They broke ranks to march up planks to the loading dock and there reformed. The floors were torn up, littered with a thousand chromium cylinders the size of summer sausages for a new conveyor system. Cargo was stacked everywhere—60 feet high in places—and some of these piles had fallen, the topmost crates burst open, lightning-struck pine stumps in the half light. A fork lift moved desultorily among the stacks like a hot ox in the alleys of an Italian hill town.

Hatchette breaks them down into squads and Gee's emerges outside on the forward ramp where they are told that now that they are on the ramp they are rampmen. On the horizon line, the dozen *Peacemakers* glint. On a Red Alert, they'd be out of sight in seven minutes. Gee wondered where they kept the Nukes. Fuck, they never tell you anything interesting.

"We gotta hold the fort til they get this automated," Hatchette drawls. "You can see we're kinder behind." He gestures over his shoulder at the cargo which towers behind him.

Gee glanced out into the sun. There were a good four acres of uncovered cargo stretching far out onto the apron surrounded by a temporary cyclone fence. Many of the boxes were broken open, equipment and clothes strewn about in pools of oil and viscous asphalt. He could make out a jet engine, crated propellers, tires the size of a drug store, a gross of moldy duffel bags, split cardboard boxes revealing household furnishings, kitchenware. Not exactly priority stuff. Near the passenger terminal, a TWA flight from Hawaii was disgorging some walking wounded, their dress uniforms wrinkled from the trip, box lunch under each arm, stewardesses gamely waving goodbye. If the commercials were in on it now, maybe things were really getting tough. Even commercial duty with all passengers almost well would be better than this.

A fighter with a nose like a gathering raindrop skittered off, afterburner leaving an orange diaphanous balloon and deafness in a film of heat waves. It banked hard to the left and disappeared through a cut in the hills.

The next day the squadron was broken down by career fields—those who were licensed for fork lift, for the 40-KG loader, for the buses, signal trucks, passenger service systems and other engines.

Gee and Gonzales lacking loading credentials were instructed to cover the exposed cargo on the apron with sheets of polyethylene and stapler guns.

Mono was naturally put to work on repax, building pallets out of spare 2 x 4s for what outgoing managed to sift through boulders of excess. He was shown how to stack a pallet on the field latrine principle; coconuts to walnuts.

Once his education was ascertained, Boyce was ushered off with some ceremony to Traffic Control, where on a series of translucent illuminated panels, he logged in the cargo flights and assigned loading priorities by slide-rule formulae with eight colors of Magic Marker.

"Why's Guam abbreviated to Gum?" he asked. "What're you saving by not writing the a? And how do you derive Sue from Seoul? . . . Ah Pilate, I salute your imperishable cargoes."

The lieutenant at the monitor desk pulled his service cap over his eyes.

Gee carried the polyethylene and Gonzales the stapler. They swathed a FRAGILE ELECTRONIC for Bangkok and INFLAMMABLE (GAS) for Pusan, a THIS SIDE UP for Taipei, a diesel for Osaka. Then they came across Col. Stargess, William P. Jr.'s household effects en route from Darmstadt to Quezon City, the carton broken open, exposing Mrs. Stargess' underthings and the children's summer wardrobe to the elements. Gee gathered the wet clothes together and stuffed them back in a box—a pair of toddler's seersucker overalls, pink beribboned minibriefs, a 36B cup bra. Gee wrapped it in the plastic, and Gonz fired one hundred rounds of limpwristed staples into her.

"Gimme a medic!" It was Hatchette yelling from the ramp. "We got a medic here?"

Gee ran towards him frantically, waving his arms with

Gonzales in tow. Hatchette looked them up and down and soon they were in an ambulance headed out to the furthest runway, Gonzales pale, coughing, clutching at his heart; Gee with his pen half out.

"No hurry," Hatchette smiled thinly. "Stretch it out, airmen."

Gee ran through the manual in his mind, there would probably be burns, don't give morphine to a man with first degree burns . . . do not attempt to remove clothing from glutinous burns . . . contrary to most first aid, if a victim is on fire, do *not* roll him. . . .

But the plane was quite intact, not crashed at all, sagging deserted on the taxi strip without visible injury, laced to its wheel chocks with orange nylon streamers. Hatchette parked the ambulance beneath the dark wing and motioned Gonzales to follow him. "OK," the sarge said brightly as he unbolted a panel in the air freighter's belly. "Here's a job for a little guy."

As the ratchet of the socketwrench swiveled the panel down, Gonzales commenced a series of badly-disguised dry heaves. Gee came over to him only to be immediately nauseated. Hatchette had doubled over with something different— a joke repeated once too often, calculated hilarity.

From his knees Gee looked up into the dark alcove of the plane; it was coated with feces, a day or more of 160 wounded or 230 infantrymen with full battle pack, excrement alternately boiled in the far east and frozen at 32,000 feet, now finding itself at midday USA slightly above sea level.

"Turn a rivet blue, huh, airman?" Hatchette croaked. "Well, just get that honeybucket down and they'll be by for it. OK, airman," taking Gee by the arm. "We need a big boy for this'n."

They climbed the crew ladder, the first time Gee had ever entered or left a plane through a door not a maw, and then they were stalking the perforated alloy flooring, Gee aware of Gonzales retching below them, struggling with the honeybuckets. It seemed to him as if blue smoke were rising through the floor, and then he realized it was only one of the blue vans arriving, emergency lights filtering through the plane entire, to relieve Gonzales of the relief.

Hatchette moved through the fuselage ahead of him, past boxed ammunition, drums of the viscous lethal, tubs of howitzer grease, a disengaged squadron's recreational equipment, then the undistinguishable boxes and crates until, in the forward cabin where the navigator may nap, Hatchette drew them up to a magnesium alloy box with brass handles. It had been strapped to the bulkhead, not with the usual nylon tie-downs, but with multicolored braid and golden tassels. Hatchette patted it respectfully.

"This here's a human remains container. It contains a polyethylene human remains pouch. I guess you know what's in the pouch."

Hatchette looked steadily at Gee and then began to recite a paraphrase of the manual in slow litany.

"Human remains containers are designated HRC on the manifest and are to be checked personally by the Loadmaster in charge under the regulations governing registered mail, fissionable materials, perishable cargo and classified documents...."

The words we use for things.... Gee was thinking.

"HRCs are to be placed in the forwardmost portion of the aircraft, with the head (marked top) towards the cockpit and raised if possible to a height of no less than six inches and no more than eighteen."

Hatchette checked the space beneath the coffin and the flooring with caliper-like fingers and continued:

"HRCs should be separated from other cargo and passengers and nothing should be stacked on any HRC, except, in the case of emergencies, another HRC."

Hatchette motioned to Gee to grab the handle. It was surprisingly, incredibly, light.

"HRCs are to be loaded and unloaded horizontally by the

Loadmaster and/or his personal designate by properly uniformed active-duty personnel, preferably qualified enlisted men of the medical service. Under no circumstances shall HRCs be handled with mechanical loaders or civilian personnel, except in those instances where HRCs comprise 50% or more by space of the total cargo. Let's go."

They carried the box back through the plane, Hatchette reminding him to keep it level as they traversed the freighter's anus. As they opened the tailgate of the ambulance and slid it in, Hatchette chorused:

"HRCs will have first en route priority on non-passenger extra-territorial flights with temperature and handling procedures under regulations governing shipment of unstable compounds, biological samples and whole blood. Upon reaching the primary destination in the continental United States, HRCs will be transported to the security cage or cold room, accompanied by an honor guard for further dispersement."

"You're the honor guard too," Hatchette flicked a salute to Gee. "Stand taller."

Gee went automatically if clumsily to attention and snapped off a salute.

Then Gonzales appeared, paler than ever, feces on his flight cap, and they were bolting across the runway, lights awhirr, where the priority cargo was carefully wheeled on a dolly to the cold room along with two drums marked "nuclear waste."

A shapeless unkempt man, his fatigues open across his chest with no visible insignia, slowly inserted a key and opened the door to the wire cage. Though he looked directly into Gee's eyes, as if to recognize a stranger, his gaze went beyond, as a car's headlights leave the road prior to a sharp turn.

"This here's Big John," Hatchette broke in. "Survivor of the Bataan Death March. Yessir. Only one out of five made it. Yessir. John's a kind of an honorary fixture round here."

Big John sat down on a stool as they passed.

After opening the envelope taped to the top of the HRC, Hatchette murmured, "Bird colonel, this'n." Then he turned swiftly to the two medics, drumming his fingers along the edge of the coffin. "Now listen. You can get court-martialed if you ever drop one of these," he drawled. "Personally, I'll just knock your dickstring loose." Then he shrugged. "Don't let it get your daubers down."

"Whatdya make of this guy?" Gee asked the room about Hatchette after lights were out.

"This man is bughouse," Mono whispered like a freighter setting anchor, "a bomb musta felled right on top his head. He gotta scar that runs from his hair to his chin. Bet it goes all the way down to his crotch and starts up the other side."

"Boyce talked to him in the chow hall; I saw him," Gonzales said.

"What'd he say, Boyce?" Gee said.

"Ah," Boyce's Boston came from the covers, "we discussed the relative merits of Chevrolet transmissions of the last decade, the motives of certain prominent athletes, the anatomy of loved ones, some indisputable causal factors in our nation's confusion, such as Mrs. Roosevelt's Negro ancestor, her husband's venereal complications, the fact that the Russian *people* don't really want another war, that the American people don't either but would win it in any event. . . ."

"Goddamnit," Mono broke in stuttering, "you know if we get over there, and we're not winning, you know what I'm gonna do? I'm gonna lead a mutiny, that's what, take over the squadron. . . ."

"That, if I may say so," Boyce continued as if he had not been interrupted, "that is a very *literary* idea. . . ."

"How do you really feel about this thing, anyway?" Gee asked Boyce in the dark.

Ah, je ne me trouve pas où je me cherche."

"You motherfucker," Mono yelled.

"Shut up," Gonzales whispered, "You're gonna get us a sentry. . . ."

"What I mean to say," Boyce took the final word, "is that the only thing I know for sure is that I'm no pacifist."

Dear Gee,

I don't know if I should bother you when you're away but Mom said you wanted me to write. I don't know exactly what you want to know. Things aren't too cool here. You know that. You shouldn't have mentioned that to Fred Tucker about maybe not coming back. You know who it got back to and fast. There's a few kids in school who still think you're a shit but we'll see what happens when they have to go. Mostly, people think you're just unlucky.

Three guys from town have been killed so far. I don't think you knew any of them. There's a sign now out near the expressway with their names on it. They were all a lot older than you. One guy, you can tell from the dates, was 41! Ricky Faricy got his leg wounded somehow. They say he wasn't even near the fighting. But now he hangs around the drugstore all day in his uniform with crutches so nobody'll miss it. Rufus said he opened the door for him once and Ricky said he didn't need any pity, to let him do it himself. Wow. Big deal.

The other night Mom and Dad had a big fight and Mom said that she was glad about my heart so I didn't have to go like you. Dad didn't say anything but I saw him trying to kick her under the table. I know she wasn't trying to put me down or anything, but it still killed me. What I really want to do is split from here but I can't leave Mom and Dad until you get back. Maybe I will anyway just to get my head straight. California must be way out. I could meet you there. I'll bet you must be really having a ball with all those chicks.

Peace, Harold

Recorded reveille is loudspoke through the compound. Mono up on his knees on the bunker bed, imaginary burp gun mowing down the troopers writhing unagilely from their morning camouflage. Dow! Dow! da Dow Dow! Mono screams, arms crushed against his ribs and Boyce obliges with a grotesque balletomane pratfall, gurgling Chinese menu curses as he crumples in his stained Abercrombie & Fitch pajamas. Down the open barracks of forty bunk beds, men spiral in morning death. Mono has a new short haircut and Gee can see the forcep indentations in his skull—according to the manual, face presentation, full term delivery with minor complications. Though Mono's hateful tracers still inscribe the air, the men have arisen and busy themselves with their packs. It's the obstacle course today. Maneuvers. Combat is imminent. Gonzales goes to his locker, removes the set of matched lipstick red luggage, opens the hatbox and takes out starched battle fatigues. He's got flat feet, a bad heart, fused spine and a feminine disposition, but that boy loves to fly. Mono lays open the weapon on his pillow and smites his head in a facsimile of disbelief. If he ever hit anybody else that hard they'd be out cold. There is a rush for the urinals. No one will crap on this training day. "Live ammo," Hatchette yells up the stairwall. Gee knows it can't go on like this and that it will. He talked to Hatchette yesterday about requesting transfer to a combat zone. Hatchette tells him they'll be going soon enough. Forgive me, mother, but I am bored. I don't care if I have a right or not. Forgive me for I am bored. Kill or be bored. I'm not gonna die in California. He studies his manual for the obstacle course, reviews the symptoms of heat exhaustion and the simple closed fracture which immobolizes but leaves adjacent tissue unharmed.

Egg on tooth, bellies distended, they are headed, herded to the juicy marshes. For the first half-mile, the spit shine of Gee's boots is phosphorescent in the ornamental flares which burst like camellias from the distant obstacle course. The heelbeat is faint but all together. They are pacing themselves.

Not bad. His knee snaps straight just as the heel wedge strikes the ground. They are probably going to set another record. Gee wishes he were not so tall. If he gets out of step, they can see his head jerk before the others. When the polished road curves he can see the other units, more than a thousand men, five times that behind. Observers line the bluffs, their cigarettes perforating the last of the dark. Like the last time they went to the Indy 500. From the pits you could look up into the stands and see the tiny winks of light, the only way you could tell the audience was *breathing*. Out of the corner of his eye, he can barely make out the eroded gullies, the zigzag trails with their brightly painted obstacles, fresh sawdust heaped at their bases.

In the sunrise, Hachette appears haggard but immaculate in a chromed helmet, scarlet honor guard kerchief, white leatherette pistol belt, holster and spats, and a pearl-handled .44. "I'll tell you about that," he says as they are put at ease for a 'last lightup.'

Gee's hands stink.

"I got a little house out on the edge of the base here and every morning I look out my window and if'n I see a jack rabbit then I take this .44 and I go out and kill that jack rabbit. You know why? For because where there's jack rabbits, there's rattlers. Rattlers lookin' for jack rabbits nests, besides the fact that I'm mighty partial to jack rabbit stew. Not to mention rattlesnake steak. Better'n chicken or a coon's hind feet. And, if'n I eat all the rabbits then those rattlers they'll have to move on. Yessir. Yesterday morning I look out my window and there I was, lookin' at myself mirror-like. But right *in* my head, I could see jack rabbits as far as the eye can see, hopping up and down, my head jes *stuffed* with rabbit like a stew kettle. So's I took my .44 and went out and I got two from the rear stoop and I then kept on going, right into the brush after 'em, for miles it seemed, I could see 'em jumpin' and hoppin' like crazy, there must a been a *million* rattlers

out there lookin' for young'uns and mamas, and I was plas-
terin' away with my .44, two snakes for every rabbit, and then
I got out in the middle of some saw grass and I realized, you
know what I realized, boys? I was still in my pajamas and
barefoot! That's *how much* I wanted those jack rabbits."

"What's he mean?" Mono whispers.

Gee shrugs.

"Absurd," Boyce says.

"That's nothin'," Mono murmurs.

Now the observers can see *our* cigarettes, Gee thinks. The
unit ahead of them starts to move out. Hatchette effortlessly
forms them up in four ranks before a six-foot wall, where they
are issued plugged-up triggerless carbines, and then whistled
over the wall by twos at thirty-second intervals. Gee and Gonz
fall prone, burying their heads in their arms as they were
told, waiting for the whistle. They can hear snorts and the
splash of water on the other side of the wall. Gee gets a cramp
in his arch and doubles up. A sergeant comes over and kicks
him in the shin. "Don't move a fuckin' inch, airman. This
ain't no game now."

The man in front of Gee kicked gravel in his face as he
cleared the wall. Thirty seconds. Then he saw his teammate
was Boyce. Gonz and Mono paired right behind. The whistle
blew and Hatchette's glare was upon them. Gee barrelrolled
the wall, breaking his fall with his forearms and came up running in full stride, relishing the gasps from the non-com observers. But after a 50-yard sprint, leaving Boyce who runs
like a girl, he is in line like for mess at the first obstacle, a
water hazard. Ten minutes later, Gee grabbed the rope as it
swung back from the man ahead of him and cleared the ditch
easily, Gonz doing the same, except after clearing it, he falls
and the rope twists back to Mono off plumb with too much
slack. So half way back, its momentum ceases and Mono hits
the muck like a defused bomb.

Hatchette fakes a kick at Gonzales' groin and then grabs

his own crotch. "Get a good grip, airman, and hold onto this next time." The noncoms jeer. "Turn it loose, airman, turn it loose. You just kilt your buddy there." Gonzales' full lips are slitted. He cannot bring himself to look back at the water hazard. He remains on his hands and knees shaking his head, ignoring the Chinese firecrackers the non-coms toss about him. Mono struggles to the bank, then lumbers past Gonzales up the hill.

Gee glided through the obstacles with only minimal effort, hurdling fences, vaulting cannisters, crawling beneath barbwire, climbing rope ladders, scaling a mini-cliff, possuming a cable across a river, leaping from platforms into piles of sawdust, passing up knots of struggling, vomiting, fainting men, the flesh stripped from their palms, harassed by non-coms with fire crackers. Finally, he negotiated a small hut of tear gas, leaping through a rear window after entering a door with a sign which read, "Russia not a signatory to League of Nations ban on Poison Gas." He tried to remember Hatchette's lecture on diagnostic anti-gas measures; nerve gas ("if you feel yerself goin' blind or can't move yer limbs"), skin gas ("if'n you gettin' big blisters on yerself"), toxic ("if'n you start gettin' sleepy or sick at yer stomach or see a big cloud around you . . .").

Occasionally, a non-com would leap out from behind a tree with a cherry bomb and throw it near him. Once, he was made to go back and crawl beneath a fence he had mistakenly leapt over. But when he was in full stride his fatness slabbed on him, impacted against his large bones; he ran with his legs apart, fullback style, not bobbing at all as when he marched, or feeling his body ooze from its carriage as when he slouched, but a fatman created to run, the fastest vastness ever, a hellcat, a blimp, a goddamn tank is right, he laughed. Before a pyramid of oil drums, Gee saw a skinny kid, the kind who couldn't do a single pull-up to save himself, and as he slowed to help him, he felt his stomach flip over his belt. His thighs began to putty, the ugly sweat that appeared underarm even through his best suit in winter, coursed into the creases of his body, his nipples burned against his shirt as his torso resumed its control over his legs. "Everybody's on his own," he heard behind him; a non-com was lighting a pack of firecrackers. "Let him *by* himself, airman. You wanna operation to get my foot taken outa your ass, airman?"

Gee withdrew his hand from the kid who shrugged and hauled himself halfway up the pyramid. "You dead, airman," he heard the non-com yell as he regained speed, "you one dead motherfucker. Them Cong 'ud have your eyeballs in their chili by now." If I'd been running full out when he said that, Gee thought, I'd have knocked his ass into old Mexico.

Soon he could hear the crack of real ammo and concussion mines. Then he was on his belly, each man to his predecessor's well-worn trough, beneath the bright golden tracers of the machine guns, one of which the now helmetless Hatchette himself fed, cowlick vibrating, hovering over the cooling apparatus like some solemn TV airline-chef. Eighty-seven per cent of fatal casualties in World War II were head wounds, Gee recalled the manual as he slithered. This was reduced to 52 per cent in the Korean conflict due to the proficiency of the paramedical team. Maybe this only meant wounds of the body were now more lethal. Out of the corner of his eye, Gee could make out Gonzales squirming like a ferret. He couldn't remember if California, like Texas, had a common border with Mexico. He stopped crawling for a moment to think. Christ, how could he forget a simple thing like that? Shit, he'd never get back into school.

They crawled forward as the machine gun crackled predictably, banally, overhead, concussion mines in their concrete mini-volcanoes exploding randomly to either side. Then they were up and running, Hatchette's curses behind them, and beyond a field of high grass, Gee would make out the bayonet dummies swaying at the finish line, strung with baling wire from splintered pine trees, groins and heads marked with Xs. "Knock out an officer and you knock out an idea," is what the manual said. Gee brought the butt of his carbine up sharply between the dummy's foreshortened legs, then barrel-whipped its chinlessness; it wobbled a bit, then sighed neutrally on its guy wires, and Gee collapsed across the freshly limed finish line into the tall grass, among the first to complete the course. A canteen of Koolade was passed to him. "That's some kind of desire, airman."

He leaned his burning lungs up against a mesquite and watched the stragglers come in. He wished they'd given them real bayonets, even if they were only medics. He saw Gonzales in the second wave, knowing that it was they who would take the heaviest casualties in any real attack. The little guy seemed hardly winded, running with his strange staid flat-footed gait. He dodged between two dummies instead of racking one up, then looked very carefully into the high grass before he sat. A few of the men gave the requisite war whoop as they struck at the dummies with their carbines, others didn't grunt as loud as the dummy itself, most managed no more than a girlish push before collapsing. Fireplug Mono was one of the last, sloshing across the sandy field, his dusk dawned totally with dust. As he had lost his weapon in the water, he gave his opposite number a forearm shiver which pinged the guy wires like an SOS.

Gee wouldn't have recognized Boyce from the others if he wasn't almost the last. He appeared out of the machinegun course in a kind of hysterical stagger, face hidden in his helmet's shadow, yet suddenly broke into a strong finishing sprint. Upon reaching the line of dummies, however, instead of faking a bayonet thrust or uppercutting with the stock, he reversed his gun, grasping it by its soldered barrel, and punctuating the air with Indian screams, proceeded to flail the dummy until, opening a slit in the capon-like torso, its various stuffings came to light. Kapok oozed from the dummy's face-place, an orison of fine sand dribbled from its cleft groin, and Boyce, spinning the remnants of the carbine above his head, finally knocked his counter clean from the restraining cables, shattering the stock with his final stroke, jerking every dummy for several hundred yards like a regiment of simultaneously hanged men. Dummy lay in the dust, no longer recognizable; its legs flipped over preposterously like those bodies which fall from cliffs and skyscrapers in movies, and halfway through a probable human spiral, began to flap against their own joints like scarecrows or amateur epileptics. In the manual it might be diagnosed as simultaneous and continuous quad-ruple hyperextension. Below the postmark on letters from Gee's hometown was the slogan, "Employ epileptics." Well, sure, OK. Let's. Boyce must have got in another dozen blows before they got to him.

A cadre of non-coms had Boyce on his back, Hatchette punching him diffidently in his heaving chest with the .44. "Shape up, airman, shape up there. Better shape up!" As they held him, struggling and whining on the shroud of his de-flated enemy, a cheer began to rise from the swale where the men lay, both deep-throated and a whistle, a cry, not of the lying crowd, but a mob. . . . And at that very instant, at the moment their anger ceased to be strategic, when they were vaguely known to each other as more than models, all possible action was sucked away, all mouths and eyes were opened and upturned as an immense shadow cleaved the field. It was a Phantom *Peacemaker,* not more than 200 feet off the ground. 3.2 million bucks, six sets of wheels revolving, alloyed skin blind bronzen in the sun, all ancient empires in a single house, entering or ending one of its endless worldgirdling circuits, engine, wingspan and exhaust completely obliterat-ing any possible animal encounter.

Gross silence filled that field, sanitizing these spent men.

Whipped was Boyce now, the non-coms holding him like a child. One shook the piece of strap and steel that was his gun to his face: "Write your fucking congressman."

Boyce spent a week in the hospital for observation. Gee tried to visit, but they had him in isolation. Tests. No putting in the morning for that boy. A Lieutenant Colonel came to the barracks to pick up Boyce's toilet kit. "Flipped," was all he said. Then they heard he was stockaded.

Hatchette wasn't around much, let a nigger march them once in a Saturday morning parade. He had delegated the unloading of all perishables to Gee. "You're a medic, ain't you?" Pretty nervous for a veteran, Gee thought. Boyce's *New York Times* continued to arrive and said things didn't look good. The strength of the enemy offensive was "surprising," they said. Mono tore the entire Sunday edition in half once. Hatchette began to miss morning inspections and another non-com had to cover up for him. Sometimes he would emerge from his '52 beige Caddy parked alongside the barracks at 4:45 precisely, his uniform creased with a few hours' sleep, and inscribing a small zero in the air with his thumb and forefinger, he would wink ambiguously at the troops, his gray eyes like slugs caught in a crimson spider web. Maybe, Gee thought, this is the way the vets get ready.

At any rate, with the Sarge hardly ever there, Gee was the man to see on the ramp. It wasn't tough. Each morning he would come in to find that the night shift had moved things around some, mostly outdoors, but even though the conveyor system was now operational, nobody was about to make a dent in that backlog. It was all Gee could do to manifest and process the incoming.

Mono took to making tunnels. There was so much cargo now that it was simpler just to disappear into it. He built elaborate labyrinthine hideaways for himself, a grid of nap-spots in the insuperable logistical overload. No way to reach him except to announce his name and serial number over the PA system, and eventually he would emerge grinning from a different portion of cargo nearly like a mole, blue in the soft damp Pacific light.

No one hassled them, and what's more, the rampmen suddently begain to get citations for moving record tonnage, and the bar graphs prominently displayed above the pinball machines in the Rec Hall indicated that they were actually ahead of schedule. Maybe it was just that they had finally learned to deal, that they *were* doing what was expected of them, that they had reached their level. Mono, by secreting himself, had learned to stay out of trouble. Gonzales now expedited the honeybuckets with dispatch, somehow commandeering a helper, a stringy silent chinless mountaineer who stalked Gonz wherever he went, Gee wondering what sort of mastery the kid had over him. Gonz had also earned the privilege and security clearance to deliver box lunches to the flight crews of the *Peacemakers*. He handed them up through the hatch; then as the Air Police escort drove him off he could see the pilots, far up in the cockpit, remove bread to see what kind of sandwich it was, then sometimes trade.

For his own part, Gee did the job. The HRCs were increasing in number, but he had them off the planes well before the unloading crew arrived, always carried with solemnity, and taken to the cold room by the long route to avoid the warehouse and possibly affect morale. The other perishable cargo usually comprised no more bulk than a single HRC, though it was often considerably heavier. Gee didn't understand why he couldn't carry the parts and liquids of men on the same load as their bodies, but he stuck to the manual, or rather to Hatchette's interpretation. Then back in the cold room he would drain the containers and repack them with dry ice—the pints of whole blood, sediment on the bottom like the chutneys his mother canned in mason jars, the vials of discolored urine, each man's piss not only a different color but consistency, the drugs, serums, vaccines, the innumerable tiny kits marked SPECIMEN. He did not understand why there was so much blood coming in, so much urine outbound.

Sometimes after checking the perishables against the manifest, Gee would sit in the cold room with the HRCs and Big John, reading the info packets, which never told of *what* or how the man died, only his rank, past specialty, and where he was to be delivered. The only item which seemed to differ was the number of honor guards to accompany the corpse; it varied from one to a dozen and did not seem to be related to rank, decoration or region. As he undid the masking tape and read the documents, however, Big John would stare at him with ever-widening eyes, until Gee could manage it no longer and replace them.

Eventually Gee stopped thinking about the men inside, why some were so heavy, some light as a feather. He wondered if they used trained medics to stuff them in the sacks—they didn't need a medic for that, any more than to unload them stateside. He fingered his tracheotomy pen and nervously wandered the cold room. He had noticed while shaving that he was getting jowly; he was over 250 now, his belt hurt him, he was constipated, even his feet seemed bloated. But of course, once over there, he would lose it. For no reason, he turned and slapped Big John on the shoulder.

"Well, John," Gee found himself murmuring. "We sure moved a lot of cargo today, didn't we?"

The custodian slowly turned his head towards him, pupils already dilating.

"Yep. I'll bet we set another record today, yessir, I'd bet on it."

The left corner of Big John's mouth began to droop and fill with spittle.

"Oh, you're probably not a betting man, John, but just put in a guess. 100,000 tons maybe?"

Big John began to grit his few teeth. Gee was sweating through his shirt, even in the cold room.

"Hell, John, we got 1,000 pounds of HRC's right in here,

don't we? And we didn't hardly work at all. Well, just multiply that by the other units. Wouldn't you say now that we done our job?"

He didn't realize he was yelling until the echo obliterated his voice. Big John had put his hands to his ears but was smiling faintly, all the pain from his ears in his eyes. Gee's head was buzzing.

"Oh we move, Big John," he whispered. "We can really move that shit."

Sometimes, he wrote Harold, *you'd be surprised the way I feel. Like the other day, I was standing on the ramp, looking out. The sun was going down coppery and it made every plane that came in look like it was on fire. At first, I hoped there would be a* Red Alert, *so I could see those big mothers line up and go off every 30 seconds, because I heard that's really something the way they do it. Their wings, see, come down, almost touch the runway, and when they get going, they straighten out and flap, just like a bird. But we been here three months now and there hasn't been any* Red Alert—*only practices—when you see the little guys in white suits run out from a concrete building and jump into the plane, and then the engines start, but they don't even taxi, because they say it's too expensive to really let them take off. And then, you know what? I caught myself wishing that one of the planes that was coming in would crash, really blow up, because I wanted to see how they would handle that, and maybe I could be in on it. Of course when they do crash, there's not much a medic can do, there's usually not much left, so I put it out of my mind right away, of course. But if they knew what I was thinking, I'd probably be put in the hospital or maybe worse. . . .*

Enclosure E:

On the evening of August 16th, on or about 2300 hours, Airman Second Class George F. Patek, Jr. did willfully and with malicious or salacious purpose remove from a shipment of perishables bound for Wheeler AFB,

Utah (NORAD) one dozen ampules of morphine of the disposable
syringe variety.

Planes were coming in every quarter hour now. As the
ramp and warehouse became hopelessly snarled, traffic ceased
utterly. Yet the bar graph of their accomplishments and the
number of unit citations increased exponentially with their
inability to cope. Only in the cold room was extra cargo evi-
dent. Gee figured they had a few weeks left at most.

Hatchette spent practically no time on the ramp, and concerned himself with new defensive measures in accordance
with the most recent field orders. The enemy offensive had
still not abated, and this resulted in redoubled sentry duty,
watching the compound, particularly in view of the fact that
it had been necessary to take on an increased number of civilian personnel. They were issued helmets, red alert flashlights
and carbines, but no ammo. Mono marched at one end of the
compound beneath the gnat-encrusted searchlight, cradling
his weapon in the manner of movie paratroops, Gee was assigned to barracks basement to keep watch over the Disaster
Pak—a crate of survival supplies in case of an atomic attack—
canned water, drugs, K-rations, burn ointment. Gee could see
Mono through the basement ventilation window as he exe-
cuted an about face at the end of the compound, Mono
against the sky, scored now with the gaseous lights of a landing per minute, then blowtorch takeoffs. It seemed to Gee that
the planes were getting older. Twin tailed skymasters built to
raid the Ploesti oil fields coursed in like puffins. The high
arched bouncing DC9s, the triple tailed Constellations, a covey
of Lockheed Lodestars, and even one extinct prewar powder
blue amphibious Catalina PBY.

Near eight someone stumbled hard at the top of the basement steps. Gee brought the carbine up abruptly across his
chest. It was Hatchette, bombed, eyes red as spaniels' after
field work, flight cap squashed on his head like the Pope's

38

beenie. He staggered off the last step, grinning, hands too large for the pockets they were in, and finally, with enormous effort, produced a dime which he dropped in the soft drink machine which fronted the Disaster Pak. Gee stepped back and shouldered his weapon.

"Hot damn," Hatchette exploded. "Hit ain't black cherry! It's that lousy Mexicali punch!"

He stared for a while at the button flashing "punch" then kicked in a panel at the base of the machine. Gee didn't know whether he was responsible for guarding the machine too.

" 'Punch' is the name of the drink, sir. It don't mean 'push.' "

Hatchette wheeled slowly, chug-a lugging the drink as he turned, "I'm an enlisted man too, Patek, don't call me sir."

"Yessir."

Hatchette crumpled his cup and stared at Gee.

"You look like a guy who's always had everything handed to him."

Gee was silent.

"I'll bet you're just dying for candy or a smoke."

Gee shook his head.

"Wal, when I was yer age we were really takin' pipe in the Pacific and for six months I got no sweets, no smokes, no poontang, no sodapop, cause sugar ruins yer eyes for nightfightin'," he was squinting now. "And ya know, after six months of that I could see a fly shittin' on a wall at a hundred yards. . . ."

Gee tried to open his face for him. He was terrified of hurting his feelings.

"And if it wasn't for that I wouldn't be alive right now and have two beautiful daughters and one woman who satisfies me the way she does. . . . So I got no squawks, right?"

Gee nodded vigorously.

"I know what you guys think a me, you think I'd be pumping gas on the outside and you resents that I'm above you."

He was looking back at the blinking machine now. "Well, that's all right. I seen what untrained hillbillies can do. At Subi Bay all the women went back in the hills and we had to go beg 'em to come out; and when they did I saw some niggers cut the titties of a fourteen-years-old girl. They were just thrown together, that army, like a lot of crap. . . ." He seemed to lose track, then, "I'll tell you that's why I respect you guys, and don't begrudge yer education . . . yessir, give one woman a chance and she'll satisfy you. You don't need ter run around. . . ."

Gee stiffened himself. "We don't resent you, sir."

Hatchette gave no indication that he had heard him.

"I'll tell you something about southern boys too, Patek, and I don't care if the northern boys know it, it's that southern boys are more mama's boys, and if you don't take sweetness away quick from a southern boy, he'll turn mean and stupid. . . ."

Hatchette staggered around again and put another dime in the machine. Then he climbed the stairs with his second punch.

"It uster be," he mumbled up the stairwell, "that a man was good because he did something he didn't wanter to. Now he's good if he don't do what he can't do." Then he was gone.

Gee was relieved at nine and went out for some air. Mono was out in the furthest shadows of the compound, squatting, a coil between his legs. Gee turned smartly on his heel to face the barracks. A recording of *Lights Out* and then *Taps* came over the loudspeakers. The radar was scanning the horizon, nodding, and Gee bowed to it between its bows; the low, sweeping courtly bows of a static operetta. He made no effort to control his paunch.

He wondered about Gonzales up there in his flannelette pajamas, pillow held tight to his stomach, filling the room with his senses, his unfocused love wrapping that room right around him, taking the room unto him.

Hatchette told them with a funny smile to put on their best dress fatigues and be up an hour before reveille. Gee figured this was it. He got out the tailored uniform with the Evacuation patches replaced by the Terminal patch and chevron promoting him to Airman First Class. But the tailor had made a mistake. The inseam had been tapered so much that it pinched his armpits, exaggerated his fatty pectorals like a girl in a strapless formal. Worse, unless he consciously sucked in his stomach the shirt spread between the buttons, emitting a series of parentheses of white flesh stashed one atop the other; the last two above the belt were also hairy. He couldn't figure out what with eating so little and working hard why he was still gaining weight; Hatchette had started calling him Blimp instead of Tank.

A bus took them out the side gate to the main intersection of a suburban town thirty minutes down the turnpike.

"Easy day, boys," Hatchette crowed. "Special duty. All you gotta do is salute! That's what you get for not fuckin' me over. You're good hardworking boys. Not like the turds we uster get."

The bus pulled up behind the defunct train station and the troops were allowed to take a smoke break on the green, where there was a tank for a war monument, lovers' initials gouged in her armorplate, vines in her treads, hatch and barrel welded up; Gee's sepulchre.

Hatchette explained that the bottom part of the moon rocket was coming through town by the old highway on the way to the launching site in southern California and that all they had to do was form up and salute it and then could take the rest of the day off. Since the town was an army town and had no high school band or Jay-Cees of their own, it was only fair to help them out.

They didn't have to wait long. A phalanx of state motorcycle police cruised into view so slowly that they had to heel and toe on the macadam to keep their machines upright.

Then a couple of open vans of soldiers, facing each other on benches, rifles upright between their knees. Then two blue FOLLOW ME trucks and finally the moon rocket on a WIDE LOAD trailer, covered and drawn taut with canvas, followed by more police horsing their cycles and talking earnestly into walkie-talkies.

It was the biggest rocket Gee had ever seen, but somehow disappointing. He'd seen WIDE LOADS before. And there weren't very many townspeople either—mostly women it seemed. He recognized a couple of hookers from the local bars standing around in their beaded sweaters and tartan skirts like reactivated reserve school girls, and what was probably a parochial school civics class, a bunch of sharp looking chicks with a priest and nun. Otherwise, a couple of slack-assed housewives with baby buggies.

Hatchette got them formed up in a single row on each side of the street, a dress right dress giving space enough for the crowd to see between the honor guard. Gee could hear the hiss of the moon rocket's semi, then it was eyes front and a salute that snapped his dickstring tight.

Because of his fixed stare Gee couldn't recollect exactly what happened next. He remembered one of the cops swerving his cycle and half tear his boot off, and then he saw the chicks and the mothers with their baby buggies out in the street, the vans locked in a four wheel drift, and the air brakes of the semi like the sirens of a Red Alert.

"Maybe the moon rocket tipped forward just a little but it was hard to tell. And right in the middle was that fuckin' priest, the only man in town, just like he was directing traffic. And the chicks were everywhere, chickens in a foxhouse; if you ever saw a girl run, really run, they can move pretty fast if they have to. Hatchette was cool, really cool, you could see how he'd stayed alive so far. 'Keep salutin' and don't do nothing stupid' he says to me out of the corner of his mouth, 'pass the word,' and I did. The cops couldn't do much except drive around in circles on those big Harleys cursing and revving, but they couldn't do much *and* keep the convoy moving. Course the chicks couldn't really stop it either, but to fuck with the moon rocket, that was something! Course she was past soon anyway, and the chicks were shoved over against us as she went by with that hiss that showed the brakes were no damn good for such a load, and I thought I heard Mono amocking me. 'You dirty cocksucker,' the voice said, but it was high and really soft, and so I looked down from under my right hand and here's this star of a chick and she had no bra on I could see, her nipples up against her satiny blouse and her hair gold billows from an afterburner and she was shaking her little white first, telling *me,* 'you fat dirty cock-sucker . . .' "

Things calmed down again right away though and that Priester if he really was one took his little mackerelsnappers back to school just like they had taken a field trip to the Museum of Natural History or something. And those women: they didn't have no babies in those buggies, they had signs. Old Boyce would have *loved* this.

Gee couldn't wait to write Harold, but he didn't know how to put it. In fact, he felt so funny that when the rest of them decided to go over to the Dairy Queen to see if they could pick up some Peacequiff, Gee ended up in the library.

He wanted to see if he could still speed read, if he'd lost his mind along with his figure. Also, maybe he could rip off some good long books, some real classics, Cooper and Poe, Victor Hugo and some of the Russians for the trip. That would be something, to take along some of those fat Russians, over there. He hadn't read anything since he'd been in but medical manuals. Boyce had told him to read Dostoyevsky, that he was a genius because though he didn't understand what was happening in Russia then, he somehow knew what was going on in the U.S. now. The later Dostoyevsky is what he said.

The librarian rose as Gee came in and while he wanted to

browse, he felt he had to go to the desk. She looked exactly like the librarian in the Wieboldt town library. Before he could ask her where the latest Dostoyevsky was, she asked him if he were stationed at Fairfax.

"Yes ma'am."

"Permanent duty?"

He was going to tell her they were set to move out fast, but maybe she wouldn't give him any books then, and maybe it was classified.

"Fine," she smiled electrically. "Then you're eligible for our summer reading program as a temporary resident."

She slid a purplish mimeographed sheet across to him. The ink was the same color as her lipstick and the flowers on her dress.

Summer Reading Program

ELIGIBILITY: Ability to read (even 1st graders may enter).
Each reader goes along at own speed and ALL readers are winners!

REGISTRATION:
One book—
Reader submits a report written briefly in the library during regular 0900-1700 hours, and is enrolled as a **"Ranch Hand"** in the club. Report is filed in manuscript folder to be given back to reader at end of summer, together with appropriate awards for quantity and quality of reading done.

ADVANCEMENT:
Three books—
Reader receives an emblem representing work done on the ranch—one emblem for each book read and recorded in permanent record book. Third book denotes promotion to full ranking **"Cowboy."**

Five books—
Reader receives emblem for each book indicating work accomplished as a **cowboy** (branding calves, roping steers, etc.). Fifth book denotes graduation to **"Bronc-buster"** class.

Eight books—
Reader receives "ribbons" for skills in rodeo competition—eighth ribbon denotes graduation to **"Ranch Owner"** class.
Ranch Owners may do **anything,** so reader will hang up his own private ranch chart, select his private ranch brand, and receive, for each book read, an emblem representing any task or skill that he wishes.

Party at end of summer for presentation of awards
and certificates

44

Gee read it with three fixations. You could tell she was surprised how fast he was. But then she just took out a long application, as long as the one he had to fill out for his security clearance, and he stared her down.

"You mean," he was stuttering for the first time he could ever remember, "you mean I got to write a report and read eight books before I can take any out of here?"

She was unmoved.

"It's our way of making sure you boys at the base learn to use the library properly. We don't see too many of you over here, you know, and it's a way of acquainting our men in the service with the total facilities of a lender library."

Gee's mouth was open. He could feel the stainless steel edge of the counter cleave his paunch as he pressed forward. His fists burned white as he clenched them over the application. He realized later he had almost slugged her. Imagine, after all the crap he had taken, he might have ended up creaming an old lady. *What's happening to me?* The counter groaned from his weight . . . she was talking, gentler now. . . .

"I suppose you saw the . . . trouble . . . this morning?"

"Yes ma'am," he dropped his hands to his sides and backed away.

"Well, it raised my confidence a notch or two. I'll tell you."

"Oh?" Gee was puzzled.

"Yes, son. Do you know who was here, sitting right in this library, while that was going on?"

He shook his head.

"The FBI. That's who."

His head had started to buzz again.

"Maybe," he said finally, "maybe I'll just look at some magazines."

"Yes," she reseated herself. "Perhaps it would be best if you started in periodicals."

For some reason he did half an about face and started for the newspaper rack.

"I'm sorry if you find the summer program restrictive," her voice came up behind him, "but you just don't give a man a gun and send him out without proper training, do you? We must maintain our standards just as the military."

He nodded but didn't turn around. He got a *Sports Illustrated* and a *Reader's Digest* and went into the "Reading Room." It was a terrific one, about the size and coolness of his aunt's parlor but with men's furniture, high backed brass-studded leather wing chairs, a firm French type sofa, a table you could screw on without it wobbling, and most important, tall lamps and shades made from old blank leather-type books. A soft and yellow light that lifted the letters right off the page. The kind of light you could set a speed reading record under. Those damn fluorescents, those spot lights, those landing lights blinkering, driving him out of his fucking mind. The ashtrays were filled with the Marlboros of the FBI. The dusty venetian blinds bore their thick fingerprints. Gee read an article for pleasure out of *Sports Illustrated*. It was about the quarterback for St. Louis who was called up by his reserve unit to active duty, and at twenty-five, with his team a contender, had to go to Kansas for two years to drill while his team dropped into the second division, and he might get in on weekend passes sometimes to throw a few, but the best part of his career was shot, and for what—to hump a few boxes that Mono could do in half an hour. It was okay for guys like Gee who hadn't made up their minds about what they wanted to do and didn't have a career or family, but for the quarterback of a contender, that was crazy. Gee himself would double his tour to keep that guy active for the few years he had left. He remembered reading somewhere that in the Civil War you could pay somebody to serve for you. That was right. There were a lot of guys besides the quarterback that he could serve for. He could save some dough up while they could play and when he got out he'd have something to show for it, and could make up his mind what he wanted to do. And he could walk up to that quarterback after the Superbowl and say, "I'm the guy who stood for you. And I'm glad I could do it. How about a beer?" And the guy would look up from the bench, squint those blank eyes, and finally understand that cat in the stands, who reads the *whole* paper, who could love and hate him so much. And they would know who they all were then.

Then he went through an article in *Reader's Digest* for practice, timing himself, practicing the single-fixation-per-sentence method his father had taught him, concentrating right on the center of the page, taking advantage of "man's peripheral vision, untapped heretofore only by athletes" he used to say, bang bang, bang, three spots a page, that was enough to get it all, "don't linger don't dwell unless it's poetry," he used to say, and sure enough he came out 1904 words per minute, though *Reader's Digest* was probably no real comprehension test.

But later, when Gee had relaxed, and the light through the FBI's peekaboo was exhausted and he had read every magazine in the place, even *House Beautiful* and *The New Yorker,* he caught something in the back of *Scientific American* that wasn't either for pleasure or for practice.

THE FIRST STATISTICAL EVALUATION OF SEXUAL
INVERSION AND TRANSFORMATION PROCEDURES

He found if he skipped the graphs and tables he could take it at 1756 WPM. It was one of those commonsensical articles about how everybody had both male and female instincts, not to mention hormones, that the shape or place of erogenous zones was relatively arbitrary, and that sex changes like most anything else was a matter of will, time and money, and that the team at Johns Hopkins could now guarantee a 65% total success factor which isn't going to get you to the Cotton Bowl but is okay for a small private school like that. "Not yet common, no longer bizarre," was the conclusion.

On the bus back to the base Gee thought out his letter very carefully, making a topic outline first, even diagramming the sentences, and got a buddy in Traffic Control to let him use a typewriter. Everybody remembered what a character Boyce was. The day before maneuvers he had filled out an entire load priority board in Chinese, and then argued with the captain about how much more efficient ideograms were. "Don't you see," he had insisted, *"That's* why they're whopping our ass?"

The teletypes and various radios were so noisy that Gee could barely concentrate, but the traffic specialists moved about the room as if they were under water, holding the incoming out over the sea for up to three-hour delays.

To: John Hopkins University
Gender Identification Clinic
1455 Terrace Drive
Baltimore, Maryland

From: Patek, George F. Jr.
AF 26411289
A1C, 104 Air Terminal Sqd.
Fairfax AFB, Nellus, Cal.

Subject: Sex change in scientific american

Having read your recent article on common sense and sex change, I am writing you about a person I know here who probably would be interested in your discovery if you approached him right. He seems very unhappy about his present "role" but doesn't know what to do about it. I am a trained medic but have never actually had the chance to use my training yet so I can not yet advise him. I thought maybe you could send me further information so that at least he could talk to somebody about it. Specifically, I would like to know, right off, that since you mention this would cost $10,000, if this operation could be performed in a military facility since this man is in the Armed Forces.

48

I guess I should also add that he hasn't done anything wrong, because of this problem, that he does his job well whatever they ask him, and that this is really about somebody else, not me. If you could write soon I would appreciate it since we may be moving out soon.

That Sunday, they didn't get their usual two hours extra sleep, and a bird colonel came in at five to tell them their new destination was now set but still secret, and though the actual departure date had been put off again, not to worry as there'd still be the traditional "moving out" party that afternoon provided by the American federal government. They were bussed out to a grove in the very center of the triangle of runways and put at ease beneath the cool mesquite and tragic eucalyptus. A strike force of *Hustlers* from Hawaii was roaring out of the hills at 30-second intervals. According to the manual, they only used them on missions in which they expected fighter resistance. The showdown couldn't be long now. An amphibious tank delivered beer and popsicles. A young lieutenant arrived in a snazzy orange Thunderbird, read them something off a clipboard called "Democrat Heritage," but with the *Hustlers* balking and raving it was impossible to hear him. Gee realized it was probably the last time he'd have the chance to see a *Red Alert.* But those golden *Peacemakers* didn't make a move. Then a two-ton ammo truck backed into the grove and stopped mysteriously before the ranks. The tailgate was flipped down and instead of a Kraut machinegunner, a crew of civilian Mexicans pushed out a load of whole watermelons and right behind them was a jazz combo, going full blast. It turned out that one of the guys in the unit was a real recording star, had even been in the top twenty. "Another guy I would have stood for," Gee thought as he watched Gene Breeze, a really quiet guy that nobody noticed hunch over a portable electric organ with his eyes closed.

For the moment there was a stunned silence, then the unit

broke ranks with a shout and ran into the fruit. Mono gathered two melons under his arms and ran to a flat place, sweet-talked a parade bayonet away from a black AP and began hacking his into cubes. Gonzales felt several professionally, settling for a smaller one, more resilient to the touch, then brought it over to share with Gee, making it bite size with the serrated edge of his dog tags, crescent moons of green/red rind beneath the full moons of radar. Gee couldn't take his eyes off the glistening dog tags, slicing there between Gonzales' bowed legs. The tags had one sharp edge in case the head was blown off the body so the medic could jam them into the body for ready identification. The manual said they should be put in the roof of the mouth, and he didn't understand if the head was blown off how that was possible.

"You like the seeds out or in?" Gonz asked him, working like a real chef.

Gee didn't say anything. He was getting that funny buzz-on again, and the kid seemed so self-assured it pissed him off.

"Well," he said, hating himself even before the words were out, "how are you, uh, coming along with your, uh, problem?"

Gonzales widened his doe eyes until they were completely round, clearly puzzled by the hostility. He began to speak, but then instead, plunged his mouth into the melon.

"Look," Gee spoke sharply, "when we move out, this is a whole new ballgame. You're gonna be in a combat zone if you do anything funny nobody's gonna be able to protect you over there. You could even get shot. Everything you do is gonna be that much more worse. I told you, you could get out on a medical. But you gotta do it now, before we cross the line."

Gonzales was chewing his melon thoughtfully, arching a few seeds into the dusty air. He held the melon like a guitar in his long graceful fingers.

"You hear me, you goddamn fuckoff, you hear me?" Gee was yelling.

When he didn't answer again but looked like he might cry, Gee decided not to tell him about the information he'd requested from John Hopkins. They'd probably be gone before it was forwarded anyway.

"Okay, I won't bug you anymore," he got up and dusted his seat off. "Just remember I warned you. And you can't count on me to keep you outta trouble all the time. I got my own problems." Then he walked away into the mesquite and sat down alone in the sawtooth grass.

Gene Breeze was hunched over the organ like a spider. Tenor sax and bongos behind him, he punched it out beyond his adenoids:

Ohh, ah, he got what he wanted what he wanted.

Gee casually took out his German pen along with the disposable syringe which it now mated, camouflaged. He had only three left. Then in one motion, as if dropping his hands in disgust, he drove the needle through the skin-tight fatigues into his thigh.

The boys were lounging in circles now; mouths, chests and fingers berry-red, making occasional forays for the last of the melon and ice cream, tossing bits of rind and spitting seeds down each other's shirtfronts. The band's bad complexions had disappeared in a soft Christmas-type light.

Oh, ah he, he got what he wanted.

Gee wanted to dance; Mono was. "Groovy," he was yelling, a popsicle in each hand, "couldn't get this band for a hundred bucks a head on the outside."

Ohh, ahh, he got what he wanted. . . .

The mountains seemed a casual rip in the effluorescent sky. The radar towers backed and filled. They were at Stop, Look and Listen. The vapor trails of Incoming had set up a grid in the stolid atmosphere. The Big Crossword Puzzle in the Sky. In the northeast quadrant the moon was still visible, a disc of petrified cumulus. Gee absently spat a melon seed into the moon and the grid dissolved.

Ohh, ahh, he got what he ah ah ah ah wanted.

A touchdown on every run? Not likely. But he had this one trick, blocking or not. Give 'em a leg then take it away. Not a question of speed or power or even picking the hole, but of balance, of minus resistance at impact. The guy comes up on you, going to rack your ass, you let your lead leg go limp, he lunges for it so he's committed himself. So when he's on the balls of his feet and driving you just relax without breaking stride and let his shoulder go right through the groin, you don't even have to give him the other leg hard unless you want to punish him, because once he takes the limp leg, the dead limb, once he can't use *your* weight, your other leg is somehow automatically by, and all you gotta do is let your hips go with *his* strength, and he ends up on his face and while you've lost a little momentum, and you don't look so hot, you still know where you're going. If you're good you can do it five, six times a game, and if you're Gee now, every play, and the fools sprawl in your wake like they were machine-gunned. . . .

But oh, ah, he lost what he had.

Gee's eyes clicked open. The sun was two feet off the runway like an old atom bomb. The band had stopped; only the sound of planes taxiing aimlessly and the distant whoosh of the machine shop testing an engine after hours. The swing shift was coming on. He couldn't remember if he was on duty. He looked for his buddies.

It was a field of carnage. Like a daguerrotype of Gettysburg he once saw in a book. The bodies stiffened and shoeless, pink gore strung from their mouths and nostrils, hands folded beneath their wrists like babies, the very grass stained red. Splayed on the ground in undramatic banal agonies, and everywhere, not smoke, not weapons, only paper; mail, citations, orders, schedules, reports, news and entertainment, garbage, personal effects . . . the containers, the packaging they had fought for.

The Commander himself showed up at dusk in a blue staff car to join the fun. He had a rum n' coke, polo shirt, alligator shoes, snap brim Panama hat, and twelve hour passes.

Gee had already packed his civvies and couldn't get at them before the last bus to Frisco. In fact, he barely had time to get into his Class A dress uniform.

"You won't even get a whore in them colors," Mono laughed at him. He had on black slacks, apricot tricot shirt with matching socks, and a large color-coordinated peace medallion around his neck. When he moved you could see every muscle, like a gnarl of kittens beneath a blanket. The bus moved hesitantly into the commuter traffic. Gee couldn't tell where the headlights left off and the houses began.

He woke over the Bay bridge where the cables reminded him of the bed springs when Gonzales slept above him. He could imagine Gonzales lying up there on top of the bridge looking down at them through the headlights and then back up at the stars. Mono was elbowing him. He had pulled out his pass and was reading: " 'Void after 8 P.M. Monday.' Is 'void' good or bad, Gee?"

Gee was surprised to see so many high buildings in Frisco; he thought there'd been an earthquake there. The bus pulled into the Tenderloin district, Gee gaping at the hookers shucking right there in front of the Hilton. In the terminal, after borrowing five, Mono disappeared before he could ask him where to meet up at. Gee saw a poster for a rock festival at the Fillmore and took a cab over. There were more motorcycle cops than even at the moon rocket. They let him in for half price, because of the uniform, and gave him the peace sign, which he gave back in spades. The double-breasted tailoring of the dress uniform gave him support and thinned him out. He'd just walk right in and say, "Bet you never danced with a fuckin' tank before, baby."

The band was really something. Gee stalked the perimeter

trying to hear the words. Looking over the crowd, he realized he was probably the biggest person in the place. "The giant's here, folks, last chance to dance with a giant 'fore he's shipped out." Everybody was dancing together but not in couples, and so wildly that Gee couldn't see how to get a girl off alone and talk to her so that she wouldn't be scared. The dope was wearing off. He wished there was some place to get drunk. He was surprised too at how many old guys there were and how young the girls looked.

Some of the guys were definitely queer, Boyce would have had a ball here, trying to guess what was wrong with who. And some of the girls looked really sick, the kind of paleness you see in the dispensary when a man hasn't been turned enough and the sheets begin to wear his heels right off. But he might even fuck a sick one tonight. And when he got over there, he'd get a beautiful sick one and feed her and treat her like she probably had never been treated before.

The music was getting simpler and harder, wordless, electric, no more silence between the beat, no more space between the dancers, a sweetness in the air. Then, as in an old musical comedy, the crowd parted for an instant to reveal a girl in military dress dancing alone and quietly to herself. Her hands went up and down precisely against the music, black hair fanning out over her behind. Gee moved around to see what she was like from the front, but her hair always floated across her face. He moved into the music as he would ford a creek, the weight of a wounded slung across his shoulders. He made out her eyes now, and she was quickly in his orbit, beckoning to him with her hands, and he began to dance the dance he had never done before, self-conscious only of his hands snapping so redundantly. How can you be ashamed of your thumbs? Then he felt as if it were raining, when you are finally soaked through and the shivering is over, and there is no difference between your senses, your sorrowing and rejoicing, another kind of life.

Gee moved closer; her eyes seem to be all iris, no white in the lights at all, and Gee wasn't dancing but running, running easily in place with a few hops in between just like the obstacle course, and he flung his chest back, pumped his knees past his waist: "Stretch it out there, airman, Crate o' eggs on your back, Glass a watta on your head!"; and then he was very close, looking right at her. Her mouth was open but unsmiling, a gap between her front teeth, and over her jeans and T-shirt she wore a Class A Air Force blouse with Master Sergeant stripes, a uniform exactly like Gee's except for the rank, a sharpshooter medal, model of his, flapping like artificial bait, the strobes glinting off the metallic thread as discs of oil floated across his eyes. The coat hung on her like a shroud, sleeves secreting her hands, unbound breasts jelloing between the great lapels, the side flap pockets nearly to her knees and bulging with grenades of oxygen. The drooping massive padded shoulders seemed to be broken in half where her collarbone ended, and suddenly she flicked up the dead man's empty sleeve, emitting darkness like a megaphone.

Then Gee was in the street, running, holding a sideache.

Mono wasn't on the last bus to the base. There was a mist under the bridge and Gee couldn't see the water.

They pulled up to the barracks at sunrise; there was a special delivery letter on his bunk.

Dearest Gee,

I'm so miserable and wish I could turn the date of this letter back. I have your last two letters to Harold where you say you think you'll be moving out soon, and though Dad would kill me if he knew I was writing this, I just can't help it. Two weekends ago, Harold was driving down to Ruxton for a dental appointment and swerved to avoid a pipe on the road and turned over several times in the Chevy. The accident fractured his skull, and nineteen hours later he died of internal hemmorhage in the brain. I don't know why, Gee, but your father didn't want to tell you, your having your own problems and all. He said that as long as you'd been mobilized and were leaving that to come back now might affect your career though I think what he meant was that it might hurt you so bad that you couldn't take it. I was angry with him but you can understand that I couldn't go against him then. Since the funeral, he hasn't mentioned it once. The school gave him a leave of absence, and I think he's going to need it. All he talks about is the war and why they don't just send the Air Force in and finish it once and for all. Dad refused to invite any family to the funeral either, and given his state, maybe it was a blessing in disguise. There hardly seems a point in burying a person nowadays. Harold was cremated. He's in the mausoleum at Ruxton where he was going and we can visit him when you get back. Dad put an ad in the paper to send a donation to the school instead of flowers.

I'm not sure if I can make you understand how much this has affected us. I've lost everybody now. As you know, your dad and I haven't gotten along for several years. Well, I cried enough for your father when he was away, and now I can only pray for the one who has left this house. Your father's drinking again, of course, and hardly says a word to me anymore, but I can't blame him. He's not being mean to me. Though he always took more interest in you, Harold was probably his favorite, in that Harold always was interested in things and ways Dad never had time for. Almost as if Harold was a daughter in a way, I don't mean feminine but secret and easy to hurt having to be protected, and enjoying things for their own sake. You and your dad always knocked something down if it didn't appeal to you, or got around it somehow, though I'm not sure if he's going to be able to get around this. Sometimes I feel that I can't tolerate this town another day, and we

should move to a city where there's more music and merri-
ment to take things off our minds. But that's an old story.
Please don't blame us for not telling you about the
funeral. It was best for everybody this way. It looks like
now I'm going to have to be the strong one. Write us when
you know where they're sending you, and don't worry.

Bless you, Gee,
Mom

Gee was lying on his bunk staring at the ceiling when the sentry came up.

"Patek, you awake?"

"Yeah."

"You got to report to the main hospital on the double. A Captain Forbes says before chow even."

Gee nodded, his eyes awash in the flashlight. He got up and began to shave, stopped after one side, scrubbed his face hard, took some aspirin and set out for the hospital. The buses weren't moving yet and it was a good mile walk.

The office number had the identification of the psychiatric section, so he figured it was about Boyce. The Captain was a heavy, pleasant man in greens, face creased from the night shift, a young voice. He glanced at Gee's chest then back at the file on the desk.

"Looks like they got your name and nameplate mixed up, Airman Patek."

"Yessir."

"That can really bug a man after a while."

"You just gotta get used to it."

"But there're things, even in war, in the service, that no reasonable man should have to get used to, right . . .?"

"I guess that's the way in everything, sir."

The Captain suddenly looked tired and sat down.

"Well, look, Patek, you aren't in any kind of trouble, I just want you to help us out. This is your letter, isn't it?" He shoved his query to John Hopkins across the desk. Gee went totally cold but didn't let it show.

"Yessir."

The Captain leaned back in his chair, the greens parting under the weight, exposing his hairy stomach. Gee figured this was a way of telling him to relax.

"Well, I'm not asking you to squeal on somebody, you understand, but it's our job to identify our boys before they get themselves or the service into trouble. . . ." he squinted at Gee now . . . "You know your unit is scheduled to move out next week?"

"Yessir."

"You know what they can do to a man who . . . affects morale . . . in a combat zone?"

"This guy isn't queer, if that's what you mean."

"Now that's the sort of thing I'm trying to get at. Okay. Don't tell me his name. Just describe his behavior for me."

"He's no homo," Gee said defiantly. "A homo is a guy who puts . . ."

"You mean he has not attempted erotic relations with any of the men so far as you know?"

"Nosir!'

"You realize that in some personalities these tendencies appear only under stress. You've had medical training. . . ."

"I told you already. If he tried anything with me, I'd . . ."

"You've indicated in your letter that sex change may be beneficial to this man."

"He thinks so."

"Why?"

" Cause he wants to be a woman he says. That's why."

The doctor was silent for a time.

"How does that manifest itself?"

"It doesn't *manifest* itself. . . ." How is that the same as what we check the HRCs off on, Gee thought, the same word?

Then he was ashamed of losing track, and then doubly so. "He, he lies in his bed and puts pillows over his . . . here . . . and he . . ." Gee looked at the floor, "he shaves his legs."

"Shaves his legs? Pillows? That's all?"

Gee nodded.

"And apart from this, all his activity is only . . . verbal?"

Gee nodded, keeping his eyes on the floor. He wasn't going to mention the small c Communist business.

"And you wrote a medical school for information on a sex change on the basis of this?

"I know what he *told* me, that's all," Gee was firm.

The doctor nodded again, pursed his lips and made his fingers into a tent.

"You're aware, I suppose, airman, that sometimes young men feign psychotic or deviant symptoms in order to . . . to gain a medical discharge?"

"But he don't want *out!*" Gee was almost yelling.

"All right, all right, calm down. It seems this whole thing has been blown out of proportion. Does he have any other disabilities you may have . . . diagnosed . . .?"

Gee was silent for a moment. Then he sighed.

"Yeah, he's got the flattest feet I ever saw, and a bad ticker. . . . Oh God," the tears hung from his nose, "my poor brother, my poor fucking brother, that kills me more than anything. . . ."

When the doctor came out from behind his desk and put his arm around him, Gee realized he thought he was talking about Gonzales, not Harold, or maybe some other kind of brother, and when he saw his bloodless face not like an officer's at all but some crummy high school teacher, he knew that Harold had gotten their asses out of this one.

He caught an ambulance back to the barracks, finished shaving, and jacked another morphine before he headed for the ramp. The fogs were worsening each day, and with the increasing incoming, the pocket of air between the mountains became so thickened that Gee found he could look directly into the sun without hurting his eyes. Out on the far strip he could see a Globemaster disgorging onto a 40,000 KG loader. At first he thought it was just the darkness, his sadness, the dope, no sleep, but then precisely as in a fairy story, a blade of light broke through the clouds and he was certain. The loader was piled ten wide and six deep with HRCs; he ran to the duty station to check the manifest. Hatchette's own initials were in the margin; "50% of cargo comprised of HRC —AFM 160-35 waived." He looked up to see the loader moving towards the warehouse behind two tugs and a full Air Police escort, a single ingot of aluminum in the dissipated light, a coffin of a giant king.

On Final Inspection Day, it rained hard. In a single night the calisthenics field had turned from beige to creme de menthe. Hatchette strode across this now, two officers in tow. The rumor was that they weren't going all the way at all but were to reopen a new Dispensary Terminal on one of the abandoned Pacific atolls. Gee thought that would be some kind of joke on the old man—he had promised himself he wouldn't write until they were out of the fucking country for good—but he also promised himself he was not going to sit and grouse on some atoll with one runway and a hamburger shack like the old man had, with nothing for him but honey-bucket duty, salting down the whole blood and giving aspirins to college kid pilots who flew too close to the water. The tank would be a real killer before that, a killer medic; a new breed. At that moment, he would have charged a machine gun as easily as giving up a seat on a bus. Not because he had become brave, but because there was no longer any difference for him between hate and fear.

The bunks were taut so that a quarter would bounce off them. Mono still hadn't showed, but instead of stripping his bunk, Gee made it up without knowing why. He hid his dirty clothes behind the Disaster Pak, scrubbed his security drawer to the white pine grain. Then he folded Boyce's mattress double to hide the stain.

Hatchette entered the bay with his officers grinning from between their battle decorations, and brought them to attention, cowlick erect as a courtier's feather. They go from bunk to bunk, and at every third one or so, an officer picks up a T-shirt, flings it against the wall to test the quality of the roll. The men stand tall, eyes fixed where the ceiling meets the wall, as the inspectors check out their creases, their boots' luminosity, search for stubble, bugs, a telltale pustule, if the fly and shirt front are aligned. Hatchette walks before them proudly, straightening a cap, flicking invisible lint from a stiffened shoulder, Gee is passed and saluted.

He didn't understand later how he could not notice. Apparently the kid had stayed in the barracks while they were forming up outside. Hatchette's jaws were working like a bird dog's, wordless chatter of surprise caught low in his throat. He fairly staggered toward the recumbent form in the upper bunk, then ripped the covers from the long curved fingers. Gonzales lay on his back, toes together and pointed like an angel, eyes squeezed shut, sweat beading on the upper lip of the faint moustache, two pillows wrapped about his stomach. Catching sight of the sleeping gown with its ruffled neckline, Hatchette finally managed a scream, the sound of shredding membrane, his tongue going crazy, sidewinding in soft jowl. Lunging against the bunk he toppled it with a moan. Gonzales lay near the bay window where he'd been thrown, eyes still shut, fingers fluttering painfully about his face. From the hem of his gown, Airman Gonzales' left foot extended at right angles to the shaven ankle, which Gee recognized immediately as a textbook example of greenstick fracture.

"Adios amigos," Gonzales said as the officers wrestled him to his feet, "pero no buenas noches."

Marched through that night's rain to the ball field, their green fatigues soon soaked and blackened. Beneath the tin-ribboned grandstand they were assembled by squadrons, a *gratis* pack of cigarettes passed down each row. The smoke and steam from their bodies rose up into the girders of the grandstand. The lights were turned on and the newly-dyed grass curled a green lip to the gums of the red clay infield.

Presently, a tall form in a white vinyl parka and a golfing umbrella, looking more like a queen than a chaplain, strode to the pitcher's mound, trailing the bronzen coil of a microphone cord. He stood with both feet on the rubber, rivulets of red clay trickling from beneath his new combat boots, holding a sheaf of papers which sagged like a bouquet in the drizzle. Still, the voice echoed with a genuine announcer's authority beneath the tin roof, though it did not seem connected at all with the gestures of this curious reliefer, steaming beneath the dais of his umbrella.

"Now men, I will be brief. We'll be seeing a lot of each other in the coming weeks. I know that I speak for the Air Force, the American federal government, your parents and sweethearts, and the Commander-in-Chief when I say that you are welcome here. But we must realize that we may not be as welcome where we're going. The nature of warfare has changed. Just ask your sergeant. He's been through this before. And he'll tell you already if he already hasn't."

He laughed to himself and shuffled his papers.

"*Orientation*," he repeated to himself as if pondering the fitness of the word. "Well, first of all, you live in a great country. I know you don't need to be told that! What you may not know is that you're on one of the largest installations of its kind in the free world. And you would be in the largest state in the union if it weren't for Alaska! How many boys here from Alaska?"

Gee looked around through the smoke but couldn't see any arms raised. The chaplain wheeled and pointed to center field.

"Boys, out there are the new weapons. Those bombers that

have awakened you in the night, those planes who've never yet dropped a bomb in anger, those slim shields who overtake the sun each day engirdling our globe, one of those planes, men, carries more destructive fire power than all—listen up—all the explosives in all the wars that all men have conflicted in all history! And that, men, that is not science. That is not technology. That is not even the wonder of capitalism. "*That*," he hushed and swallowed his own acoustics, "that is where religion begins. . . . As it says in *Revelations,* 'Cleanse us, oh Lord, from secret faults.' . . ."

"And if this machine is so efficient, so terrible, you must be thinking, why are we here? We are here," he paused, "we are here to keep that plane flying without anger, to keep that plane *from* anger. I believe you know this by some way or other. Christ himself came with a sword, it is true. But He also came with humility. And He also came because 38% of his followers were incapable of defending themselves. Show the sword so as not to use it. God is neither to be ignored nor enlisted in such a situation. As much as we would like, we cannot choose Him captain. For we are more powerful than He in destruction, though not as wise in creation. And if we destroy God's handiwork, we destroy God's idea, and God's idea is God's mind, and God's mind is God, and we are in God. In order to continue to worship Him, we must be willing to protect Him. . . . I hope I have not stretched a fine point. . . ."

"So when you see 'men as trees walking,' when you ask 'to what purpose is this waste,' remember the consequences of war for God. While justice is denied on earth, we must nevertheless be just with the Lord. And that, boys, *that* is the message of the Sermon on the Mount. 'We are in the wind and earthquake; but God's hand is not in the wind and earthquake. God is the still point. But we must endureth all to preserveth all.' We are the big stick."

The chaplain was rocking back and forth on the rubber

now, the microphone cord slathering in the mud like a water moccasin.

"Naturally, the question remains. 'Nations go from strength to strength . . . can a man take fire in his bosom and not be burned?' To that, we can answer, assuredly, we cannot act on faith alone. 'We shall not all sleep, but certainly, we shall all be changed!' and the Prince of Peace is possible only and for the first time as we defend the Lord. No. We shall never hit first. We shall be 'an astonishment among nations.' You perhaps resent being only a number, a tiny part of the whole. But it is your existence on paper, boys, as that number precisely, which prevents the holocaust. Like the great martyrs, a vital statistic in the eyes of God. Not to mention the enemy. They do not fear the Lord. It is He who fears them. And God's fear is the beginning of our wisdom. . . .

"For this, you will not be very well understood in the world. It is difficult to be a hero without a chance to be brave. But that is the burden of the miracle of being part of the Big Stick. It isn't a task for those who are not sticklers for pride. Or a task to be taken lightly. So peace be with you, and you with it. If you have any problems, either official or personal, my door is always open. 'To obey is better than sacrifice, and to hearken, than fat off the rams. . . . For we wrestle not against flesh and blood nor even against powers, but against spiritual weakness in high places.' I'll be seeing you boys at our next destination."

Heads drooped about Gee, and this excited him. The bowed backs of his compatriots steamed as the chaplain left the mound, his rainwear spattered with red gobs of clay. He walked deliberately with one arm extended, looping and coiling the microphone cord about his shoulder, disdaining the wind and rain.

Gee was surprised he slept so heavily. The man who'd moved into Boyce's bunk shook him up. It was raining; each hole in the screen filled with a squared-off raindrop. The interval between the planes was as short as he had ever heard it, sound preceding the plane like the light before the bomb. He went down to the terminal to say so long to Big John. The HRCs had been integrated into the conveyor system and John was stationed at an intersection upon a high stool. Sometimes a HRC would come off the rollers slightly crooked, and John would give it a solemn slap with his forearm to get it retracked. Gee fingered the fountain pen in his pocket, and wondered if a tracheotomy would have saved Harold. He couldn't have relieved the pressure on the brain, though; only an expert could have done that. If Harold had only gotten a mortar in his stomach, maybe he could have saved him. But he probably got the best help available. Gee was getting dizzy. The trouble with morphine is that a man can't piss, it depresses the pisser along with the pain. The piss comes right to the end of the pisser but it won't come that final centimeter. The stomach blows up and you have to catheter them. They would rather not have the morphine than be catheered, most of them. Pain is repeating, pain is being sent back, doing it over, not being used. Keep it moving. Suspended over the hatch of a shuddering helicopter, Gee's hand on the hoist winch, ratchet clattering like a printing press, the jungle stops like a newsreel below, whirlwind of green whorled in the hatch's frame, the cable's pendulum stroke diminishes, unknown hands in the clearing grasp the body, strap him in the loading basket, hands across his chest, basket spirals up from the trees, spins clockwise laterally while rising vertically, a slow propeller launched from the verdure. The body rises towards Gee, the real wounded. He is waiting, the needle pointed down to meet the arched chest winched up to him. His decorations are in order, his hair has been brilliantined, parted down the middle, slicked along the bruised temples. Blood on the brain. Greasy weapon beside him, the basket rises up through the hatch. The helicopter moves out through

65

plumes of shrapnel. Skinny for an infantryman. Gee sops the oozing field sutures, plunges the hypo into the odd C-shaped laceration on the breast. But the syringe gorges forth only a pellet of pure honorific air. . . .

He ducked instinctively as the garbage pulper with a Stockade Detail slammed to a stop at the edge of the ramp where his feet dangled. Several men jumped off and began to wrestle the refuse drums into the hydraulic maw of the pulper. On top of the truck, Gee could make out Hatchette, capless, cowlick erect, telling the men to get the cob out of their ass, sweating profusely through his gray unmarked prison fatigues. Not knowing what else to do, Gee stood and saluted him.

He got a hitch with the Perimeter Patrol down to Operations.

"I don't have to do this, you know," the driver said to Gee. "We don't have to pick you guys up, y'know."

Gee nodded assurance.

"I didn't have anything else to do. That's all."

Gee nodded again.

"So what the hell. I picked you up. Right?"

"Right."

The Base Commander was at work in his glassed-in office, lightning embroidered on the bill of his cap, like the conductor of a sight-seeing bus crouched over his wheel. "Maybe I'm no stickler for pride," Gee was thinking, "but I'm no chicken either, and I ain't bored no more, Ma, bored no more. . . ."

The air attaché gave him a hard time, but after a discussion in which the Commander looked up several times glowering through the glass, Gee was admitted, his heels meeting as the salute pinked his forehead. He was offered by hand signal the sofa, which he recognized as the chintz one which they had accompanied from Texas. On Colonel Pompillo's desk was a walnut triangle upon which was mounted a brass coated nut and bolt. Below, an inscription, also in brass, read, "No, not without a washer." Behind the Commander, through a waist-high window, if you squinted, the planes appeared to be taking off and landing on his bookcase. Even sitting down, the Commander's hips slanted away from his shoulders like a pyramid. A tracheotomy in that man's neck would be a dangerous business. *He* wasn't fat. It was the Commander who was fat. Patek was just big. For some reason Gee sensed he was actually afraid of him.

"What can I do for you, Airman . . . Gaptech?"

"Sir?"

"What do you want?"

"Oh, about the transfer. I can't go."

The Commander pushed back his cap with the lightning on its bill. His face was smiling before his mouth.

"Now look. . . ."

"Yessir," Gee interrupted, "I was afraid, sir, I wouldn't have the guts if we were already on the plane and packed and everything. I mean, I'm not scared of getting killed or killing. But you got to know that you really can't trust me. I don't mean to be disrespectful, sir."

Colonel Pompillo rose up and did a kind of scenario strut before the windows, a ruler clasped behind his back like a swagger stick. He was altogether human now, splitting out of his uniform at every remove. He stopped before the window, back to Gee, took off his wraparound sunglasses and tilted back his night cap with its built-in fifty-mission crush and the lightning across the bill. Then he put the sunglasses back on and took his cap off.

"I can overlook this, airman," he said softly, just as if Gee had insulted his wife, "because I'll tell you a little secret. It'll be announced tonight anyway."

Gee stiffened on the sofa. He didn't know whether to come to attention or not. Another cargo transport landed on the Commander's book case.

"You see, airman," he went on without turning around,

"you've noticed the increase in traffic, of course. Well, it seems we've won a great victory, yessir, and in any case, you see, we're not going into a combat zone. We're being transferred to Hawaii! How about that! Did you know that there are whole beaches in Hawaii, miles and miles of beaches just for the military?"

Gee's mouth had dropped open. The eternal dampness appeared across his chest. The Commander had still not faced him.

"The boys over there have done their job, airman. Not that they had much help from our politicians. They did it, and we're going to need willing hands and all the support we can get to finish it up right. Believe me, this has not been a pretty business, and I can understand how you feel, but thank God, most of us have stuck it out, and you can be proud of yourselves. We can't let them down now. . . ."

The Commander was squinting at a Starfighter's touchdown when he felt the pain in his hip.

"Don't you move," Gee whispered from his knees, "or you'll break it off in you."

The Commander looked down in horror, saw the hypo professionally emptied through his uniform. His pelvis was filled with light.

"Don't you worry now," Gee said solemnly, producing his Red Cross identification card. "You're gonna feel just great. You got a double."

Gee eased the Commander into his chair. Already something like a .15-calibre grin had spread across the face.

"Maybe you better put your hat back on," Gee said. But as he reached for it the Commander had already begun to scream foggily.

The APs were actually very polite, letting him sit in the front seat between them on the way to the stockade. Gee asked them if they'd heard they'd won a great victory and everybody laughed. Maybe they thought he was crazy. He wondered if Hatchette would still pretend he was angry, if Boyce would still be winning all the arguments with the wrong answers, and if Gonzales would have had the shit beaten out of him by this time. Maybe they'd have rounded up Mono too. That would really be something.

Then he thought of the Commander, his first patient, all his worries gone for twenty-four hours, dreaming his life over on that dope so it was perfect, a touchdown every play, knowing that nothing could sabotage him. All victorious. Each plane chock full, cruising contentedly into the sun; total transport.

He thought if he was ever wounded he'd refuse morphine as long as he could stand it, not only so he could piss and wouldn't poison himself, but that if he had to die, he'd rather go like Harold, without a reason, upside down in a ditch, teeth in his hand, body filling up his brain, late for the dentist. He'd refuse it not to be brave, not to act like that, just to show how stupid being killed felt. He didn't know, of course, how much pain he could take. Nobody knew that anymore. Or how long you have to live before you can speak for the dead.

The five-thousandth baritone

A masque in five parts

Synopsis

GERALD FOX, a frustrated burgeoning young artist in questionable health, involved against his wishes with

HAROLD SCHMAR, clever and jealous Associate Professor of Aural Literature, who can manipulate the moods and feelings of others, and is despised by all, especially

DR. HELMUT SELLE, *D. Mus.,* respected and venerable teacher, his promising performing career cut short by Fascism and his faithful wife

NELLY, who also hates

DEAN LAWRENCE NOBILE, a comic functionary and gentleman of the town, who introduces Gerald to

BONNY BAGINSKI, Music Education Major, daughter of

ED AND EMILY BAGINSKI of Berwyn, forsaken by their daughter but infatuated with the ministrations of a reluctant Gerald

ASSORTED PRIESTS, STUDENTS AND BURGHERS

The situation is a hopelessly confused affair in which everyone feels neglected. Schmar's help proves more of a hindrance to Gerald, who becomes entangled with the Baginskis through a misunderstanding which defies solution even though they are all reunited in the end.

I

All that we know definitively about Henry Purcell's history is that his voice broke in 1673 ... beyond that lies the territory of invention.
Mr. Westrup, 1947

HE'D SUNG THE HALL BEFORE, though never in recital. The stage was set for Henry Purcell's *Dido and Aeneas,* the curtains half drawn across a line of aluminum foil columns which supported a highly problematic horizon. The baby grand had been set in a fold of the curtains, and throughout the mandatory section of *chanson,* not one phrase of which could match the composers' collective names—Bachelet, Massenet, Chabrier, Fauré, D'Indy—Gerald Fox never left its deep ebony curve.

Certainly not in his best voice, he'd loused up the Glück, unable to sustain the low tremulos, but his projection was awesome, and the applause at intermission had been more than dutiful. Done with the Monteverdi, Dowland, and Thomas Linley, the latter whom Dr. Selle claimed would have been the "English Mozart" had he not perished in a boating accident, Gerald turned to his accompanist and gave the signal for the surprise finale. Then he left the piano, ascended the next night's set, as Schmar, all claws and elbows, began the ground bass. A few heads dropped perplexed to their programs, and then, necking reflectively with a glistening pillar, Gerald launched into Dido's *Lament*—but in full baritone.

75

Gerald saw Professor Selle grin in spite of himself in the balcony, and while he was for that moment in perfect command, Gerald noted the composition of his audience as he sang:

>   *Ah,*   *ah,*   *ah,*
> *Peace*   *and I are stran*   *gers grown,*

In front, as usual, were the graduate students, dressed in the russet, olive, beige and black of phlegmatic earnestness. Further back, spilling out into the aisles, sprawled the gaudier, paisleyed and striped undergraduates, umbrellas and rainwear steaming in piles at their feet. In the balcony, he could make out what must have been a visiting high school band class, restless, jaunty; girls smoothing tartan skirts about their knees, in serried rows assembled. How he loved girls who wore high socks.

Within that spectrum, Gerald looked in vain for the only faces he desired, those creased angular visages that turned up at only the most unique University functions—one found them at the afternoon organ recitals, a small group, unknown to one another, spotted about the massive loft of the chapel like prechristian plinths, or slowly masticating lunch in the shadow of some modernist, featureless anomaly in the sculpture garden—figures of life dwarfed by secular sepulchers. Their crusts and rinds were dropped into paper bags and never left behind. Then you would encounter them again, the same grim, alien western race; teeth, hair, everything imperfect except the essential bone structure, whereas the undergraduates' perfect teetheyeshair seemed set in formless crowns of flesh like sequins on an Easter egg . . . you would encounter them as they sold you a book, or filled out your library slip, or handed you a menu . . . those freakishly expectant faces which Gerald dreamed might one day be gathered in his name.

> *Peace and I are strangers grown*
> *I lan   guish till my grief is known*

Again the applause was more than perfunctory. Gerald left the stage and met Professor Selle and Dean Nobile in the foyer.

"Pretty gutsy, Mr. Fox," the Dean said, "slipping in that transposed soprano bit."

"Gerald has the greatest range of any student I have ever had," Professor Selle said stiffly. "Gerald will one day do an entire program of great female arias in the baritone."

"It'd make a great LP, don't you think?" Gerry said, "Imagine, all those terrific songs never sung by a man. The man always declares his love in some idiotic recitative, then the lady gets to *sing* about it."

"Everyone *young* sings songs originally written for other voices," Dean Nobile replied matter-of-factly.

"They're not written for other *voices*," Gerald said rather too seriously to make the point, "they are written for other *roles*. If I can pretend I'm an 18th Century Italian Duke, why can't I pretend I'm an 18th Century Italian Duchess? If I can go *Ho-Ho*, can't I do the *Fa-la-la* as well?"

"Ho Fa, la ha, I suppose then," the Dean hummed and strode airily from the foyer lined with florescent oil portraits of former deans in robes.

Schmar was suddenly at their side, mincing the congratulatory. Harold Schmar was the best accompanist and the worst director Gerald had ever experienced. He was forced to be featured in Schmar's productions—everything from *The Mikado* as an attack on Neo-Colonialism to a production of Handel's *Xerxes* with the entire cast, including the chorus, suspended from guy wires, illuminated by strobe lights—so that he might be assured of a suitable continuo on those rare occasions for the single voice.

"Perfect as always, Schmar," Gerald said grudgingly.

"What did you think of that fi-finale?" Schmar addressed Professor Selle, "Next time he ought to do it in c-counter-tenor and d-drag."

"You go too far, as usual," Selle said. "Gerald innovated *just* enough. And what's all this about *Dido and Aeneas* as an allegory for Fascism, Schmar? I lived through Fascism. I can tell you those fellows were not merrymaking courtiers. They did not go Ho-Ho-Ho. They went *Tod, Tod, Tod!*"

"D-D-Dido is the State," Schmar rejoined, "she commits suicide when she ca-ca-cannot subjugate the Individual Hero, Aeneas, na-naturally."

"Oh, bullshit, Schmar," Gerald broke in, "She doesn't kill herself anyway, she dies of a broken heart . . ."

"No one has ever died of a broken heart!" Schmar said firmly. "Anyway, modern audiences couldn't understand that."

"The story, Mr. Schmar," the professor said, "is, I believe, after all, Virgil's . . ."

"Purcell was completely defined by the court he lived in," said Schmar, surprisingly articulate. "Had he lived in Mussolini's time, he would have been a Fascist."

"In England?" the Professor said in disbelief, and stalked away with Gerald in tow, inviting him for cocktails in a whisper, indicating with the folds of his enormous forehead not to bring Schmar on any account, then he sped up the elm-lined street on his fifteen-speed Czech bike.

"Imagine," Schmar said petulantly, "in a world of starvation and genocide; to talk of a pure aesthetics!"

Gerald turned quickly and walked off without a word. Schmar's speech defect was as calculated as his ideology; it seemed to have no pattern or principle, a half-baked stutter giving an appropriate form to fragmented ideas, deployed as a strategic vulnerability, contrived to gain compassion, and allowing him a governance of outrageous talk which would never be tolerated from someone with less obvious self-hatred.

Gerald arrived at the Professor's before five and found him cutting the lawn.

78

"I'm early," he said, "I guess I should apologize for Schmar."

"Mr. Schmar is a *luftmensche manqué,*" the Professor announced, without looking up from the whirring blades. "Ten years ago he would have been a life insurance salesman. In Weimar, a brownshirt."

Gerald walked behind the professor in the newly mown stripe; the clippings fell to each side of them as from the prow of a boat. The mower led them around the house to a small terrace, where his wife, Nelly, was stirring a pitcher of kir. And then they were toasting, Nelly's eyes misting over and the Professor actually gave a short bow. Gerald realized they had worked together now for seven years.

"I've got to go to work," Gerald mumbled.

"Oh no, Gerald," Nelly cooed, "we must celebrate!"

"Celebrate what?"

"Why your degree, your . . . appointment," Nelly turned quickly to her husband who was staring into his drink.

"Gerald," the Selle announced, "has refused the appointment. He will not want to teach."

"Well, we have always taken ourselves quite seriously, haven't we?" Nelly flared. "Is not teaching a noble profession? Even at Schiller?"

"It is a question of loyalty to a discipline, not institutions . . ." the Professor trailed off, "as I understand it . . ."

"Gerald can speak for himself. And where will you go then?"

Gerald gulped his kir.

"I don't know."

"Gerald," Nelly said, "you don't know what the competition is like. There are 5,000 good baritones in the world at any one minute!"

"I know."

"You have always been self-preoccupied and stubborn, Gerald, but never sullen."

"I know."

"Vocalism is not like physics or the ballet. You are a young man . . ."

"Twenty-seven."

"He is saying something, Nelly," Professor Selle stood erect and reasserted himself. "This fall will be the first fall in what, sixty-one years, that I will not be in a classroom or a detention camp."

Nelly glared at both of them. Gerald apologized and excused himself. As his van backed out the drive, Nelly spoke sharply to her husband.

"You taught him discipline and self-respect, Helmut. Did you teach him to feel sorry for himself too?"

"I can assure you, Nelly, that I am as disappointed as you. But you don't understand. These young men have nothing to *blame;* what Gerald is resisting is an eternity of *Dammerschlaf!*"

"Still, it is *he* who must have the character to decide . . ."

Professor Selle began to mow again. "I am 65, Nelly, and it's a fortunate thing. Because I do not love my profession anymore."

Gerald Fox had inherited his sales position from another student, a surly southern lyric tenor who had taken his Doctorate in Applied Voice back to the Old Dominion where he quickly rose to become a county superintendent of public schools, and thus it was that Gerald had become Regional Representative for the Cranach Cutlery Company. It was not a difficult job, certainly, and Gerald figured if he had to go into it full time, he could easily clear more than $20,000 a year. More, it suited him, not only because the commissions had paid for the better part of his various degrees, but because while driving his appointed rounds, he could practice with his tape recorder.

The monthly instructions from the industrious Research

& Development Dept. of the Cranach Company had arrived that morning, in cassette form, and he put this, along with several BurgerKings, a Coke and a tape of *Dido* in the front seat of his van.

Between the company's cassettes, and the tapes he had made of Schmar's accompaniments, Gerald had a total educational setup. Cranach, in fact, complemented him as perfectly as Schmar. They supplied lessons in General Salesmanship, even model dialogues, which invariably worked better than whatever Gerald managed to make up on the spot. Having computerized all possible questions and objections, they had fashioned a rejoinder for each. And once the programmed patter had begun, it was as in bad taste to embellish it as the practiced spontaneity of a Mozart aria. Recently, the Cranach Company had even provided maps of metropolitan areas, charting in red ink the biannual mobility flow of those consumers who had somehow blundered through the American seasons without a set of Cranachware. The newest routing did not veer into the inner city as usual, but struck out directly into the westernmost suburbs, the red felt pen taking the discretionary temperature of Gerald's as yet unknifed countrymen.

Gerald swung the van out on Holton Avenue, passing the bunker-like Administration Building with its false campanile, which told the time with electric chime and vented the bombshelter. Behind loomed the Music School, like an enormous Victorian lady in a filagreed whitelace hooped dress leaning upon a filing cabinet.

The street was fully canopied in maples, and further fleshed out with retirement condominiums, white wroughtiron balustrades, estates surrounded by miles of cyclone fence, enormous homes by disciples of Frank Lloyd Wright with sunken living rooms, sunny loggias, and Byzantine friezes about the cornices; doctorlawyerville. Gerald noted on the map that the initial portion of the route had been crossed out with a jagged line, and he looked up to find himself in a narrow corridor of the negro section, the large homes broken up into apartments, laced with a scaffolding of stairways, a dozen cars parked in each front yard. 'What the hell, don't blacks buy knives anymore?' Gerald thought. 'Well, maybe not in sets.'

He reached the edge of the Sanitary District and crossed the first ring of expressway into the next township, an artery of radar burgers, frozen bialys, private brand gasoline, foam rubber, Mrs. Bagel, Mr. Donut, bowling, a synagogue hovering like a flying saucer, your poodles cut, your dry cleaned, your 27 flavored, and long lamentatory lannonstone homes of rose, puce, and magenta.

When he had first started, Gerald had sold a goodly amount of Cranachware in this sector, but as the area became increasingly fashionable, the ladies of the house were less and less at home, their daily dispersal quotient finally unacceptable to the Cranach Computer which declared the artery varicose and directed Gerald westward.

Once or twice he had tried to sell in a parking lot or along a median strip on a car-to-car basis, which he saw clearly as the coming thing, but the Chamber of Commerce put an abrupt halt to this after a woman had reported that a man had threatened her, not only with a knife, but seven of them, in back of the Piggly Wiggly.

Gerald passed Foxcroft Drive where Schmar lived in a small brick English Tudor job with his wife, two big lipped children, neurotic dog, her two grand pianos, his jazz collection, time plan Italian Provincial furniture, the patina of which he imagined Schmar improving with chains, blunderbuss and horrible augers, that very unlikely house from which issued notice of the coming Apocalypse, the Devolution of Imperialist Western Thought, and the deserved demise of Faustian man.

The single family dwellings ended abruptly at the second ring of expressway, and at that point, the modular pastel Bauhaus of insurance companies, shopping centers, mental hospitals, and a Catholic high school complete with a lunar observatory and enormous chartreuse playing fields took the landscape unto them. Gerald glanced at the map. He was not even halfway to the target area, and he reminded himself to have a look at the most recent Cranach earnings statement. Either the company was suffering or its prime consumers, it seemed, were all fleeing westward. There was also the possibility that he had done his job so well that his perimeter audience was truly saturated.

At the fourth ring of expressway, Gerald realized that he had passed even the airport. The Moorish style motel towers glittered in his peripheral vision, the planes fell heavily, vacously, from clouds of oil across the road ahead of him. He emerged from an underpass beside a pasture bulldozed into the interlocking figure eights of a fetal subdivision, and then, suddenly, he sensed he was *there*—a doughty area of permanence and amiability—pre-war bungalows, expertly manicured, and turned with some diffidence, if not precisely dignity, upon one another. On the horizon, a perfectly rectangular haze rose from the airport, and the van waffled a bit as another jet barged over, wheels aspin. In a cloverleaf of the expressway, an enormous white apartment complex, square and opaque as an ice cube, with a Mansard roof at the sixteenth story, was nearing completion. But here, in the labia of what must have been a drained marsh, even the truckwhine was muffled. He turned off the ignition for a moment and listened to the curves of airliner roar and tractor trailer drone intersect at F sharp. He checked out the map again, the small area encircled in red, and noted from the mailboxes, that most of the names were central European. Even a few which retained umlauts and diacritical marks. Börsi. No, too recent. Vaclav. No, too forbidding. Verititcheff; too aristocratic. *Ah ha!* Gerald snapped the map together joyously as he noted a mailbox with the name, "The Baginski's," the 'i's' of which waved tiny hand-painted American flags.

Emily Baginski, who would have been superstunning if only our race stood in barrels, opened the door almost immediately, as if she had been waiting for him. He took care to look straight into her eyes and gave her *Thought Provoker #7*, designed to create 'potential areas of agreement.'

"Afternoon, Ma'am, I know you're busy, but I just found myself in the area. Frankly, I'm a salesman, and I want you to know that right off. But I've got something here I think is just terrific. I won't stay a minute longer than you want. But if I could show you how to save a lot of money on quality cutlery, wouldn't that interest you?"

This being Gerald's own improvisation, it did not seem to have immediate recognizable effect, though Mrs. Baginski smiled like Dido herself, her hair pulled heroically back from her fine temples.

"We usually buy at the store or through the mail."

Gerald advanced upon her, the Larghetto of the Queen of Carthage still resounding in his ears:

> *Shake*
> *The cloud from off your brow.*
> *fate your wishes does allow,*
> *empire growing,*
> *pleasures flowing*
> *fortune smiles and so should you!*

"Of course, I see I've caught you, Mrs. Baginski, when you were busy. Here's our brochure and dial-a-message number, and perhaps on my next time through . . ."

"Oh, that's all right. Come in for a minute then."

"Thank you, Mrs. Baginski. You won't regret it."

Once inside, nothing was odd except to touch. In the living room, they trod runways of ribbed and mottled plastic across the carpet to sit in swivel chairs also sheathed in polyurethane. *Let Dido smile and I'll defy/the feeble stroke of des-*

tiny/Aeneas has no fate but you. The off-white vitreous poodle, excreting somehow from its eye sockets, takes a three-corner shot off the living room ensemble and then goes to eat catshit out of a box of kitty litter. *Cupid throws the only dart/ that's dreadful, dreadful, dreadful.*

The victorian coffee table appeared to be marble, but through the lens of a Venetian ashtray, Gerald could make out the fecal depression of a cigarette burn. He put his attaché case down on the arm of what appeared through its wrapping to be a sofa. Everything was protected by plastic, even the shade of the Biedermeier lamp. The doily beneath the lamp was encased in amber like a driver's license, the drapes were polyester, and did a number in the breeze, simulating a rustle. In a corner on a pedestal, was a bust, for some reason, of Nefertiti. Perhaps a prize or bonus of some kind? And in an enormous glass breakfront cavorted a collection of porcelains; shepherdesses, Hussars, strange mustachioed hunting dogs loping across heavily cut crystal—figures, even at the time they were made were already corrupted remnants of a mythical monarchy.

Gerald had stumbled upon the Kingdom of Opera itself.

Emily poured a sweet liqueur for the Trojan Prince as he fumbled with his score. All that plastic made Mrs. Baginski even more appealing; her jet black hair, strong neck without a crease, the cheekbones of Tartary, the flat but upturned nose of the nomad Slav. She lacked only bracelets and spear to put him totally off stride.

"What's on your mind, now, son?" she smiled warmly.

"Well, er, Mrs. Baginski, I'm going to tell you a little bit about this now. Of course, you're not committed in any way, just *listen* to me, see, and if you like what you hear, well then, we can go from there. But whatever you decide, you get a free gift for allowing me in your home. Here's a real nice salt shaker. It's made of special wood, and it'll pour right through the dampest of times. Of course, if Mr. Baginski buys something for you, I'm going to give you a pepper shaker, too. Ho, Ho."

Gerald noted that Mrs. Baginski laughed more spontaneously than he.

"Well, I'll get out my cloth here and show you what this is all about. The first thing I'd like to point out to you, Mrs. Baginski, is that all our salesmen are bonded. Triple A Dun & Bradstreet. We're no fly-by-night operation. Our Home Office is right downtown, same as General Motors . . ."

"But what's your name, dear?" Mrs. Baginski said.

"Oh, uh, Gerald, Gerald Fox, I'm sorry . . ."

"Have you worked for this company long, Gerry? Gerald?"

"About seven years now, Ma'am."

"You don't look like the average salesman, if I may say so."

"Well, actually, I'm doing this to put myself through school Ma'am. But that doesn't mean that the merchandise . . ."

"You don't go to Schiller, by any chance?"

"Why yes Ma'am, I do."

"And what are you studying?"

"I'm in . . . uh, a singer?"

"I just can't believe it."

"Well, I can assure you, Ma'am."

"Oh, I didn't mean I don't believe you, Mr. Fox. You see our daughter goes to Schiller too, and she studies music!"

"No kidding." Cripes, Gerald thought, could the Cranach computer have become *this* sophisticated?

"Well, to get back to the merchandise, you know that before any product can be popular, Mrs. Baginski, it's got to be advertised . . ."

"Do you enjoy it there, Mr. Fox?"

"Well, I don't work out of the office, Ma'am, you see I'm on the road."

"I mean at the university, of course."

86

"Oh, well, . . . it's a complicated business."

"Ziviale, that's our daughter, she calls herself Bonny, why I don't know, doesn't seem to like it, Mr. Fox, and she isn't doing very well either, I'm afraid. All she talks about is going to California."

Gerald was suddenly reminded of Cranach Stratagem #17.

Never give the whole story to only half the team.

"I know you must be busy, Mrs. Baginski. Perhaps I could stop back later in the evening when your husband is home?"

"Well, yes, that would be nice. I'm sure Ed would like to talk with you and hear about the school, and, what is it you're selling, exactly?"

"Knives, Mrs. Baginski. The best set of matched cutlery in America. Let me tell you what it takes to make a good knife. First of all, you need the finest steel. Most knives are hard on the outside but soft on the inside . . ."

"Then come back tomorrow evening. Ed won't be back until late tonight."

"Whatever you like," Gerald left too humbly and hurriedly, he thought, but Mrs. Baginski nevertheless smiled and waved him off from the door. "My Ed loves fine tools," she assured him.

In the crush of rush hour he tentatively recrossed the four rings he had traversed and upon re-entry at the campus, Gerald blasted forth in both bass and falsetto:

Our plot is took,
The Queen foresook.
Ho ho, ho ho, ho ho.
Our next motion
Must be to storm
Her lover on the ocean.
Ho ho, ho ho, ho ho,
ho ho, ho ho, ho ho!

Gerald went over to his girlfriend's house, had sex, went to a bar afterwards, got drunk and in a fight with somebody who countered his gentlemanly collegiate left jab with a kick in the balls, gimped deflated to a White Tower where he had four toasted bagels with cream cheese and chives to counter the cheap bourbon, urged the van home with one eye, fell down on his bed alone, dreaming he was singing four parts at once, his fine legs those of the swain, the tremulous lithe upper body of a soprano, the vocal chords of a baboon perfectly trained in Transylvania, *Elissa bleeds tonight and Carthage flames tomorrow/ Destruction our delight, delight our greatest sorrow,* gets up, puts himself through 75 grueling pushups, and after a slug or two of brandy, presents himself at the Selle's at 1:30, hungover and highly strung, but this is more in preparation for Ed Baginski than another class. 'Ed, we heat the steel to 850 degrees then drop it to 100 below zero. In other words, once you get a Cranach knife sharp it'll stay sharp . . .'

Doctor Selle woke him from his trance.

"Gerald, you have been abusing yourself again. Your fine face will melt, your facial bones will jello, your cheeks will pustrate and sag. Your nose will vein over and pock, you'll be susceptible to every banal virus."

Then the professor jerked his protegé roughly down to the basement studio, which he had paneled in resonant tulipwood with his own hands, and where Nelly usually joined them, a mark of respect the professor reserved for few, though his wife was a decidedly inferior accompanist.

Above the piano was the sign which Gerald stared at through—what, a thousand lessons?—

OPEN YOUR THROAT

**The Four Basics of
Successful Singing**

Respiration

Phonation

Resonation

Articulation

and above, a blowup of a transverse section of the human face, the nasal scrolls like some worshipful Mayan design.

Nelly entered, and without a word, began to play the exercises to warm Gerald up.

The tone begins with a tightening of the buttocks, flushing it upwards from the liver and spleen by the contraction of the unconscious diaphragm, past the ubiquitous heart, hung like a pork belly in the flared ribcage, and as the nasal ports and trachea valve flips open, twenty-two fibrous muscles raise what is by now nearly a vowel into the voice box, from whence it rebounds off the palatine arches and pharyngeal walls, and is transmitted to all the tissues and bones of the head. The soft palate is raised, the larynx lowers, the tongue goes forward, the lips vibrate as reeds . . .

"No, No," Selle screamed, "You're guessing, you're looking back for the source. Drinken your breath! Open your throat! As if in astonishment or Vunder!"

Gerald began again, but the Professor cut him short, pacing a closing circle about his protégé; "How many times muss I tell you! The voice is like the penis! It is just a special muscle! There is no *mystery* about it! If it doesn't work, the problem is *never* local, as it appears to be . . . to call attention, for example, to the fact that your jaw is stiffening, as I do now, is only to make matters worse. The problem is *else-where*, Gerald."

Gerald began a scale again impatiently.

"Pretty hooty, reedy, white and thin, Gerald. Pretty breathy, throaty, greasy too."

89

Nelly excused herself somewhat peremptorily on the pretext of the doorbell.

"You are just not 'categorizable,'—a vunderful American word," Selle went on more softly now, "you have too many possibilities of range to settle on a *tessitura* just yet. You have mastered my inhalation/expiration system. Your throat, when you do not abuse yourself, is completely open. The resonance in your epigastrium is that of a man twice your physical size. These are positive gifts. In some ways nearly unprecedented. One day your voice will settle, find a conventional range. and you will have, I am sure, a brilliant career. You also have what no one can teach—a sense of The Long Line."

Gerald was all staring, ballfisted despondency.

"*Your* repertoire has yet to be written, my friend. For you, now, in one direction lies only gimmicks. In the other, extreme specialization. I have been thinking, frankly, of perhaps your concentrating on the Heldentenor—limited roles, perhaps, and for that matter, mostly oratorio, but it would mean a small career you could build on."

"Listen, Professor, I never told you this, but sometimes I find, when I'm not really practicing, in the car, in the shower, sometimes I can make two tones, even a third, simultaneously. Now if I'm going to be stuck here, why don't we work on that? Think of it. One-man polyphony!"

Helmut Selle, still standing, began playing a fugue at twice its signature speed. "Freakishness," he interpolated, "not many people can do that, but so what? My boy, you cannot put tone before the idea. If you have the *idea*, the *tone* will be automatisch."

Nelly was standing in the door. "Helmut, your next student has been waiting in the yard for half an hour."

"Oh, Great God. Listen, Gerald. Calm down and get some rest. Come back tomorrow and we will have double lesson. But please, stop drinking, don't worry about jobs. You are young und single. Think of yourself as an athlete! A fussbal player must know the fundamentals of blocking and tackling, the tennis player, the serve and volley. Just as the baseball player must spear line drives, so the vocalist must know his rhythms, pulses, his intervals. Basic techniques first. A successful golfer does not begin on concentrating on where he wants the ball to go. First he must learn to grip the club. At first, he doesn't even use a ball."

But Gerald was already ascending the stairs.

"You know, Professor, the only thing I've ever minded about my education, is having it explained to me."

In the interstices between lessons, Dr. Selle played for himself a little Delibes, cut short by Nelly, posture-perfect, arms folded severely in the stairwell.

"I didn't know you were taking up golf, Helmut?"

Gerald Fox lopestomped cross campus, his palms deeply marked from his finger nails, grinding his teeth. Warm and dry for March, the crocuses were burgeoning. Squirrels also. And seated on the swale before the library, which, with its foreshortened towers, appeared as a tortoise flipped on its back in neo-paleolithic desuetude, clustered the first "outdoor' classes of the year; namely Schmar with a section of *Music I* beneath a profusion of dogwood and redbud. A few of the girls had on skirts, which they were smoothing. Not a sullen or unlovely face among them, a lot of Speech Therapy and Theater majors no doubt. As he passed, Gerald caught Schmar's familiar stacatto stutter.

"We are m-monsters, all of us. C-c-criminals!"

II

First speech, then rhythm, and finally tone—
and not the other way about . . .
Mr. Caccine, *Nuove Musiche,* 1602

IN THE VAN, between the second and third rings, he did Selle's exercises:

> *Ma-la-mi-do-do.*
> *Ma-la-fi-ta-doo.*
> *Ma-la-sha-bon-si.*
> *Me-poo-go-fe-roo.*

Steering with his knees, Gerald inserted both forefingers in the softness below his sternum, and as the hum became a vowel, he felt the abdominal wall catapult upwards, the tone vibrating his nostrils, lips, tingling the soft palate—then plucking his lower lip, the darkened syllable floated off into his cheekbones and the whiskey dark wells of the brain cavity.

At the fourth ring, he felt sufficiently resonated to give it a try, and sure enough, the two tones came simultaneously, a perfect major third, and he thought he detected somewhere in that harmony the echo of yet another potential note. Peering into the rear view mirror, he opened his mouth to see if his tongue was relaxed, and suddenly slammed on the brakes in horror. Pulling over onto the shoulder, he pushed his jaw against the mirror and gaped again. No doubt about it. Right on the tip of the uvula, that most ladylike pink and glistening stalagtite, there was a white polyp, a *growth.*

Gerald checked the time and set off again for the Baginski's, somewhat chastened. He cut off *Dido* off the stereo rig and pushed in a virgin Cranach tape, *"Intangible Areas of Exploration: Some Fine Lines."* The slick baritone spoke:

There is a fine line between being creative and tricky.
There is a fine line between persistence and being a pest.
There is a fine line between being confident and cocky.
There is a fine line between a champ and a chump.

And then a chorus:

OPEN YOUR MOUTH
Remember
The Four Basics of
Successful Selling
Aspiration
Activation
Inspiration
Perspiration

He arrived at the Baginski's just before six, and Emily showed him her rock garden with the extraordinary number of stone animals and elves among the hooded begonias.

"Ed's a little late. Let's have a slivovitz."

She produced a bottle of the amber nectar with a long, bright weed floating in it, and filled two tiny syringe-like stemwares. Gerald is finding he likes this unflappable woman enormously, though Cranach had warned him repeatedly of the consequences of getting "involved with your clients."

But just as Gerald raised the glass to his lips, the front door flew open, and Ed Baginski entered, as if a buffo character from Rossini had got his evenings mixed, and blew in on a Tchaikovsky *pas de deux*. The Man-of-the-House had on a red polyester outfit; crimson monogrammed sport shirt, red and white tattersall slacks, and maroon vinyl slip-on loafers with black buckles. Emily rose to kiss him, and he hugged her as if he had just returned from the Great War. Then he sat down on the sofa next to his wife, and to Gerald's utter amazement, took her hand in his. Pouring a slivovitz for himself, Ed raised a mock toast, nodding deadpan towards Gerald, "Is this the boy you've been cheatin' on me with, Em?"

Gerald suckled on his heavy breath as Dido's temples were garnished with flames.

"Just kidding. Em says you're studying music like our Ziv, . . . I mean Bonny."

"Uh, yes sir, but actually . . ."

"Knives, Ed," Emily saved the day, "Knives! Mr. Fox here is selling them to work his way through school."

"I remember. Well, what the hell. I wish Bonny would get off her little fanny and cooperate like that."

"You see, Mr. Fox," Emily interjected, "Ed and I never went to college, so perhaps we expect too much . . ."

Gerald felt his sales control going. He recalled the seminal Cranach tape, *Finding the Achilles Heel*. And what was the Baginski's Achilles Heel? Of course. They wanted "recognition of their sacrifice!" That it was all worth while! Gerald blundered ahead with the scenario.

"I was telling your wife, Mr. Baginski, that most knives are hard on the outside, but soft on the inside. The reason is . . ."

"Cause they're made lousy," Ed guffawed.

". . . is advertising, sir." Gerald gagged, realizing he had left out an entire stanza, though Ed did not seem to regret it.

"You know, Ed, they tell me some of those TV spots cost $50,000 a minute. How would you like to get paid like that for an hour's work?"

"Tell you the truth, I'd like to know what some of them professors get."

"Well, it's the same thing, isn't it? Most people don't realize who pays the bill, but it's you and I, isn't it, Mr. Baginski?"

"Boy, you said it."

"For the advertising, I mean. That's why *we* put our money into the product. Because I'm here instead of your seeing some guy on the tube, you're getting better merchandise for less money. Now, the program I'm going to show you, Mr. Baginski, is so good you won't believe it. But please correct me any time you don't understand what you're hearing, won't you?"

Ed began to speak, but then apparently thought better of it. Gerald knew he had him slightly off stride.

"I'll just get us something to eat," Emily excused herself.

"Of course, Mr. Baginski, there's a few things we'd like you to do for us also. I mean, in return for the saving of all this money."

"I'll bet."

"I'll get to those in a few minutes." Gerald saw that Ed was settling dutifully into his role and would not challenge him for the moment.

"I know you understand that we can't talk to *all* the people, so we just talk to the best prospects. One at a time, face to face. In other words, Mr. Baginski, I won't be around here bothering you again. You might put it this way; if you like the merchandise I show you this evening, like it *this evening,* OK?"

Mr. Baginski refilled their glasses and seemed to nod.

"Great," Gerald went on, "Now most men realize the importance of good tools," and then he noticed as Ed drank that he was missing a thumb and half a forefinger. "Incidentally, what line of work are you in, Mr. Baginski?"

"I'm Chief of Service Maintenance at Brentwood-Harwell."

"I see. Well, tools certainly make your job easier, don't they, no question about it. What most men don't realize is that a woman has a knife in her hand more times per day than even a skilled craftsman has his tool in his. And her job is seven days a week, 365 days a year."

"And," said Emily, re-entering with an angel food cake, "You don't get to retire from it."

The Trojan Prince was in full gallop approaching the Deities. He opened the attaché case and removed the set of knives from its purple slipcase, ultimately brandishing the large bread knife.

"Our steel is the best, tempered through and through. It's known as the 'million dollar baby' in the industry. It will stay sharp 60 times longer than any knife on the market. Just watch this."

Gerald flicked the knife three times through the angel cake.

"Isn't that something, though!" Emily cried out.

"I'll bet even an excellent housekeeper like yourself, Mrs. Baginski, didn't know that handles are the basic cause of bacteria in any home."

Emily was appalled that she had not, for all her day to day experience, been privy to such a fact.

"Well, we've tried everything in the handle area, believe me. May I smoke?" Granted his pleasure, Gerald lit up a cigarette and snuffed it out dramatically and without apparent effect on the handle of the bread knife.

"Man-made petrified wood, soaked seventeen times in resins and secured by three German silver rivets, Mr. Baginski. Now as you know, your hands are usually wet or greasy when you go to use a knife, but a Cranach handle will sit in your palm perfectly whether you're right or left handed. Just take aholdt a one there."

Ed and Emily sat side by side, each obediently holding a butcher knife while Gerald entered the *adagio*.

"Well, folks, I hope I haven't given you the impression that our cutlery isn't expensive, because it is." Gerald spread the rest of the knives on the coffee table and opened the ring binder to a colored photo. "You know, our statistics show that a woman, cooking just for two, mind you, spends 1,482 hours a year preparing meals, and if a job of this size doesn't require the finest equipment, no job does."

"Yes, I'm just cooking for the two of us now," Emily said absently.

"And of course, if you had a beautiful set of tools like this, you certainly wouldn't put them in a Fibber McGee drawer, would you? That's why we have available the finest home for Cranach home cutlery. I mean, you reach into a drawer and you want to know just what you've got ahold of, right? Isn't this a good looking knife house?" He pushed the ring binder towards them. "You'll notice that we have them in two colors to match our choice of handles, natural or ebony."

Ed poured another round of slivovitz without looking up, and Gerald noticed that they had already emptied half the bottle. The weed in there, whatever it was, was drooping from lack of liquid volume. A brief intermission was in order.

"Mr. Baginski, do you mind if I ask a question at this point?"

"Hell, no, son, you're doin' just fine."

"What's that uh weed, or is it an herb, in the bottle? That's quite a flavor there."

"Beats the hell out of me. What is it, Emily?"

"It's from the old country," Emily said. "It translates 'Buffalo Grass,' or something of the sort."

"Well," said Gerald, "I prefer the natural, but many like the ebony. Which one do you all like best?"

Emily was slightly flushed. "I think the natural."

"Well, Ed, I guess we'd better stick with the natural." Ed gave a single sharp nod, rather like a pheasant.

"Well, you know, it's really been great talking to you folks, and in my time, I've seen an awful lot of people and done a tremendous lot of research. And I found out that most of the women, since they've been just about *this* high, have always wanted a set of real fine china. Have you folks looked at china recently? Priced it or anything of this nature?"

"Not recently, I guess." Emily smiled, and gingerly putting down her knife, held on Ed's nearest knee as if it were a circuit breaker.

"You know where china originated? Of course, it might

not surprise you. China. Now we've been unable to duplicate the real China china because we don't have any real white clay like the Chinese do in our part of the world. Of course, only in China do people possess the meticulous skill and patience to make China, but that's another story. As you probably know, the English people took old old bones, ground them up, those bones, and they were able to get their china white. But that just increased the problem of chipping. Am I right, Mrs. Baginski? That's why you keep your most treasured pieces in the breakfront."

"And to keep the dust off," Emily smiled.

"We Americans make some good china too, of course, but it's always shown to you on a cream colored cloth because it's creamcolored, not really white."

"Jesus!" said Ed, snapping to, "I didn't know that."

"I honestly didn't either," Emily blushed.

"Well, you know though that most women want an eight to twelve place setting, I don't care how you make your money. And when you start to multiply eight to twelve times 75 dollars, it starts running into money pretty fast, doesn't it?"

Gerald noted that Ed had begun to sweat.

"Well, I know you'll find this hard to believe, but here's what we've done. We've combined the skills of creative artists oceans apart, an American designer to get the taste of the American women, and Oriental craftsmen to do the work. We started with thousands of patterns and boiled them down to six, Mrs. Baginski. They are the only patterns we have or ever will have, so they'll never be out of date. This china has been fired twice just like our knives. If you wanted to, you could take a TV dinner, put it on our china, stick one of our knives into it, and heat the whole thing to 450 degrees and serve it. And the handle would be right there on the knife and the pattern would be right there on the china . . ."

Emily looked a little puzzled so Gerald increased the tempo. "Now the first pattern I'm going to show you is one where you think of *Peacefulness*, the turquoise of a high mountain lake with a fleecy cloud floating right in the middle of it. Isn't that something, though?"

The ringbinder crackled as Gerald flipped the pages.

"Now the next pattern is more symbolic—of our *Country of Plenty*, that is. Where anyone who wants to can get out and earn a good day's pay. Notice, it's wheat, and it has a falling motion sort of, just after it's been cut, but just before it hits the ground. Isn't that something, though? . . . And listen to the bell tone, *Ping*," he sang. "Isn't that something, though? Which one do you like best?"

Gerald paused only for a second, a breathy caessura in his final aria.

"This next one here is really just incredible. Think of a real clear night, looking up into it. The stars, constellations, the heavenly bodies, look, there's Orion! You get a special booklet on how to read the stars with this one, tell your future right as you eat. I can see you really like that one. Oh, I almost forgot. Here's another dandy. You know when the frost just hits the leaves? Well, here's *Frosted Leaves*. You can almost feel them, can't you? Those leaves won't ever come off your plate! Do you like the *Holy Stars* or *Frosted Leaves* best? *Holy Stars*. OK. Now here's a very traditional pattern. I shouldn't say traditional, maybe, formal or classical would be better. This is the one, anyway, that's dignified, like if you were going to have the Senator or the Governor in for dinner, say, but when you get right down to it, Mr. Baginski is more important than all of our elevated elected representatives put together, isn't he? This one has a simple platinum-type ring to be symbolic or remind your guests of marriage, purity and love. Isn't that something?"

"There're so many I'm getting confused," Emily said.

"That's why I've been saving the best for last, Mrs. Baginski. Of course, your favorite may not be mine, but this is the one that's our most popular even though it's the most expensive. I call it . . . *Polonia Rosé.* Some of our customers call it the 'rose that grows,' because, well, you know how a rose works. It's closed in the morning, so the bud is closed on the coffee cup. Then you get your bread plate for a nice sandwich or one of Mrs. Baginski's homemade goodies, I'll bet, and it's open a little farther, and by the time dinner rolls around, *zowie,* it's in full bloom. You always know what time it is when you eat on this. Now which one do you like best? *Polonia Rosé.* Well, it's a beauty, no question about it . . . Well, Mr. and Mrs. Baginski, this is our cutlery, this is our china. The Cranach miracle. Did you enjoy seeing it? I certainly enjoyed showing it to you. Now we'll get right down to business, like I like to do for everybody, and then I'll be on my way. Now . . . Oh, Mr. Baginski, you have a question?"

Ed was shaking his head. "That was beautiful. Just beautiful."

"Well, I told you the products are . . ."

"No, I mean the presentation. I never heard anything like that before."

"Well, let me ask you this, sir. If I left all this with you for a full year and then came back and found you completely satisfied, thousands of meals prepared and served effortlessly, and I asked you for five dollars rent, that would be pretty reasonable, wouldn't it?"

Ed nodded incredulously.

"I really have to start supper," Emily said. "I'm sure you men can decide what to do." And then she smiled right through the swinging door.

"A really lovely woman, if I may say so. Anyway, if the average family kept the set for fifty years, then $250 would really be a fair rent. But if you have only one setting, you'd have to eat on it alone, right? So we'll start you with eight. Now Wedgewood, if you bought it, knowing half a setting would be broken or chipped in a year, eight of Wedgewood would cost you $100 a setting, or $800 a year, if you follow me. Our china is not only tougher and whiter, but I'm going to surprise you now. I'm going to give you this eight place setting for only $250. So together with the knives, you have $500 worth of retail merchandise right there in front of you."

Ed Baginski blinked.

"Here, shake hands with that." Gerald pushed a paring knife into Ed's good hand. "And that," pushing a coffee cup with a closed rose into the maimed one. "That's a man's cup, one you can really get ahold of. And 25 years from now, if you drop it, there'll be another one waiting for you, Mr. Baginski. And even if it's stolen and you have something from a law officer, we'll replace it at half price. You can't be much fairer than that."

Ed was nodding now, wondering where to put the knife and cup down.

"Now, remember I told you that there was something you could help *us* out with, Mr. Baginski? Fine. If you had this quality merchandise in your home, wouldn't you want to tell your friends about it? I know that as nice people you must have many friends. Nice people like yourselves who will sit down and offer me the courtesy you have. All I would like is five names. Here's my card. Just write a little message on the back, like 'take a look at this' or 'let this man in your house and listen'—any kind of little note of that nature. The other thing I'm going to save for a moment. But if you'll do these two things, for us, I'm going to take the $250 cutlery set *and* the knife house *and* the $250 china set, and we're not going to ask you to pay $500 or $475, but an unbelievable $299.95. That's only six cents a day, and I'm sure you'll agree that's a bargain. However, like I mentioned, there is one other very important thing we want you to do for us, and we're willing to make it worth your while, and that's this: We don't want you to discuss this special price with anybody else. We want to keep this just between the both of us, not even your wife. This should be a surprise, don't you agree? You know the names of these people that I mentioned? Well, when I go to the area where they're at, I'm going to make those people exactly the same offer that I made you right here this afternoon provided that they're home, of course. But you see, you don't realize how many times they've gone over to the ocean fishing or to the mountains skiing, and well, Mr. Baginski, I'm just like you, I have to do my work. The company expects me to make so many calls every day. So I'm going to call on someone else in that area. And I'm going to make *them* the offer. Well, you see, at some future date, your friends, your relatives, they'll come into your home, they'll see your cutlery in its nice house, they'll see your china, they'll like it, they'd like to have it, but I'll have to ask them $200 more than you paid. And it would make it impossible for me to explain it to those people. Now does this make good sense to you? Well, I'm going to tell you how much good sense it makes to us, Mr. Baginski. Because if you'll do that for us at this time, the company actually allows me to include along with the knife house and the knives and the china at no extra charge to you whatsoever, over $80 worth of real stainless steel flatware, a complete service to match your china. This flatware is made out of forged steel, it'll never loosen, rattle or collect moisture, and you couldn't go down to a jewelry store and buy a set like that for any $80. As I say, this is going to cost you about 6¢ a day. That certainly wouldn't bother you financially, would it? Fine. Let's see now, if I were to guess your age, Mr. Baginski, I'd have to say about 45. Is that right? And who could you give me where you've had previous credit references? Sears Roebuck? Penney's? That's fine. And let's see here. Of course you're married. Well now, if you'll just put your OK right here, Mr. Baginski, we'll work this whole thing out for you."

At this point, Ed Baginski lifted up his large torso, glanced over his shoulder in the direction of the kitchen, and motioned Gerald out to the sunporch, where they sat on hassocks amongst the purplish glow of Emily's gro-lights, trained intently on a number of African violets.

"Mr. Fox," Ed began somberly.

"Gerry, please."

"Gerry, I really like the way you handle yourself. If college can teach you that, then by golly I'm all for it. And I'll be glad to take you up on your deal. As a matter of fact, I've got a poker party coming up this Friday night where you can meet some real good prospects, and have some fun. It'll be better than writing on any card, I can tell you that. Wouldn't that be something, though?"

"Gee, Mr. Baginski, I don't play cards."

"Hell, that's all right," Ed slapped his red leg like it was a bad pet. "God knows we need some fresh blood. And you can do your presentation again. I could listen to that like it was on the Top Ten."

"Well," Gerry said, "if you'll get me the five prospects like I ask . . . but you have to promise to remember about the price stuff."

"Oh yeah, sure. I get the picture. But there's a couple of things I'd like you to do for me, Gerry. It'll pay off for you. You want to listen?"

Gerald stuttered an OK.

"I just want to be frank and straight with you like you been with me, Gerry. Emily wanted you to come, so maybe, well, she liked you right off, of course, but then . . ."

Gerald fixed a stare on Ed's head. Out in the kitchen an exhaust fan suddenly went on, as if to provide them cover.

"See, uh," Ed went on, nearly in a whisper now, "Ziviale's our only child, and we always, well, brought her up thinking she was the best, you know, she was always the perfect little lady. I don't think we were that strict, we were just honest with her about what would hurt her, see. She always got straight A's in everything and went on to college. Not many do that from around here. She didn't get a scholarship. I make just over what the limit for a scholarship is, they tell me."

"Mr. Baginski, I don't see what this . . ."

"Now let me finish. I didn't interrupt you, did I, Gerry? Now since she's been at school, she's changed a lot, see. Not disrespectful exactly, but critical, you might say, particularly to her mother. It can roll off my back, of course. But a woman like Emily, well, I can tell you she's done nothing but cry for the last year every time that child comes home. First I thought she just missed Ziviale, but then she started praying for her. Lord did she pray. And God did she cry. Now how would you feel if a woman like Emily cried all the time?"

Gerald squinted into the gro-lights. "I would despair, Mr. Baginski."

"Well, that's what I'm doin'. And something's gonna get done about it! I got to find out whether it's her, or that damn school, or even us that's changed. God knows she's always had everything she wanted. She's always been better with older people or children than people her own age. Never did date much. Maybe she needs a boyfriend, I don't know. Maybe, God help us, maybe a head doctor. We've always been real outgoing people, party people you could say. Maybe she didn't respect that. Maybe she ought to go out and get a real job. Maybe she ought to travel. Gerry, it's gettin so a man doesn't know what to do!"

Gerald was near exhaustion, and against the explicit instructions of the Cranach manual, he reached out and touched Ed Baginski on the shoulder.

"You want the lowdown on Bonny, is that it?"

"I just want to know what's comin' off a little. To find out what's on her mind. She'd respect you, I know. She won't talk to her old man. I hope you don't think I'm puttin' my nose where it ought'nt to be, I just want to know why she acts unhappy. It ain't right for Emily to have to suffer like this."

Gerald realized he was cornered.

"Okay, Mr. Baginski, I'll see you on Friday; I'll try to find something out for you by then. And I'm looking forward to meeting your friends; but not a word about those prices."

"OK, my friend," Ed stood up. "Now look, you can think what you like of me, the idea is; we put a silver spoon in that little girl's mouth, and we're going to keep it there!"

Emily called out goodbye from the kitchen, and at the door, Ed reached quickly across with his good left hand to grasp Gerald's right wrist. "See you about nine or so, Gerry."

III

*I do not study Eloquence or professe
Musicke, although I do love Sense and
affect Harmony, my Profession being,
as my Education hath been, Arms; the
only effeminate part of me hath been
Musicke which in me hath always been
Generous because never Mercenary.*
Mr. Tobias Hume, *Airs,* 1605

IN THE VAN, Gerald Fox was furious. This was no decent tradeoff. If it were a simple matter of a brief violent servicing, listening to a sad untrue story, then what the Hell. But this double agent stuff was something else. And he was exhausted from his presentation—one of his best, he thought—particularly because he knew the Baginskis were not your average listeners, and because, yes, he genuinely admired them. Their mutual concern, their toughness, their won serenity; the enormity of Ed's frustration and Emily's grace, which somehow didn't contradict each other. Ed could be sold, but only on his own terms. Ed knew you get what you pay for, and when you always get exactly what you pay for, products cease having intrinsic, even relative value—only the *act* of selling or consuming matters. Like an opera, sort of; it didn't really matter who got killed or married, or whatever, in the end, it was only the arias between interstices—that manic overblown entertainment between predictably brutal, banal, and unnecessary transactions.

He tried again for the two-tone, but got nothing for his efforts but a squeak, a black and white wingtip golfshoe kicking a cow pie in the rough. Then he fumbled in the console for the mandatory Cranach tape, *Self-Criticism Following a Good Prospect*. He crossed the second ring shuddering to the deep-voiced, oblique narrator.

Were you a good listener? Did the prospect have the authority to make the buying decision? Was it possible that you badfully qualified the prospect? Maybe his very qualities oversold you? What's going to happen if he finally refuses? Maybe even is insulting? Lets you waste a couple of evenings preparing for that final sale? Lets you build up a lot of false hopes and then lets you fall flat on your face?

'That son-of-a-bitch had better come through,' Gerald thought.

Remember, there's no need to go back if you failed to overcome their initial objections. No objection is a true objection! Either they need more information, or their reluctance was brought on by your own sense of failure. Did you listen with your third ear? Did you practice eye-control rather than staring? Were they those 'I-don't-need-a-thing' sort of customers? If so, next time remember, if you can't always be right, you can always agree . . .

Gerald flicked off the tape and tried the two-tone again. A triad to be sure, but with neither resonance nor resiance.

'To Hell with the Baginskis; There's plenty of fish in the sea, in the sea.'

Then Gerald Fox pulled over and illuminated his maw with a penlight. The uvula glowed red, and as he two-toned again, he noticed the polyp vibrate independently. Then he slammed his fist into the dashboard, realizing that he'd left his sample case in the Baginski dining room, now three rings behind him.

The next morning, the eyeearnose & throat man's brow furrowed behind his little round mirror. "Well, isn't that something though? It's a growth, obviously. I doubt if it's malignant, but of course we can't tell until we cut it off and do a biopsy. I'm afraid, Mr. Fox, that the uvula is rather an uncharted ocean."

"Uh huh," Gerald said.

"And whatever," Doctor said, rummaging for a scalpel,

"You're going to have to cut out the smoking immediately."

"But I don't smoke," Gerald said, rising to a sitting position, slipping the plastic napkin from his chest. "And I think we'll let the cutting go for a while."

Doctor said something as he left, but Gerald was humming *Dido* to himself and couldn't make it out. *Remember me,* he sang, *but forget my fate . . .*

Friday morning, Gerald Fox's uvula hung like a limp windsock at an abandoned airstrip. Each attempt to produce a note only energized his gag response. He trotted about the campus dryheaving, and finally entered the Faculty Club, hoping to get some tea, realizing the enormity of his error when he caught sight of Schmar and Dean Nobile at the buffet. He dove to disguise himself in the coat rack, but Schmar had already waved him over.

Of all Schiller institutions, Gerald hated the Club most of all; its broiled hamburger patty plate, the kraut snob of a headwaiter, the placemats with *mice* cavorting in mortarboards and gowns—most of all he hated watching Schmar eat his cottage cheese with ketchup and the Dean his red jello and three bean salad. He wondered if Ed Baginski could hate Brentwood-Harwell as much as he hated Schiller.

"Hey Gerry," Schmar said, his mouth full, which somehow attenuated his stutter, "hey, guess what Shakespeare's mother's name was?"

"You know I'm pratically illiterate, Schmar."

"Elizabeth Arden."

"No shit."

The scarlet veil of the Dean's eyes parted as at intermission. "Arden?" he muttered, "There's a forest of Arden in what— the Tempest?"

"My, my, how Freudian," said Schmar.

"Schmar," Gerald interrupted, "Do you have a student by the name of Baginski? Bonny, I think?"

"Yeah, I think so," Schmar said, "blonde, fuzzy-fucky type?"

"I don't know what she looks like, Schmar."

"Well, I'll check it out. What's up?"

"Oh, uh . . . I saw an ad for private lessons, but I want somebody who's well, you know, motivated."

"What the hell, Gerald, they're all the same. That's their beauty, don't you see?"

"That's not true," said Gerald, "and it's not beautiful either."

"Come on over, Gerald," the Dean said, folding his napkin. "I've got to get back to shuffling the old papers. Obviously Schmar is going to be of no help."

Schmar, in fact, had some things between his teeth.

The cornice of the Dean's office was thumbtacked with *Playbills* from apparently every performance, musical and otherwise, he had ever been to, which seemed to include a good deal of summer stock.

"Don't mind young Schmar," the Dean said, somewhat surprisingly, "You know we're not too strong in musicology."

"What do you mean we're not *strong?*"

"You know," Dean Nobile said, holding up a small white fist, "Strong."

Gerald sat down disconsolate, while the Dean unruffled a computer printout, like a gypsy displaying a bit of embroidery.

Except for the alcoholic's eyes, his face was child-like, framed in a crew-cut and bow-tie. "He looks," Nelly once said at a reception after only one sherry, "like something you would find under a seat after a Frank Sinatra concert;" which was pretty astute for a woman who was in fact eating turnips in a Leipsig cellar when Frankie was busting them up at the Aragon.

"B, hmmm," Nobile muttered, "Bacon, Bader, Baddy,

110

Bator, Baginski, there 'tis, Z. Bonny B., voice major, junior. Bonny's been on probation twice; I recommended a switch from Performing Arts to Education. In fact, I've just finished a letter to the graduate school, and you may want to add a reference. Here, take the dossier and be in touch with me."

As he handed the manilla folder over, the red velvet curtains of Nobile's eyes closed again while somewhere in his spiraling cortex, the set was changed by some phlegmatic union laborer. Gerald caught himself staring. The man had flies on his tie. On the tip of each bow, there was hooked a trout fly.

"If you want to stay around here, Gerald, there's always a place for you in Administration," the voice was foggy, "You've got the seriousness it takes."

"I gather," Gerald said, "that Miss Baginski is a rather mediocre student?"

"Well, yes, average, but then again, Gerald, we're not in the business of producing geniuses here; we're creating the audience of the future."

Gerald lost and regained himself in a single instant, murdered and swallowed the murder, and so from an observer's viewpoint appeared only slightly stunned.

But the Dean was going on. "If only you had put the energy you do into performing into the institution, Gerald, you'd be right at the top by now you know."

"Wrong again," Gerald replied abstractly, "I'd have a Ford agency."

"Oh, I know, you chaps always think we're not moving fast enough. But we're making progress, Gerald. Enrollment and endowment are up." The Dean then patted a pile of manilla envelopes on his desk.

"You know what these are?"

"No sir."

"Alumnae codicils. Don't worry, Gerald. They're dying every day."

Dizzy in the hall, Gerald paused at the bulletin board, noting a memo from the Dean, that repeated discoveries of phlegm in the basin of the third floor lavatory required that it would henceforth be restricted to tenured faculty. "Is somebody sick?" it concluded. Then he found the sign-up list for practice rooms, and noted that Baginski, B. was scheduled M W F, 5-7 pm. Three hours to go.

As Gerald descended the central stairway he thought he heard Schmar calling out to him. But the voice floated, just out of earshot. Ordinarily, he would have feigned deafness, but the insistent hectoring tone finally got the better of him, and he retraced the hall until he finally located the voice in the central lecture hall. Then he recalled that Schmar was in the habit of taping his lectures, and replaying them in afternoons and evenings, in the unfortunate event that one of his charges had missed their class. He pushed open the swinging doors into the three-story amphitheatre. The chandeliers were full on, and upon a spotlight lectern, sure enough, was a small tape recorder, addressing the blazing, empty balconies. And below the machine, in the first row, head folded in arms, a single androgynous form.

> "If Rimbaud wa-was a composer
> and l-lived in Chicago . . ."

Outside on the steps, in the wavering light, Gerald breathed deeply and opened the dossier. He skipped the transcript, having long forgotten how to interpret the numerology of the test scores. Her "Statement of Purpose" was typed on yellow stationery, with a rose etched in one corner.

Scholastic Objectives

In going onto Graduate study (M.A./Ph.D.) my field of concentration will be Post Modern Music and the teaching of Music Education. I myself am an actress, musician and singer, and am interested not only in all the Humanities and Social Sciences but in the way people influence and especially relate to one another. . . . While I intend to continue to perform I will also continue my researches into other relevant interdisciplinary fields, and learn Greek and Latin. I am interested in a realm of discourse where both forms and meanings achieve an autonomous existence, but which have also created a truly Western ill-definedness of role problem. Being against Solipsism, I feel the scholar must produce enabling conventions so that a new communal consciousness can come into being, and make autonomy, responsibility.

.... In my studies I have dealt with these problems in various modes, artistic, cultural, literary. The problems have been examined inductively (empirically) and deductively (conceptually). Anything that I teach or discuss will be viewed, not only in its purest form, but also, in the light of this problem of communication ...

Z. Bonny Baginski.

Gerald was beside himself with excitement. If good old Ed tried to pull a fast one on him, all he had to do was produce *that* little document and Ed would again be dependent on his interpretation. Four more years of school, Mr. Baginski, at *full freight.* And hadn't she learned her *Schmarese* well, though? *Quello Pedogogica!* But Gerald's hilarity was cut short by the Dean's pithy recommendation.

To Whom it May Concern:

I am writing on behalf of *enthusiastic* Bonny Baginski. The subject of her *joie de vivre* is creative imagination. She approaches all her endeavors with consistency and discipline be it a new chord progression in her voice improvisations, a new poem or critical essay, and generally (as in a five voice fugue) attempting to integrate a number of voices; each of which has its own beauty and formal independence, yet must needs come together to create a meaningful whole. So in Bonny, there is a contrapuntal moving forward ... a perpetual cross-pollination of elements, which in my judgment have been brought to a high level of fruition for someone so young.

Bonny is one of those soon-to-graduate whose desire to go on for further professional study seems the best, most logical step, not only because she could handle the "intellectual discipline" but because such a stimulating environment would best prepare her for her future creative/recreative course.

I feel I know her and her ideas very well, as I was willing to dialog her a number of times over the coffeecup.

If I can be of further help, contact me.

Cordially,

Lawrence Nobile
Dean of the School of Music

Gerald went sullenly to the Registrar's office, xeroxed the

dossier, and kept his lesson with the Selles only because he still had time to kill before Bonny's rehearsal.

Nelly played much better than usual, smiling while the Professor stalked Gerald as if he could see the resonance slipping from his body like incense. He felt confident and full-throated, and then, slipping from a glissando in the *Evening Prayer,* he decided to let them have it on the last run. The two tone came, actually hurting the roof of his mouth, but nonetheless, a perfect third. Nelly's fingers stuck to the keys. The Professor stared, but then quickly resumed his pacing, running his fingers up and down Gerald's diaphragm, and then playfully plinking his Adam's Apple.

"I taught you to sing and now you want to be an instrumentalist? Picasso drew a horse before he threw those blobs of paint around."

"Professor, I'm not a painter. I'm not a golfer . . ."

"You're a sourpuss."

Nelly was musing. "I heard that once. I think it was in Dubrovnik. About 1925, a Rumanian basso. He sang a folk song in two parts, gutteral and falsetto, but still, yes, that same tone. His name was Coudrescou, or something like that. He had an equal combination of the head and chest registers. Each vowel had two rates of vibration. A true *voix-mixte.*"

"Never heard of him," the Professor snorted. "Gerald, Schröeder-Deviant is coming to town. Go hear him. He never tries anything fancy. The man is a master."

"I want to do things that Schröeder-Deviant never dreamed of," Gerald said.

"Gerald, you will recall that Guido D'Arrezo discovered in the Hymn to St. John, written in 770, the hexacord *ut, re, mi, fa, so, la.* Since the 11th century, all that has basically changed in music is that we have changed the *ut* to *do,* and finally *si* to *ti.*"

Gerald stared hard at his mentor. There were beads of sweat on the Professor's high forehead.

"He who behaves as a tissue behaves," the Professor spoke to the ceiling, "becomes free . . . you may have many voices, but only one throat . . . ."

"It's an angel's voice, Helmut," Nelly interrupted curtly. "A strange, dark angel, perhaps; androgynous, superhuman, uncanny."

Gerald left them remonstrating each other in *Hochdeutsch*.

To get to the practice building, he had to cross through the new Student Union, an octagon worthy of Mussolini with color-coded carpeting and modular offices, impermeable sealed windows, fixed executive swivel chairs, a cafeteria and gift shop, provided to ease the students' passage into corporate America. Then he passed through a series of vaulted arches into the queerly lit American gothic quadrangle of sororities, where a herd of sweet-seated bicycles were corralled in the sunset, then across the parking lot to rumpled Hynes Hall. It was in the middle of that parking lot, when Gerald was an undergraduate, that he would stand for hours wedged between the autos, listening to the interminable practice sessions of clarinet, belabored cellos, saliva-filled tubas and moaning damp violas, straining against themselves with such determination, those fragmented melodies, precise, brief, and extreme; that sum of severe atonalities that Anton von Webern must have heard when he walked out into the Salzburg night, lit a cigarette, and was shot through the head by an over-vigilant American sentry.

Gerald waited until the campanile's digital clock blinked 5:15 and then entered the building through a fire door and climbed the stairs to 246.

He pushed his ear to the crack and could hear Bonny B. going through what appeared to be an Englished *Die Winterreise*, accompanying herself pretty well, a surprisingly big voice but without technique or feeling or control, barely competent for a good chorus. Gerald was despondent. Now what to do? He visioned himself in the ocean at the water line of a marvelously clear iceberg. Above him, Schröeder-Deviant at the icy summit waving affably, Coudrescou, the unknown Rumanian basso sporting a Tyrolean hat and shooting stick, a dapper mammoth frozen at the center, and next to Gerald, treading the numbing waters, Professor Selle, remonstrating Gerald for having his lifejacket on backwards, his fingers leaving bloody scratches on the obdurate ice—and then a wavelet fills Gerald's mouth, he spits salty mucous, and looking down into the waters he sees a young girl with a baton directing a band consisting of little fishies, playing mainly flutes before scrolled music stands, no sound track, but lots of bubbles rising . . . and then Gerald watched his fist gradually obscure the doorknob.

Bonny Baginski gripped the piano bench in terror as the door snapped open. "Oh God, thank God," she whispered clasping her hands, "I thought it was one of those crazy niggers."

Gerald's mouth was open, his uvula twanging like a tuning fork. "I'm, I'm, sorry, there is probably a mistake."

"It's all right. I recognized you right away."

"We've met?"

"I mean all the teachers say to go to your recitals and everything."

Gerald's authority, purpose, humor, and civility slipped from him all at once.

"Well, I'm sorry. I thought I had this room reserved."

"That's funny. I've had it this same time all year."

Ziviale 'Bonny' Baginski, sad to say, had the beginnings of her father's body and already the remnants of her mother's face. His large bones in her arms, nose, wrists and ankles, but without his anchoring muscles, or the guywires from hipsocket to trapezius to cheekbone, and high forehead to accommodate them. She had none, to use her own phrase, of the 'enabling conventions,' which Schmar had undoubtedly transposed from Beethoven's 'ennobling convictions.' Her appeal, as it was, lay only in her age, which would likely double at the first sign of neglect, since roccoco beauty, her potentiality, can be achieved only through thoroughgoing decadence or unremitting labor. Her chin was still firm, but her second stomach threatened immediate laxity, and for some unknown reason, Bonny B. wore a halter to expose that doughy expanse, hiphuggers which emphasized only the seams of her panties. Her dark blonde hair was frosted at the tips, and she wore a goodly amount of blue eyeshadow sprinkled with sequins. What would have been valued as a Bloom-of-the-Mouth-Club selection in Lodz or Rekjavik, here was only a red operatic gash, very like those porcelain shepherdesses of her mother's; in short, the sort of girl you wanted to hug or slap, for precisely the opposite reasons that one usually does such things—the first to punish, the second to clarify.

Gerald's weathered eye searched for some object which could serve as a pretext for the next sentence, and seized upon her metronome, a small copper plaque at the base of which commemorated the services of Ziviale Baginski as choir captain at Berwyn High.

Gerald took it in both hands, as Boris Gudonov takes up the chalice before he falls from the throne, locking the pendulum in place.

"*Ziviale,* what a beautiful name!"

"My friends call me Bonny."

"Well, *I'll* call you Ziviale."

"Look, if you want to use the room, I'll get out. But I don't think it's fair."

"No. no. There's been some stupid bureaucratic mistake, and anyway, it's late. Say, have you eaten yet? I'm famished."

And while she had, she wouldn't refuse a pizza.

"Thanks a whole mess, Mr. Fox," she said, and Gerald's temples glowed with shame.

Act III, Scene IV. *A darkened Pizza Hut, crowded with wan Indian Theological students in western dress, and black*

*caballeros striding aimlessly in and out amongst a desultory
citizenry.*

Gerald had vanilla ice cream to deflect the odor of Bonny's
massive pizza. He asked her what she intended to do when
she graduated, curious how Schmar's rhetoric would be fil-
tered, and more puzzled than ever as to what to tell Ed. She was
prettily to the point.

"Grad school, I guess. I don't know what else to do. What
I'd really like to do is bum Europe."

"So why don't you? I'm trying to save up to get to Munich
myself."

"Are you kidding? There's no jobs here an artist would
take. Besides, I don't know any languages."

"So is grad school going to be any better?"

"Better than teaching a bunch of brats out in the sticks or
getting raped in the city. Look, I just want to grow! The shit
they put you through here is unbelievable. Grades, tests, has-
sles. Why do you have to write a paper about a book when
you've already read it? Do you have to take a grammar test to
sing German? Shit, a lot of great singers can't even read music, I'll bet."

"Right on," said Gerald, throwing himself into the role to
prevent the ice cream from igniting his nostrils. "These guys
around here just aren't interested in creativity."

"A bunch of creepy old cockers. They remind me of my
parents."

"*What?*" Gerald cried out.

"Yeah. Fuckin' pigs on a bummer."

Gerald's uvula, etc. was killing him. How many roles could
the kid play? She had gone in one hour's acquaintanceship
from a structuralist critic to an admiring vulnerable teenager
to a pizzeria anarchist.

Bonny took a big bite of pizza; a strand of mozzarella
drooped, inscribing the air with tackyness.

"You know what my mother thinks is Culture?" she continued with a Schmarian full mouth, "Dolls. Fuckin' china dolls. All she does is clean and cook all day and when Daddy comes home he just turns on the TV and drinks."

"Well, maybe, uh, maybe he's tired," Gerald said hopelessly.

"They're just . . . you know the expression—Pollacks? Well, that's just what they are!"

Then she performed a quite charming tight-lipped grin. Gerald could simply not believe his ears. But somehow he had to get more acceptable information for Ed and Emily.

"Well, what do you want to do, uh, after your P-H-D?" he spat out.

He realized that he wasn't even listening to her reply and caught only the last sentence. ". . . marry somebody rich so I don't have to work and can practice all day and perform when I want to."

Gerald was not shocked by the actual comment as he was reminded how self-absorbed and unobservant he was. "Are all the girls already looking for men?" he mumbled. "I mean, do you consciously look for certain kinds of men? I thought that sort of think was passé."

"Are you kidding? Every girl in my dorm has a crush on some professor. I don't care what they say. They all want to get married as soon as they graduate. See, when you're a freshman you're looked down on if you fuck, when you're a sophomore you ought to talk alot about it but probably not do it, but by the time you're a junior, you ought to be fucking somebody or they look down on you. And then when graduation rolls around, all that freedom, all that bullshit, just gets lost, man; they get desperate!"

Gerald smiled thinly and resumed negotiations. "Oh, uh, do you have a professor?" Certainly Ed and Emily would want to know that.

"Oh no, just a boyfriend. He's Chinese. In Physics. Boy,

would my parents die if they knew."

"Uh hum."

The pizza crusts lay scattered about the pan like shrapnel.

"Do you by any chance know Professor Schmar? Like, is he involved with any student?"

Bonnie laughed, almost delightfully. "Oh, Dr. Schmar. He's brilliant, he really is. But, you know, he's not too attractive, and he comes off as just too horny. He's married too of course."

Gerald smiled to himself, smug for the first time in many months.

"God," said Bonny reflectively, "have you ever counted the number of times in a year you do it?"

Gerald at first didn't understand. Then finally blushed.

"My parents would *die*," she mockmoaned, "if they knew what goes on around here."

Gerald concurred with a nod and asked for the check.

He walked Bonny back to her dorm and although he had seen enough to make his report, went along dutifully when she invited him up.

It was even worse than he anticipated. Three girls crammed into two small rooms. The two roommates pushed perfunctorily past him in robes and hair curlers. Bonny didn't bother to introduce them. Her room was papered with a pastiche of headlines, posters and Sunday supplement pictures. Gerald found the bunkbeds terribly amusing, a true sculpture from antiquity.

"I got the single, thank God," Bonny said as she kicked the door shut. The room was puce, airless, redolent of hair spray. Hundreds of cans and bottles were piled up on the pine desk which served as a dressing table, and both closet doors were open, unshuttable, actually, stuffed as they were with so many clothes—more expensive clothes than Gerald had ever seen. Agog again. Hundreds of dollars worth of cosmetics, thousands of dollars worth of clothes—cashmere sweaters, tailored lined slacks, pantsuits, evening gowns!—it was absolutely incredible. The entire Brentwood-Harwell Corporation pouring its capital, siphoned through Ed, into this pea green room and its chubby ingrate whose forehead Gerald was now kissing for lack of anything better to do, seated side by side on the bottom bunk, the cool iron railing of the upper jammed against his neck. Over the top of her mirror there was a large poster with Uncle Sam pointing out from it, and below the headline.

TAKE YOUR PILL

Wasn't that something, though? And the zipper on those hip-huggers was tight all right. He raised her buttocks up, jerking the slacks off, a leg at a time, the flesh ballooning as the casing was removed. *The tone begins with a tightening of the buttocks and is flushed upward past the liver and spleen* . . . Gerald was in a frenzy, though hardly sensual. What he desired was to somehow *stop* her, cancel her out . . . she offered neither resistance nor acceptance. And utterly silent. Was this some passive trick her Oriental engineer had taught her? And Dean Nobile, look at this! Cotton panties. Now wasn't that something, though? And bad breath. My God, could anyone have bad breath anymore? Amidst all those grenade shaped cosmetics, was there no room for a packet of Sen-Sen? And where do you buy cotton panties? How would you ask for them? *Cotton* panties, please? A Peck & Peck tweed suit and cotton panties? All those bottles and still bad breath? *Anchovies, oregano, green pepper, bacon bits, Hegel, degradation conscious of its degradation, Engels, Ravel, Biedermeier, Louis Quatorze, Victor Emmanuel, Trompe l'oeil, Glinka, Dos-toy-ev-skeeeeee!*

He loved her like a first violinist applauding himself, his conductor, his colleagues, the piece just concluded, back of his bow rapping the neck of his instrument, wishing to strike harder to show his appreciation, but mindful of the long-term consequences.

Then she was glistening beneath him, and she spoke.
"Hurts," she said.
"Yeah," Gerald replied. "I know."

Back in the fog of the gothic courtyard, his buttocks creased
with the imprint of the upper bed springs, Gerald revealed
himself as a shark pressed up against the glass wall of an
obsolete Aquarium. He felt no shame, but only that what had
happened was somehow both fully appropriate and totally
unnecessary. It was clear now, however, that he would have
to forego the Baginski Prospect, and most probably relin-
quish the Territory completely. But how to get his samples
back? Cranach has required him to place a considerable de-
posit on his Presentation Kit.

Gerald grabbed a Charburger and soon had the van out
beyond the second ring in the heavy acidic rain. The dossier
had served its dramatic pretext and activated his adrenalin.
But what the hell was he going to tell good old Ed? That his
daughter thinks she's sexy, but isn't? That she thinks she's
talented, but isn't? That she's no bombshell, no sir, and that
she's screwing a Chink? And that not very well? That she
thinks *they're* dopes? That she doesn't have a chance to make
it? Diagnosis: *Common*, Vulgar even. Could anyone possibly
be vulgar anymore? Was that possible? Was it possible even
to consider, much less call anybody vulgar?
God forgive poor Bonny. Gerald was beyond shame. The
entire nation had become a gross artifice, an opera in which
words were only pretexts to be engulfed in tone and texture,
silly little words which had only the most cursory effect upon
the action, a little snow fence to give the blizzard of tonalities
a name, a frame, a price . . . but no matter how ridiculous
when examined isolate, no matter how eventually obscured
by spectacle and ingenuous polyphony, still, those little words

once tugged everything *back* to them. And now those words, entire rhetorics, jargons, librettos, were flying out *away* from the poor singers; Schmar, Selle, Bonny, each with their great balloons of metaphors, clots of locusts, lemmings, dirigibles of stale lozenges, hoofing it out over the horizon, dotting the landscape with great blobs of reprocessed mucous and simulated lava, while "the audience" could only watch in a kind of dignified slouch like Ed Baginski before the *Evening News* gripping a cool Pabst like a grenade, hidden from his prophets and governors, even his progeny, sonic booms of language *preceding* their fragile aircraft. *Boom,* the windows rattle, the septic tanks groan; *Boom* and you look up and *Boom* there be no starfighter, no lunar beauty, but a great balloon of gaseous residue, and quite a while later, taking its own sweet time, comes your Spad, or blimp or pigeon, or maybe the Queen herself astride a bridled swan. And Gerald saw himself then in the robes of an exiled prince, brandishing a barline, a section of the iron fencing which surrounded the campus, flinging it through the great clots of text, the flags of German, the ribbons of French, the strands of Italian and the grand motes of English, poems without music, poetry without poets, and then Gerald thought, unlikely for his practical mind, that it is only the sickest societies which let language get out that far ahead of them, and he thought again of Bonny, *Die Winterreise* racing away from her, and for the first time since his bad car wreck, Gerald Fox cried.

How could such an exceptionally human couple produce such a monster, a monster mediocre even in its monstrousness? And finally, who was he, unrecognized parasite, slick purveyor of housewares, debtor and professional student, exiled to the drudgery and indignity of performing in churches and colleges, to tell *them* anything? And even if he was Schröeder-Deviant himself, shouting from the top of the iceberg, what authority would that have provided? Did he not share Bonny's cynicism and frustrations if not her sloth? Who was Gerry Fox to push anybody out of the boat? He attempted to deflect his thoughts with a Cranach tape.

Will you go the final step? Ask the question directly, if all else fails. 'Do you mind telling me what's standing between me and your order?' Tell them any Bad News before you close, but don't discard your Standard Story! And don't feed your ego! Sell the prospect. The only real question is really— by rail or by truck. . . .

IV

*Nations do not always express the
same Passions by the same Sounds.*
Mr. Addison, 1711

JUST BEFORE TURNING into the Baginski's driveway, Gerald
pulled over, took the penlight from the van's console and
illuminated the roof of his mouth. The polyp had grown
measurably larger, perhaps due to his recent exertions, or perhaps the jalapenos on the Charburger. He tried the two-tone,
sottovoce, and it was firmly there. He resolved never to examine, nor reflect upon the growth again.

Emily met him with a hug, her hip crushing her daughter's
most recent dampness into his abdomen. 'Well, I just don't
have the light touch,' Gerald thought, 'I'm a huggermugger.'

"This being the boys' night in," Emily giggled, "I'm going
to make myself scarce. But I think everybody is pleased with
your things. Maybe you ought to let Ed handle it. Don't come
on too strong, you know? Sometimes, it hurts more than it
helps."

"I know."

Emily had on, incredibly enough, a blue Empire gown, no
makeup, not a jewel, with that black hair tied severely back
from those fine temples. *Fear no danger to ensue/The Hero
loves as well as you!* And when she opened the folding door
to the dining room, Gerald could only suck air.

The table had been set, not for dinner, but a kind of mock
buffet to display his wares. Each of the laminated photos of

plates had been garnished with a different strudel or tiny fruitbread, placed precisely so the patterns were still visible. *Polonia Rosé* was in full bloom. Each Cranach knife had been placed on a Damask napkin, and a set had been constructed into a pyramid in the center of the table, as halbards were once stacked in baronial halls. A photo of an entire place setting of *Holy Stars* was set off with a service of some strange alloy; the forks had tines of carved bone, on the handle an imperial crest.

"Oh, Emily," he sighed, "that's just incredible."

"Let your hair down a little with our friends, Gerald. I'm sure you'll get on just fine." Then she disappeared into the kitchen.

Gerald feigned nonchalance as he marched to the sunporch. The News was on, and in the theatrical glow of the gro-lights, all of Emily and Ed's fine friends seemed to be uniformed. "Sorry I'm late," he said softly.

"Hey Gerry, there you are." Ed jumped up and gave him the left hand. "Great you could get here." Two others struggled up from their chairs, each keeping an eye on the tube.

"This is the fella here I've been tellin' you about, guys. Studies at Schiller with our Bonny? Real fine boy, and working his way through too. You don't hear much about that sort of kid anymore, eh? Gerry, most of the *Berwyn Wolfpack* is what you're looking at."

They were all huge men, big as Ed and perfectly at ease in the claustrophobic sunroom in the moonlight. And all standing now, except for the oldest man with an enormous pocked nose and a goiter on his neck, who remained slumped in what was, apparently, a place of honor. 'They are all superior people,' Gerald thought to himself. 'They are all grown up.'

"This is Asa," Ed went on, pointing to the seated old man, "our president elect."

"Glad to meet you, sir," Asa said, but his gaze remained steadfastly on the TV. "Or what's left of me is glad, anyway."

"Just call me Gerry. I was an enlisted man myself."

This brought an enormous guffaw from Wally, who was introduced as the best machinist in the city. And then RC who is in 'insurance,' with a Prince Valiant haircut, striped slacks, vinyl boots, and finally Ron, wrists as thick as Gerald's calves, a little distant from either confusion or awe, who Ed said was in recapping.

"Really?" said Gerald, wondering what it was.

"Boy, just look at that guy," Asa waved at a flickering Walter Cronkite, "Now there's a real man for you. He's seen it all. But he's got no emotion one way or the other."

"He's a good old boy," RC intoned.

Walter C. finally got around to the Dow Jones and an exemplary anecdote, and Ed reduced him to a star which whooshed from sight. "Let's get started," he said, and the chips and cards enfolded magically. Ron got Gerald a chair, and clapped him on the back. "I hope Gerry here's no pro."

"I'll watch for a while," said Gerald, "maybe I'll catch on."

Gerald had been fully prepared to feign enthusiasm, but in fact was fascinated by the effortless intensity, the sinuosity, of their game. And now he could see that while they were not exactly uniformed, each had on a khaki shirt with flap pockets and epaulettes, and over their hearts, each bore a custom patch of the *Berwyn Wolfpack,* a great seal upon which a golf club was crossed with a fishing rod; embroidered in the interstices, were a scarified grouse, a bowling ball, a die, and a frothy mug of beer, across which, the slogan, *Preserve American Heritage. The Right to Bear Arms,* gulls.

The table glittered with small change. After each hand, one of the players would show Gerald his cards, encouraging him to regard his strategy, the others explaining patiently what had gone right or wrong. All of them had hands big enough to hide their cards, except for Ed's right, of course. Cards were flipped in the air or dashed to the table amidst curses, false threats, bad jokes, monologues which trailed off into guttural oblique name-calling, all that is wonderful precisely because there is no point in recording it, excited Gerald—the harmless irrelevance of it all thrilled his compartmentalized disposition. Their heavy thighs jarred his when they lost, and in gleeful victory his knees were gripped beneath the table. Slivovitz smuggled in by Polish submarines alternated with an aluminum keg of chewy beer sweating in the corner beneath Emily's gro-lights, the African violets going through their second coming of the day. Only a single card showed, the one behind Ed's missing index finger. Diamond, heart, jack, queen, spade; they all looked like cunts to Gerald.

He was amazed that no matter how much they drank, the men never seemed to lose either their intense concentration or self-control. Perhaps this was due to Emily's swift, silent entrances with plates of steaming *pirogi*—as if the melting crust insulated their collective medulla, effortlessly transforming alcohol into translucent triglycerides which charged out like Hussars, achieving a rapid series of small victories, securing the always vulnerable, historically contested state borders of the liver.

And suddenly Gerald realized that the enthusiasm he had so carefully prepared and then so unconsciously lost, was exactly that of those tuxedoed entrepreneurs hauled by their silver-haired wives to the opera, and more, that the *Berwyn Wolfpack* was performing for him in the same way and for even the same reasons he wished to *provide* for them—the exuberance of watching someone else play, utterly self-absorbed, by rules only vaguely apparent, but actually as complicated as they were strict; to play *at,* as well as in spite of, an arbitrarily pronounced role, to play in a way that whoever was watching, couldn't.

The slivovitz caused him to drowse. The game had become static as Berlioz. Ed was losing badly, RC was winning big, and suddenly after folding on his draw, Ron leaned back and putting an arm around Gerald, mock-whispered, "Hey man, is it true that you artists get more ass?"

Gerald glanced across to Ed who was pushing his chips away from him as if they were scraps of fat from a roast.

"Well," Gerald muttered, "enough I guess."

"Boy, I'll tell ya," Ron went on, "I used ter work for the phone company, and I used ter go up to Schiller in the fall to those dorms and install those little pussies' phones, and I'll tell you, I just about creamed in my pants, out of my fucking mind, I'll tell you. You could hear those pussies snapping in the halls like a fishmarket."

Gerald couldn't repress a silly giggle.

"Hey Gerry," Ron slapped him on the back again, and now in public voice, "You ever eat pussy?"

Gerald tried to think of something funny, but nothing was going to stop Ron now. "Tastes like shit, don't it?" Ron the recapper grinned.

The table quieted. Ed glanced out to see if Emily were in earshot.

"Yawk," Ron yelled, slapping his knees, "you just took too big a bite, little boy!"

The table dissolved in tears, and Gerald wept for the second time that evening.

Ron hugged him tight again. "You're a good old boy, Gerry, you're all right."

Asa's mouth was open in a soundless apoplectic roar, and Ed raised his hands like a referee.

"Allright, let's take a break before I got to get a new mortgage," and they filed into the dining room past Emily's Cranach buffet.

"You got some pretty nice equipment here, some pretty nice things," Ron said, "A quality line."

Gerald's role had been revived. "Yeah," he said picking up a cleaver as the cassette slid into neurological contact, "Here's something your grandma didn't have. This is for real heavy work, Ron. In other words, if you're going to really whack into a corn cob or a melon, that's what this is for."

Asa broke in, "I remember my mother having to take an axe to a Hubbard squash."

"Oh dear," said Emily, "I don't think we have a squash."

"That's all right. I believe old Gerry here."

"Well, it's all guaranteed, Ron, I mean, except for misuse. I mean don't try to take your hubcaps off with it."

"Haw, you're a good old boy, Gerry."

"Now look at this beauty," Gerald brandished the carving fork, "No more chasing your bacon all over the pan with this baby . . ."

But just as he was about to hit the lyric strain, Gerry glanced up to see Ed waving, winking, grimacing to him from a half-opened bedroom door. "Hey Gerry, let me show *you* something. What I built myself."

Gerald's mouth was open at midpitch. He couldn't believe it. He *had* them all right there, and now the crazy son-of-a-bitch was sabotaging it. But the spell had been broken, and he had no choice but to exit, slumping off stage right, with a small wave of resignation to his audience. Ed backed into the bedroom, shrugging apologetically, and finally grinning like a small boy caught out, pointed at a gun rack with glass door and a brass lock, but for some reason, painted red. "I antiqued it," Ed said helplessly. "I shoulda left it natural."

"Mr. Baginski," Gerald took over with a good imitation of the Dean's tone, "I've made the acquaintance of your daughter."

Ed Baginski stood still and sane as a tree, staring into his guns.

"And I have heard her sing."

Ed Baginski put his hands in his pockets without moving.

"And we have talked . . . spoken . . . I believe I have a fair sense of her situation."

As if he could stand it no longer, Ed wheeled, "Well, whadya think? Have I got problems or not?"

And now Gerald Fox dropped the Dean's tone, switching into *Schmarese;* the Schmar who was not only the hit of Faculty Firesides, but had even been asked to address Alumni Luncheons! "These are new and complex times. It is difficult ..."

"Just tell me the facts."

'The Facts?' Gerald reflected. 'Where to begin? With Copernicus, Darwin or Freud? The relationship between the sexual revolution and the automobile, the desacralization of art, labor theory of value, the impossibility of classical tragedy in a Democracy? The ambivalences of the Middle Class? Consciousness raising, the dissolution of the nuclear family? The conspiracy of intellectuals against the laity? Which of Schmar's florid categories could best satisfy Ed's quandary here?'

"Well, you see, Ed," Gerald began, clearing his throat, "Adolescence in America is prolonged."

"How long?"

"Well, that's the problem. And there are natural strains in the family fabric where the adolescent hasn't a defined role."

"You mean, like a job?"

"Yes, or marriage. Things of that sort."

"Is that why she don't clean up her room? I mean if you're mean to your mother and sloppy, if you can't even make your own damn bed, how you going to hold down a job or be a nice wife?"

"Well, you've got a point there."

"What if she were *your* daughter?" he blurted. And Gerald was so moved that he reverted to the classic Schmar/Nobile defense.

"Maybe it's just a question of believing in something; all of the old gods are dead . . ."

"Yeah?" Ed snorted. "What's that got to do with Bonny?"

Gerald knew he had lost the sale. A Cranach reminder was appropriate. *Don't leave a bad taste.*

"Mr. Baginski, I think we should look at this as a problem to be solved. It's hard to diagnose. If it makes any difference, I don't think Bonny is much different in this respect than her peers."

Ed had slumped down on the edge of the bed.

"I tried to get her to go to pre-dental school. Wouldn't she be better off there, Gerry?"

"We'd all be better off in Dental School, Ed."

Ed wiped his nose and almost chuckled.

"Look . . . but what the hell do they *do* there?" Ed barked. "Why are they all so goddam unhappy there?"

"Ed, it's just too complicated. You couldn't really explain to me how Brentwood-Harwell *works,* now could you?"

"Well, I see your point . . ." then he paused, "Well, but really and truly, how about travel? You think that might help?"

Gerald had to restrain himself. Yeah. Travel for Z. Bonny B. *A lot* of travel, that might just be the ticket. Put the bitch on the road. Let her shack up with some weird dude and come back home with her buttocks stuffed in her ears. She'd make her bloody bed then. But he felt his hand moving to the xeroxes in his coat pocket. Which one should he hand over? Bonny's application or the Dean's recommendation? Should Ed be lulled, bemused, or should he be provoked into deserved, righteous wrath?

"I think she's made other plans," Gerald said, and handed over the Dean's letter, as hopelessly, helplessly, as he had received his own certificate from the same small white hand.

Ed read it carefully, quizzically.

"It's no guarantee she'll be admitted," Gerald mumbled, "and he doesn't say anything about a scholarship."

"It's a nice letter," Ed said, extremely pale. "So she's gonna stay in school, huh?" Then he took a deep breath. "How many years *is* that, Ger?"

"Around . . . four," Gerald found he was losing his voice.

"Four more years?" Ed sniffled. "Just like the Presidency, huh?"

"Ed," Gerald had hit rock bottom, "Ed, if she fights with you, it's just because she loves and respects you so much that she can't deal with it. See?"

"Yeah, sure. Well thanks, sir. I mean Gerry. I can see you went to alot of trouble . . ."

Gerald thought he might weep again, but Emily had gently eased herself in the door.

"Ed? Whatever are you doing? Our guests are just milling around."

"OK, OK, Em. Just showing Gerry here the old artillery."

"Well for goodness sake, Ed, this isn't like you," and she took two fingers and slapped him on his good wrist.

As Ed hustled out, his polyester slacks screeching with each step, Gerald tried to catch a glance at *their* closet, but it was Emily who was now in the door, giving the cue, winking, pointing, gesturing with her head to come on *out!*

Onstage again, Gerald saw that only a real *tour de force, a succès d'estime* would gain his commission.

"Hey RC, shake hands with that," he took up the patter, pushing a carving fork into RC's hand. "Isn't that something, though? Generally speaking when you buy a fork like this, 99¢ of every dollar is in the handle. You know, I had one lady tell me that the fork was worth the whole set if it prevented just one burn in a lifetime. Did your Missus ever pick up a roast and have hot grease spatter all over her arm?"

RC looked at him aghast. Then Gerald realized he had confused RC with Ron of recapping.

But he had regained the general attention now, by the traditional method of holding a note too long. The programs and wraps had ceased rustling, the house lights were dimming. He could sense the front row of faces gazing up at him attentively, through the glare from the pit.

"Our spatula is heavy enough to pat a hamburger patty," he bellowed, "yet flexible enough to flip a link sausage."

"Quiet, everybody, quiet now!" Emily cried out.

Gerald regarded her incredulously as if the prompter had suddenly ceased mouthing the text and began to sing himself. 'What in the hell are they trying to prove now? Damn her eyes! Bonny was right about them. They *are* creeps.'

Gerald grabbed RC's arm in desperation. "Now tell me, RC, we'll just work this whole thing out for you. How do you like to do business? Cash? Or is it on credit like myself and the rest of the people in the US of A?"

Emily continued, utterly unruffled.

"You boys have had your game now. I thought we'd do something a little different tonight. Gerald? Wouldn't you sing something for us?"

Gerald's Cranach face folded like a camellia blasted by frost. His uvula filled his throat. His long delicate fingers became the flipper fists of a demon.

"Hey what a great idea!" Ed boomed, though Gerald was unable to detect any similar enthusiasm from the balance of the *Berwyn Wolfpack*.

"Bonny won't sing for us you know, Gerald," Emily went on softly, and with considerable dignity. "She says she only wants us to hear her in recital."

"Well, some artists are that way . . . you know, persnickety," Gerald mumbled. "But I don't really want to interrupt . . ."

"Please, Gerald. I had the piano tuned yesterday just for you."

"Emily, I'm no good at accompanying myself."

"I know. Of course, I know. Frieda, come out here."

The kitchen door swung open, and a thin nervous woman

in a patterned housedress appeared, physically a dead ringer for Wanda Landowska.

"Frieda's one of *my* friends," Emily announced. "She studied in Cologne before the war, and she gave our Bonny her first lessons!"

Frieda wrung her hands. "I haven't played professionally, Mr. Fox, since I was a girl, and my arthritis . . ."

Frieda would not meet Gerald's stare. For Christ's sake, the poor woman hiding in the kitchen for hours, waiting for Emily to ask him to sing. He took her long veined hands in his. They were somewhat stiff and clawlike, but he could feel the vestiges of practiced ligaments in the elongated swollen knuckles. Frieda brightened immediately, "And vat will you sing, Mr. Fox?"

What would he sing? The Cranach singspiel? *A hand is only as good as the knife that's in it. When they think of a knife they should think of you!*

> *Oh, cut clean to the plate*
> *You'll get a nicer slice.*
> *Of all things we peel and pare*
> *They're all 'round aren't there?*
> *No, you've never seen a square vegetable*
> *Except maybe frozen peas.*
> *But what if you want only half a package?*
> *Against the grain*
> *You'll get more tender meat.*
> *Try it for yourself,*
> *Just draw the blade across* here!

"I got some music in the car," Gerald mumbled as he backed out, humiliated.

As he fumbled in the briefcase out in the van, he found two of the recital pieces, the Handel and Purcell, and at that moment, he recalled Cranach rule #8:

Master Salesmen say that the awful silent moments may be the most fraught with sales-making potential. *So make the quiet moments pay off.* Today's hole-in-the-wall operator may be tomorrow's biggest buyer.

He re-entered the Baginski's home by the back door, through the statuary garden, for reasons unknown to him.

The *Berwyn Wolfpack* was seated in folding chairs about the fine old upright like the Budapest string quartet. Frieda was busily adjusting the stool between her legs. How many scales Bonny must have tossed off on the old instrument, her hardened netherpuss driving that screw stool right through the linoleum. Gerald handed over the Handel to Frieda, who exclaimed something favorable in what Gerald presumed to be an Alsatian accent, and they went right to it, the opening aria of *King Xerxes.*

> *Frondi tenere e belle del mio platano amato,*
> *Per voi resplenda i Fato . . .*

He found that given the exertions of the evening and even without warmup, he was nevertheless in good voice.

> *Ombra mai fu de vegetabile cara*
> *ed amabile soave piu*

And Frieda, sight-reading brilliantly, had the tempo exactly right. Gerald finished, flushed, and Frieda gave him a small pinched smile, obviously afraid to bow and applaud in such a democratic milieu, but after Emily had clapped politely, everyone relaxed, and RC laughed, "I think you got the wrong ghetto, Gerry. But I like the tune."

Ed was still applauding unconsciously, interminably, with his head cocked to one side like a hound dog just exposed to a new whistle beyond human range.

"Hey, Ger, translate it for us," RC said.

"Well, uh, the scene is a Persian summerhouse in the courtyard of which is a plane tree."

136

"A *what* tree?" Asa demanded.

Gerald was suddenly terrified, as he did not know. The one time he had seen the opera—he recalled that it had been staged less than a dozen times since its opening failure in London in 1738—the set offered something which looked like a rubber tree.

"If der is und American equivalent," Frieda interjected tersely, "it vould be the Hackberry."

"Oh great," muttered Asa.

"Well, anyway," Gerald went on desperately, "this is a late work which strives to be both funny and sad at the same time."

"I don't understand how that can be," Asa whined.

"It's vat *you* are," Frieda snapped.

"The song," Gerald continued hurriedly, "is about a king, who is declaring his love to . . . a tree . . . you see."

Asa suddenly bit on his hand to stifle a laugh, and Frieda gave him a furious stare. RC hugged himself tight and he looked at the ceiling.

"You are paying too much attention to the *story!*" Frieda barked.

"And the king," Gerald went on, "also wants to build a bridge across the Hellespont to unit Asia with Europe . . ."

"Why?" asked Asa.

Gerald ignored him, fearing Frieda would explode. "He is declaring his love to the tree because the tree is so beautiful, the shade is so soothing, and because he feels slighted because his declaration of love is answered only by a rustling of leaves. That's why it's both funny and sad."

Asa nodded. "I get it. OK. He's a king, after all. If he wants to love a tree, nobody can tell him any different, right?"

"Why don't you sing something in English for us, Gerald?" Emily said, not so innocently.

"Just one more then," he said, and after a brief whispered conversation with Frieda, they heaved out Purcell's *Evening Prayer*.

Now that the sun
Hath veiled his light
And bid the world goodnight
To the soft, the soft bed
My body I dispose
But where, where
Shall my Soul repose?
Dear God, even in Thy arms
Can there be
Any sweet serenity?
Then to rest, Oh my Soul!
And singing, praise the Mercy
That prolongs Thy days,
Praise the Mercy that prolongs Thy days.

Hal-le-lu-jah, Hal-le-lu————jah!

"Hallelujah," cried out Asa, and *Hallelujah!* the group joined in. There was a brief moment of collective awe which obviated the ritual applause, a kind of spontaneous calm out of some forgotten, pure athletic respect, as if for the revered air into which the notes which lay so harmlessly upon the page had disappeared, as motes. And thus Gerald Fox concluded his peripateia.

"Now that's one helluva song," muttered Ed.

"Whatta pair of pipes," confirmed Asa.

"You haf," said Frieda, standing up and giving him a short bow, "a fine future. *Warum sich schwere, Gerald?* Danke for this evening, Emily." And then she disappeared back into the kitchen.

Gerald suddenly felt faint. Both the roof of his mouth and his groin burned. He asked Ed for the bathroom, and Ed turned on the light to the basement stairs. "Emily's been washing underthings in our tub," he explained the detour.

As he descended, he could hear Ed: 'Hey Em, we're going to have a professor in the family."

Once in the basement, Gerald urinated convulsively, and

then against his vow, examined his mouth in the mirror of the medicine cabinet. The uvula was fiery and the polyp seemed to have increased in size. But after a couple of gargles, the burning subsided and his throat seemed to open up again. Exiting from the bathroom, he headed for an open basement window to get some fresh air, and fearing a fall, flicked on the fluorescents.

The room was apparently an ongoing remodeling job of Ed's. Half a wall was paneled with scraps, half of the floor tiled with multicolored squares, half the pipes painted in dayglow colors; the framing for a bar jutted out from a vinyl scroll of water softener tubing.

And above the place where a sofa would be were pictures of *Bonny's Progress* from a bebanged sailor-suited little twat on a tricycle to a graduation picture with rouge-tinted cheeks and a page boy. On either side of the photos were two large display cases, one with a collection of knives hung against green baize; including a German SS dagger, a Norwegian fishing knife, a Balinese ceremonial curved dagger, a Samurai sword, a machete inlaid with mother-of-pearl, and a buffalo bone handled skinning knife. The others he couldn't label. *Viva il coltello!*

And in the other case was a set of the most exquisite Herend hand-painted porcelain he had ever seen, in a Chinoiserie pattern, obviously once too delicate to be used even in a great Polish country house, once prized, now only to be parodied, its rigor now pretentious, its outrageousness mere sentimentality, its history obscured, its uniqueness a burden. He thought of his own poor wares upstairs, he marveled at the accuracy of the Cranach marketing computer, celebrated the well reasoned resistance of his clients, and finally, he resolved never to forget that mote of silence—that sudden break in routine at the end of his brief recital—not recognition specifically, but the shared perception that there exists forms to get you back the world.

Higher than he had been in years, Gerald Fox turned off the lights and ascended the dark stair to gather up his wares. His first missed sale in some time to be sure, but over all, he could hardly be resentful.

The *Wolfpack* had retired to the sun room, and as they took up their choral interlude, a storm came up. The windows flashed with lightning, and as the power went on and off, doors throughout the house were opening and closing; then utter darkness and terrible thunder.

When the lights came back on, Gerald saw that Emily had already packed his sample case.

"Maybe you'll run across our Bonny at school," she said, handing him his order pad, "and if you're not too busy, maybe we could have an evening here when you could both sing."

"Wouldn't that be something, though?" Gerald muttered.

"Well, I hope you enjoyed our friends," Emily said.

"You're very lucky," Gerald replied as he backed into the storm, "and you deserve to be . . . Oh, I don't have a pepper shaker, Emily, so keep the butcher knife as a free gift."

And thus it was that Aeneas left Dido holding the dagger to her breast and sailed off to his destiny.

Back in the van, the wipers undone by the torrents of rain, Gerald checked out his little futuristic polyp. 'Someday those fuckers will read my name in the papers, and they'll put up a fucking plaque on their door . . .'

> **Here in the house of Baginski**
> **Gerald Fox**
> **gave his first salon recital**
> **for the**
> **Berwyn Wolf Pack**

'That's what the fuckers deserve, to hear me on records and never see me again.'

140

Then obediently, he put on the Cranach *After Sale Selling* tape.

... failures are measurable and therefore manageable. Be honest with yourself. Did you observe the fine line between the Enthusiastic and the Bombastic, between Dedication and Fanaticism? Did you wear your smile upsidedown, or like a cat in a canary cage? Did you avoid puffery, use short words and avoid worn out ones? Did you top your customer's stories, or interrupt them? Did you practice your silent selling ... ?

Gerald snapped off the tape in a fury, tried to cram his order pad into the console, but he noticed that it had been meddled with, and fearing for the integrity of carbons and serial numbers, stopped the van to examine and smooth the hexacordal layers of manycolored tissue.

Inside he found six sales contracts, each filled out in Emily's charming lucid hand. The entire *Wolfpack,* it turned out, had each taken a set of cutlery and china. Asa predictably had chosen *Peacefulness.* RC, *Frosted Leaves.* Ron of recapping, *Holy Stars,* and mute Walt had reaped the *Falling Wheat.* Not to mention Emily's full set of *Polonia Rosé.* Almost $2,500 in commissions alone. Maybe a record. No, he would spread it out over time. If it were a record, Cranach might make him take their prize two weeks in Honolulu.

$2,500 would get him to Munich, get him out of Schiller, beyond Schmar and Selle, beyond the conspiracy of Bonny B. and Dean Nobile . . . Cranach might even be persuaded to open an overseas branch . . . and in the great hall of the *Statsoper,* before a real audience, Gerald would dedicate a third encore to the *Berwyn Wolfpack,* and might even slip in an old two-tone, the voice of the future, in Emily's memory.

The van slipped through the storm like a stool from a baby.

V

Is that someone singing about me?
Mr. George Handel, *Xerxes*, 1738

SCHMAR WOKE HIM early with the phone.

"Got a gig for us, Gerry, fifty pieces each."

"Where at, Schmar; I'm really not up to much."

"The fucking cathedral, where else? Some memorial service. And I've got better news than that. Pick you up at three
o'clock."

Gerald went over to the Holiday Inn and had a lumpish
buffet brunch. Then he cashed the checks, sent the sales contracts off, made a plane reservation on Lufthansa, and spent a
good part of the afternoon staring into his mouth. The polyp
was subdued. He probed it lightly with a ballpoint, but
gagged before he could see the reaction. He recalled the base-
line of a Renaissance motet: *'If ye exorcise my demons, what
of my angels . . .'*

Schmar was nothing if not prompt. His enormous station
wagon smelled of soiled laundry, pet food and kidsmucous.
In the coming Apocalypse, what would become of Schmar's
station wagon!

"Got great news, Gerry. We got the grant for the Sympo-
sium. $35,000 bucks from Rockefeller. Can you believe it?
I've already got a title. 'What's Wrong with Music.' Or maybe,
'What *is* Music,' or 'Whither Music.' Anyway, I can commission you to do a gig."

"Jesus, Schmar, that just takes the cake."

But Schmar was burbling even further than usual beyond insult. "How about a panel on 'my favorite characters in opera' then? If you don't want to get into theory."

"There are no more characters, Schmar. Only virtuosi."

"Yeah, yeah. Well, how about 'the death of opera?' You know, art as ridiculous people in privileged positions."

"An artist now, Schmar, is simply someone who controls the destiny and price of his product, that's all."

Gerald wanted badly to tell Schmar about that mote of silence at the Baginski's. But how to explicate? Perhaps he could give a lecture on The Baginski Syndrome, or 'What, in fact, is in our Basement.'

"I got an idea," said Gerald testily, "I could give a lecture on the music that hasn't been written for me yet."

"How about something more p-positive? The Art Song as the Culmination of Bad History and Bad Poetry—alone at the bend of the piano, solemnly progressing through four centuries and five languages, a trial for all concerned . . ." Gerald shook his head venomously.

"What do you want me to do," Schmar cried out, "Get down on my hands and knees?"

"You know what I hate most, Schmar?"

"What's that?"

"People who try to kiss my ass. And miss."

They pulled up at the rear delivery door of the newest university cathedral which had so mystified the community that it had been billed, "built not by human hands." Its "contemporary gothic" was faced with that curious lannonstone quarried apparently from the very same pit which built Baginski's block. The stained glass abstract picture window at the front entrance, "symbolizing the universe" ("the swipe of red in the left hand corner represents God's love") in contradistinction to all Christian theology, was hidden from the worshippers by an air conditioning unit, and so rather than casting a roseate glow upon the congregation, shone only *out,* assisted florescently, for the benefit of the cruising rush hour traffic, visible *both* night and day, they advertised, incandescent through the severest storms, giving off, Gerald just realized, the very same tint as Emily's sunporch.

Dear God, even in Thy Arms
Can there be any sweet serenity?

'Oh, Christ, nice new cathedral, couldn't they just leave you alone? Couldn't they have just settled for a nice toothpaste box of a building with some counseling rooms, a snack bar, maybe even a little bowling and Savings and Loan, rent it out to Kiwanis and Speech Therapy conventions to pay off the mortgage? How come, cathedral, your spire's so squat? Is that contemporary? How come your flying buttresses are straight? They didn't put rooster weathervanes on Chartres, you know, those are *gargoyles,* fellas, *make-believe* animals, you know—but you wanted a *real* church, like the front window says, 'this is *a* cathedral, *our* cathedral!' So how come you foreshortened the choir, converted the presbytery into lavatories, the sacristy into a coatroom, bleached the pews blonde, installed brushed aluminum tapers, lopsided the cloister of Christ's boat with folding vinyl doors and padded the ceiling of our nave with acoustical tile . . . *Great minds against themselves conspire| And shun the cure they most desire . . .*

"So what's the scenario?" Gerry asked meekly as they walked into Edith A. Perkins Memorial Chapel.

"Beats the hell out of me. All they want is a Prelude and a Recessional. That's what they said. You got some music with you?"

In short order, they agreed on the Handel and Purcell and donned their robes.

"Don't worry about the tempi, Gerry. Just watch me,"

Schmar said, "I'll give the signal, and remember, I got the brakes and the accelerator right up there." And he disappeared up the stairs to the organ loft.

Gerald seated himself in the small anteroom off the Choir which contained several chairs, a washbasin, reserve candles and a commode. He realized he was past exhaustion. To hell with Munich. What he ought to do is hit the Riviera, abuse and indulge himself in every way possible, and then hole up in a deserted resort town at the end of the season and clear his head, perfecting nothing but the *two-tone*. With that mastered, a good agent, a couple of talk shows—who knows? . . . another, deeper John McCormick? Except that he would sing his own accompaniment as he sang the song, that pure one man monody with figured bass—before polyphony had obscured the word, and the vocal and instrumental were indistinguishable.

Then he heard some chimes strike, and Schmar began to fill the House of Worship with the great clots of solemn chords and *ritornelli*. The crowd had apparently begun their entry. Suddenly, the door to the anteroom flew open, and Gerald recognized the fine gray curvelinear temples of the University Chaplain, an Academic All-American tackle at Schiller a generation ago. The Chaplain did not acknowledge him, however, and lifting his purple and white cassock, slipping off his beltless bellbottoms, he plunged down, like some tropical waterbird, on the commode. As the cassock settled to the floor, so did his expression, and Gerald studied his score redundantly. When the Chaplain arose and silently beckoned Gerald unto him, they emerged onto the Chancel as one, and then like stunt planes trailing their colorful airbags, veered out of formation, the Chaplain to the pulpit, Gerald to the choir, where he had the best view of Schmar hidden from the congregation in the loft.

He sang the Handel with almost pop casualness, without

the score, hedging where he usually bore down, concentrating instead upon the audience in an attempt to determine the the ritual in whose name they were gathered.

There were no more than fifty people out there, scattered randomly in the shampooed pews, a respectful well-dressed older audience, a center slice from the great pink double-cured picnic ham of real life, gripping their telltale programs, glancing from their glistening shoes up to Gerald and finally up to the semi-vaulted ceiling into which his notes disappeared like buckshot into bread.

What in hell was on the program? Maybe it was a memorial service for the guy who built the place? But he recognized not a single face, academic or administrative. Had Schmar somehow gathered together his "Generalized *Other*," the respectful mute, to certify Gerald's futility and isolation?

He pulled his robes about him and seated himself in the choir. After a series a jaunty transitional soapopera chords, the Chaplain arose. Gerald glanced up at Schmar—who was giggling uproariously as the organ swelled with requisite fatuity, the perfect mockery, the apotheosis of Schmar's brand of anarchism, perfect because it was both riskless and appropriate, inoffensive to anyone powerful enough to punish. Nevertheless, Gerald found himself engulfed by uncontrollable laughter, and fearing he would appear an embarrassment, slunk back to the anteroom where he realized that he could not hear the *Invocation*, and so was denied any further clue to the purpose of the occasion. But the *Sermon and Benediction* were apparently concluded in only a few moments, and in the midst of a nightwatch of his uvula, Gerald was startled to hear the funebrous chords suddenly break into the continuo of the Purcell, and it was necessary to stride rather too dramatically back to the choir. He was furious now, his skull and entire frame buzzed with the Recessional text . . . indeed, the congregation which had arisen, suddenly looked up, and slumped, slinked back into their seats.

Gerald stared down the nave at the rubies of the *Exit* signs, the walls hung with liturgical banners:

> I was sick, and you visited me
>
> Treat the Living as though they were dying
>
> I was a prisoner, and you came unto me
>
> Go to the ant, thou sluggard, consider her ways and, be wise
>
> A false balance is an abomination to the Lord; but a just weight is his delight
>
> He that withholdeth corn, the people shall curse him; but a blessing shall be upon the head of him that selleth it
>
> Here I stand, I cannot do otherwise

and the ten side stained glass windows, those great abstracted metaphors which were their only common environment, a plaque below each to decode the allegories, to the left:

Commerce   Space   Communications   The State   The Races of Man

and to your right,

Healing   Law   Discovery   Literature   The Arts

Look here, if you squint a little, and use some imagination, there's a lamb's head signifying the Lamb of God, and a stalk of wheat representing *food,* and a bunch of, yessir, grapes, representing the *Communion,* folks, and four little fish, each with a cross on their backs, an ancient symbol, no doubt, and, Great Scott, here comes a horse, symbol of *Dignity,* and following a turtle of *Patience,* as opposed to, of course, that serpent of you know what, and the two test tubes there, symbolizing both the *Age of the Atom* and the *School of Pharmacology,* ranked third nationally, and all the doves of course; a little dove symbolizing the *Unborn Child,* a bigger dove, the *Spirit of the Law,* a hunkering dove, the *Creative Spirit,* a dove on the wing, *Freedom,* and the biggest, grayest V-shaped

147

swooping Dove-of-All, bearer of God's Love to Earth . . . hit
those brakes, Schmar! . . .

> *To the soft bed, to the soft, the soft bed*
> *My body I dispose*
> *But where, where shall my soul repose . . .*

A few members of the audience seemed for a moment to
break out of character; one rather portly man in a three piece
suit at the rear stretched his arms out to Gerald, just as when
in the London autumn of 1734, the unremarkable basso,
Girolamo Senesino, while playing "the tyrant" to Farinelli's
"captive in chains," was so moved by the castrato's lament
that he forgot his role and embraced him—*When they think
of a knife, hey, they should think of you!*

To finish off the Handel with Purcell became all the more
appropriate, as the purity of the Air swelled above the ground
base, as Gerald realized that the entire history of the sung
English tongue had been irrevocably deflected the moment
the simplicity of Purcell had been abandoned to Handel and
the *Royal Academy:* those florid, loaded adagios, the vulgar
athleticisms, the extraneous deviations, the absurd entangle-
ments, the cheap psychology, the visual spectacle, and above
all, those obsessive metaphors which even the King James
version couldn't save which had culminated in the secularized
stench of Schmar's theory, like those cornfed Venetian clouds
which burst forth heavy choirs of marching, badmouthed
eunuchs.

Against the respectful and dutiful silence which now surrounded him, he would have preferred the girls' prep school
where Henry Purcell could at least marshall a manners which
was also a discipline. He would even have taken his chance at
the Royal Theatre of Turin, where the boxes extended onto
the stage, each equipped with fireplaces, card tables and beds,
where the performer would have to overcome the incessant
drone of social conversation, political negotiations, grum-

bling and lovemaking issuing from the mansion which engulfed him. Where he could be hissed for taking offense at a waiter who dropped a tray of roasts and sack in the middle of his otherwise unbroken *legato,* would endure his colleagues breaking character and talking to friends in the audience, joking with the orchestra during *his* aria, and when their turn came, sabotage the drama by singing an aria from *another* opera, one which more suited their voice, emptying his exacting acting of any meaning—all entrances, exits without regard to probability or motivation.

If you'll just put your okay right here, folks; we'll work this whole thing out for you.

Gerald completed the cadenza as well as he had ever done in public. And now that "public," thoroughly confused, all continuities broken, fumbled for their programs where they had dropped them, the Chaplain glaring at him with each mounting crescendo, and then Foxo let him have it, on the last syllable of the first *Hallelujah,* a perfect two-tone of *voix mixte,* and while lost upon the congregation, Gerald heard the organ stutter as if in disbelief, and he glanced triumphantly up at Schmar who was literally openmouthed in amazement. Gerald Fox finished with a silent selling series of false echoes and embellishments from the chest which made the "organ" seem a mere word.

He noted that a few people who had originally begun to leave had moved down a few pews, no doubt to get a better look.

But no sooner was the Evening Prayer finished, than Schmar *restarted* the Continuo, ad lib with variations as the player pleases, and on this unprecedented run, pulled all the brass stops and accelerated the tempo. Schmar in effect had challenged Gerald to follow, and our Hero, our King, our Regional Representative, did not hesitate for an instant; indeed, even improvising a trill on the first redoubled cadence.

149

Schmar matched him with an enharmonic embellishment of oboe, and then his ultimate fillip, the seldom used banks of two thousand Ruckpöstiv and Brustwerk pipes.

But Gerald responded effortlessly with a roulade of one and a half octaves of stunning rapidity. Taking off from a D-E flat, he hurled the notes to the loft, neither words nor sounds precisely, but distended spheres, mucoid globules of energy unattached to anything . . .

He spat his Hallelujahs into the framed and named allegories, shat Pure Phonics into the Symbolics . . .

There's something for ya, *Commerce, Space & Communications;* and here's lookin' at ya, *The State & The Races of Man;* and hey, hi, *Healing, Law & Discovery,* wasn't that something though? And for *Literature & The Arts,* Gerald reserved a *sforzando* attack, holding the dominant notes a touch overlong, thus winding Schmar's tempo down, down . . . down . . . and so the duel was concluded without the audience suspecting it, or even appreciating Gerald's triumph.

Despite his exhilaration, Gerald was only further infuriated that Schmar and he were merely performing for one another, business as usual, The Harry & Gerry Show. He found himself wandering the bare chancel like an empty bar when the last girl has been picked up. As he regressed into the prow of Christ's boat, he could hear only the recess of his audience, the crackle of their programs, and suddenly as he reached the plexiglass Holy Table, looking up through the oily crisscrossed tints of *Creation, Redemption and Triumph,* he saw the outline of the great cross of whole timbers, anchored in the Franklin E. Parks Meditation Court, and whirling about, robes flying from outstretched arms, shouted out, and not *bel canto* either, a translation of the Handel they deserved:

> *Look upon Xerxes!*
> *Inflamed by an ordinary tree!*

And whose love is answered
only by the rustling of leaves . . .

The Congregation had not yet dispersed, though most were already milling in the main aisle. A few turned out of puzzlement, removing the program once again from a vest pocket or purse, some wandered aimlessly, and one stout lady with custard gloves to her elbows seemed to scowl at Gerald's final and undeniably desperate attempt to prolong their encounter, if only to be able to identify the nature of the transaction.

Schmar slumped silent at his defeated instrument.

Well Folks, that's our program! Fabulous, wasn't it? I wasn't kidding you, was I? I won't ask you which one you liked best. Because I really have two jobs. The first is to explain the program, interest you in it. I feel I've done that part of the job. The second part is to work out a way so you can have this in your own home. Do you mind telling me what's standing between me and your order . . . ? Oh, I see, I see; now that's a dandy choice . . .

The doors of the House of Worship have opened. Headlights of the roseate rush-hour halo the Congregation. The great window is blinkering orange, issuing a Driver's Advisory. Gerald dropped his arms, disdained Schmar's incredulous stare, noted that the upstaged Chaplain had stalked off somewhere, undoubtedly to file his report, and suddenly both his condescension and paranoia evaporated into the spongy ceiling with his song.

For Mr. Gerald Fox realized that this was no longer just *his* problem. For while he had achieved a kind of purity—emptying the room of everything except the text, the solitary singer and his page—that now, to take offense, was no longer sufficient. For in his triumph, he realized that *whatever* he had sung, sold, whatever outrage he had committed, that the audience's reaction would have been no different. Their pliancy, equanimity, even their constitutional reasonableness, had been programmed to absorb both his expertise and rage.

Fickle Gerald Fox stalked the chancel as King Xerxes

paced the bridge of his bark as the Greeks destroyed his bridge of boats across the Hellespont. 'And so this,' the King thought, 'is what all our wealth and ingenuity have brought us to.'

Gerald vaulted the Communion rail, and seating himself in the first pew of the emptied mansion, turned the score of the opera from which he had sung only the opening aria, to the final page.

"My friends," he hummed Xerxes' last royal words, *"have pity on me for my anger and rejoice in your loves."*

A perfect ending, of course. Bridges burned and forgotten. Losers look for other lovers. Forgiveness. But this was not the time or place for yet another perfect ending.

A dolphin in the forest,
A wild boar on the waves

A requiem for Christmas future

We must act AS IF *we were lost, desperate beings . . .*
—Van Gogh to his brother

WE'LL START WITH MOULTON. He's my brother and the important one in the story, which is also about Mom and Dad and poor big sister, Rita. I'm known as the genius of the family because I remember what everybody else says. But I'm no genius. I never made up a thing in my life! I simply remember and wonder, like most people. They think *I'm* brilliant because I can repeat what *they* say. And recite for guests, of course. My teachers say I've got a photographic memory, but with all due respect that's a sloppy evaluation, since a camera can't hear. Certainly I can remember whole pages of what they tell me to go read, and whenever anybody talks, the words go across my eyes like on a movie screen; so it's seeing what you hear and then repeating it that I'm really good at. Please remember that what I'm saying is what other people said—something I've read or heard somewhere—and a lot of the time I honestly don't understand it myself. I'm just thirteen, after all, and just because I got straight A's doesn't mean I know everything. But don't get me wrong either. I do love all those voices in my head. It's just that I don't love one more than another. The other thing to know is that people think I'm not only smart, but cute—and I have the feeling that I'm going to pay for that. Everyone I ever knew who was cute, smart or not, has.

At any rate, when Moulton came home from college for Christmas this time, he was really sullen. Maybe that's all you really have to know about him. There were some sporadic fires in the city, at least there were coils of smoke on the horizon. The airlines were grounded, and Moulton had to take the overnight train, then hitch with a security patrol to the National Guard camp. Moulton has changed a lot since he has been to college, and because Mom and Dad never went away to school, they probably exaggerate it. But having, as I do, a better memory, as well as less to remember, I think it's fair to say that nobody can say just how Moulton has changed, and if they try, they get pretty confused. Mom and Dad aren't against change exactly, just any more change in their own lifetimes. And if you want to know, I don't blame them one bit.

Moulton always had to work for what he got. I don't mean in the way that Mom and Dad did, but he studied five times as long as I ever did for good grades, and made himself into a "competent," as coach says, football player. He was not big or particularly agile, but was born to a certain leverage, an ability to anticipate holes before they open, and in that he could usually beat a bigger man. His specialty was blocking extra points. Invariably, Moult could find the hole, break through, and throw himself onto that foot. His fingers are all broken from it, the knuckles bend both ways. But each frottaged finger signals one less point for *them*—and gains these days are always, coach has said, are a matter of inches! The defense catching up to the offense, if you need a handle for the age.

Because of my talent, my problem, this linotype of words slipping across my cute cobalt corneas, I have always divided people into those who are able to write and those who should be written about. Moulton, for better or worse, falls into the latter category. You and I think more clearly, more demandingly, perhaps, than my brother; but we think almost exclusively about people like him.

It could be argued that no man has been more generally

156

disappointing (and none, certainly, more forgiven), but Moulton gained his distinction from giving the impression that he was lost in a world of his own making. He alone had no excuse but Providence itself. And no matter how maddeningly self-assured or curiously impotent he might seem at any one moment, he always retained an almost ethereal balance. That, I suppose, is what the Founding Fathers were getting at in the *Declaration* when they gave equal weight to the dissonant voices of justice and consanguinity.

When Moult went away, he was wearing a lovet green suit and a yellow tie. His hair was carefully brushed and he wore horn-rims, black and amber like a coral snake, with which occasionally, when you were talking, he'd remove and poke you. Girls took this for vanity, but gradually I saw what he was accomplishing. Not knowing whether he was near- or far-sighted, you didn't know whether he wanted to see more or less of you. He was one up already. He just stood there, slouched in what girls called "conceit" and he called "empiricism," beautifully tentative—the pioneer stance—a man who pays lip service to nature but finally stands in awe only of his own will.

But when he came back, his hair was standing on end as if in the first moments after electrocution, his glasses were rose-tinted and rimmed with golden wire, he wore an old Prince Albert which he had once refused to wear to a debutante cotillion, its velvet lapels spattered with an undistinguished sauce, a $35 Viyella shirt which had been ruined after one washing (explicitly against the instructions on the label, words in a red saddle-stitch which still move across my somnambular gaze), and Lord, our Dad's old white bucks which he could never bear to wear, too big for Moulton, naturally, for Dad is very large indeed, larger than life as they say, but I'm afraid unSanforized. Beauty has gone out of the world, the poet says, and the instructions come to the eye's mind:

The soft tartan will glimmer in the sunlight. But not if you wash it.

As I was saying, Moulton was more withdrawn each Christmas he came back: bittersweet, perspicacious, but reluctant to exercise his perfect control. My own theory, having been forced by circumstances to scan much serious literature, was that his fine preparation had merely begun to lose its dazzle, that his *potential* had become a cumbersome and slightly ridiculous bearward. He no longer fathomed either the sources or the uses of his considerable power. He was becoming more invisible, or rather *hazier,* by the day. I shall never have such power, but I will never be so alone.

"What are you going to do now?" he was frequently asked, and this was not simply a paternalistic question. It was asked by badly acned sailors with whom he had sat by chance on public transportation, by girls with a page boy's hair and function who at parties held him by a single finger of his hand like a child crossing the street, by businessmen who slipped him their card, invited him to lunch, so that he might resist and confirm their lack of prejudice. They all had high hopes for him. They all had their investments, had devised strategies for his better knowledge, and very soon, they insisted, any minute now, he would *go and get it.*

So, as it happened, Moulton was the unacknowledged arbiter, the administrative cement for the irregular shape of our family, and perhaps Mom and Dad secretly believed that he would take care of them properly one day.

I have no further comment on the matter.

Mom and Dad looked up from swabbing out the turkey and rifle, respectively. The air was flecked with beads of oil. Moulton was stomping around, cursing silently. Then he went to the closet, slipped on his parka, flipped me mine, and thumbed me toward the back door.

"Take your gun," Dad said.

"Mind the frostbite, hear!" Mom chorused.

One thing I have always admired about Mom and Dad is

that they almost never scream for more than five or ten seconds. Moult slung a bandolier of shells over one shoulder and strapped the .30-.30 across the other. My .32 was where it always was, in my parka pouch with the hand-warmer. The message across my eyes read: *Get me out of this fucker house!*

Out in the back yard, the wind had frozen the snow solid, and we walked upon it without sinking. It was so cold and clear that you noticed the sun only when you looked straight into it. Mere light. The creek was inseparable from the land. That wind had fossiled everything.

We walked down the middle of the creek toward the "Weeds," blitzing the delicate sewing-machine tracks of fey, lighthearted animals. Moult's heavier feet kicked away more snow than mine, and in his footsteps I could see black water surging beneath the ice.

The Weeds are forty acres of despoiled copse bounded by the creek and a piquant railroad cut. We have lived near here all our short, totally recalled life. The creek is lined with willow, clumps of hemlock, and wild privet. This latter bush is always brittle from either fierce frost or malarial heat, shattering upon our thorny touch. It grows green and flexible only in our forty-eight-hour spring when the creek burgeons and makes the copse impassable. Because of the flooding we had always believed it safe from development. But it was filled with homes now, long low homes of lannon stone and aluminum, sporting wrought-iron trellises, a *fleur de lis* or American eagle on the front door, and garages with percale curtains in the windows. It still floods over, nonetheless, and when the husbands come home on either of our spring evenings, their Oldsmobiles throw a wake like PT boats. The doors rise upon an electric signal, the curtained windows enfold and disappear into the roofline, the scarlet brake-lights reveal walls beaded with the sweat of the comatose. The houses jut from long, whiskey-dark puddles—cork tile, bits of colloidal forest, and hundreds of indestructible styrene toys which span the generations bobbing about—toys older than me!

They still have more money than we do.

Many years ago, once each week, before I could read, armed with ball bats and lengths of pipe, Moult and I went to tear the real estate signs down. It was rather stupid, as I remember, the clanging and fume of sparks as we smashed them down. The first signs were wood; we simply threw them in the creek. Then they erected strip steel; we bent them double. Finally, they set anodized aluminum poles in concrete; that was when we had to smash them down.

I am not at all sure what we were up to.

What is certain is that they have relinquished what we would have prevented. The California redwood oozes orange from their unmaintained casements. Their yards, slabs of yellow mud, are inching their way into the creek. Moonbeams dive beneath rivulets of mud in the middle of the night. The mud suffers in the sunlight where quince once bloomed and wild iris prospered amongst gnarled roots. Through the word SPRING, I can see the old creek running to rise, and between the white eddies our heavenly detritus: tires, cans, bricks, bottles, and great stationary eels of toilet paper.

The moss hung in the willows along the creek has been cut away, and floodlights installed so that lawns, once glazed white for guest arrivals, are now illumined for the unprescient prowler who shall be blasted from the night.

Nobody outside today. The men are home, yes, all home. From each house, headlights peer out from the curtains; thick smiles of pumpkins, rushing the season.

Moulton arched a snowball onto a front yard. I remember when he thought, not so long ago at all, that he was better than they were. I asked him about this, but he didn't answer. I am beginning to suspect that Moulton thinks too much about his life to think properly at all. Maybe that is his problem. The hardest thing to understand about this world is that nothing is true to the extent that it is widely understood. And I am developing a theory about people like Moulton. It's that everybody normal is born with this ribbon of words in their heads like I have, but they stop seeing it after a while because they worry about themselves too much. They stop seeing what they're listening to; sending or receiving. Maybe it's true that people get overwhelmed by their "feelings," but all the people I know have been worn out by "long-term planning," as the President terms it. And I wouldn't have minded Moulton giving up so much; it was the self-important way in which he was doing it that bothered me. The truth is, mister, you have to be loved or hated more than ordinarily to pay attention to that telltale tape. And I have been loved a-plenty. I suppose, eventually, it soon dissolves into the red webs of one's eyes, and comes out, if not as tears, then as that yellow stuff in the corner. Or somewhere else. Who knows.

When you're in the Weeds at night now, and the headlights crash back from the picture windows, I remember the only house I loved as a former child—before I learned what the words meant on my "window to the world," as the newsmen say. It was just a white cement-block shoebox of a house with windows running all the way around. The poor guy had put it up a year before the expressway was built, and they arched a cloverleaf right through his front yard. After that, every time a car took a turn, its lights flared up in his living room. You would have thought he'd thrown up a hedge, got out, but he never planted anything and stayed. He must have had a lot on his mind to do that. He must have just sat in his living room sipping brandy with a big dog at his feet, just leaning on back with neither book nor fire, studying the patterns of light sweeping the wall, and not a little warmed by the glare crackling through his glass.

And I wondered what he did now with no traffic, no snarl and thud and haste and honk, no lights save the blue strobes of the patrols. I remember watching Dad when you could go to work in the city, when the expressway had just been finished, watching him from the ridge, his big puce car caught between the other sealed and waxen commuters, exhaust fumes rising over the splattered dogs, asphalt seams smacking, smooching, popping, as they went to get the money before it got too dark.

We're in the silent trough of some gigantic wave.

We followed the creek until it dodged into a culvert beneath the expressway. The traffic was sparse; the orange light for general security was lit. Only an occasional coal truck, weaving to avoid the potholes. Pretty soon the old green Zenith would be plowing along the median strip, her upper windows busted out for machine-guns, the bar car filled with monitoring equipment and a complement of security patrol.

In the dark of the culvert, Moulton again stomped and cursed. No ice here, the water coursing over my boots, and light, nothing save light, such blinding light, at both ends.

As we emerged, Moulton reached back and took my hand, but instead of continuing into the Popular Forest, he turned up the embankment, back toward the expressway. We then crawled beneath the barbwire and jumped the restraining barrier. The four lanes were badly buckled and faulted. I looked both ways out of redundant habit, and then, as my brother again took me by the arm, I knew what was coming up. Chicken.

Chicken was a game. We had played it with the Zenith when she was still a commuter.

Moulton led me over the northbound restraining rail and out onto the median strip. His hands were cold as the tracks we knelt over. I gave him one hard look and then lay down. I hadn't forgotten how. The tape was wet and blurry. I was damned if I would cry. I knew the rules. Moulton pressed my head onto the rail and turned my face in the direction of the Zenith. Then he lay down solemnly behind.

I tucked my scarf in, the rail was cold, and I could hear the hum of something not such a long way off after all. I wondered about the patrol and if they might take a pot shot at us. I wondered who they might be carrying besides the usual army officers, priests, doctors, and dreary journalists.

The humming became a dull recognizable beat; then it began to syncopate. I looked down the rail like a rifle barrel and could see a boggling light. It was coming fast, this one. Maybe VIPs, or wounded. I was not yet either curious or scared, and this surely didn't recall our good old times together. The way things were now, it seemed a little, well, "self-indulgent," as Dad says sometimes, probably too often actually, and the other voices in my head were fogging over, diving under water and gurgling echoless.

That converted tank of a green streak was closing in, and the rail whanged my cheekbone. Whoever took his ear off the rail first was the Chicken, so I reached behind me to grab Moulton. But he was too far, I couldn't reach him.

"Moult," I muttered, but no answer. Bluffing, the son of a bitch. It was mean of him to pull this. I hadn't survived all his petty bullying for nothing. So I stayed put, my jaw aching, the snow soaking through my jeans. The light was in my eyes. I was the smallest of his lies. It was like looking down through the ocean at an old console TV with plankton glowing where the picture was. It wasn't like it was when Moulton used to lie on top of me until I gave; it was as if he were trying to punish himself through me, his only brother. So I thought then I would really scare the pee out of him and lie there right until the last moment, until he screamed and screamed.

But only the train and me were screaming. And that train wasn't socking on the brakes like she did in the old days. If anything, she was speeding up. I still wasn't scared, mister. But I did feel a little stupid. That rail was shimmying right along the ties now, and then my legs were scrambling even though my brain was welded to that steel, and then I saw my cheek was frozen to the rail, and I flashed on a newspaper clipping about a dog that got his tongue frozen to a street-light in Lebanon, Indiana, and the whole town gathered around him, and finally, they cut the streetlight down and carried the dog and the streetlight, still connected, into the fire department until they thawed.

Moult!

The scream didn't come from my mouth. It came out of my whole body and *that* scared me. The Zenith wasn't twenty yards off now. My head was an inch off the rail, my cheek skin ripping away, and then a piece of the lower lip. My tongue was thick with blood. I had been waiting for Moulton to be grabbing at me, to be screaming too, to be helping me, to be calling me chicken, you're the chicken, but then my body saved my brain, popping me off that steel like a band-age off a wound, and my ears were full, the words had stopped and I saw the scream as I rolled.

Er, Er, Er, Er, EEEE

And instead of my life all over, which, of course, would have been so boring, brief, and inconsequential, there was time in those few seconds to run through the alphabet a few times, as the carriages clacked monotonously along the tracklets. I kept my eyes closed in the ditch, but through the slits I saw the guards' helmeted heads go by me upside down. They wouldn't waste a bullet on a corpse when there might be real trouble ahead. I spit out a lump of something. Still no Moult. I waited until the sound of the Zenith was gone, and then the funny thing was, I crawled up the embankment to look for my flesh on the track, but it was shiny, shiny as a gun barrel, "Clean as a whistle," as Dad says, a phrase which I have never understood.

164

I put my hand to my face, the only manly thing to do. I covered one eye to take my mind off my bad lip. And then, something like a pirate, I looked around for Moult. His tracks crossed the tracks and were headed across the southbound lanes toward the Popular Forest.

Obviously I should have gone home right then and told Mom and Dad, but they wouldn't believe that my own brother was trying to bump me off. For one thing, there had been so much killing lately; easy, unpunished killing, along with what Dad calls "unjustifiable melancholia," that if he wanted to do somebody in, it didn't have to be me.

I followed Moult's tracks as they entered the Popular Forest. A cut of trees had been taken out for a fire break. Down the cut, across a junk pile of old radios, the railroad and the expressway, you could see straight through to town. On top of the bank was a sign telling the time and the weather. No clock or thermometer, just numbers changing every minute with the new time and cold.

It was 10:45 and 9° when we went in.

The creek was tangled with dead vines in the forest, slow going. Besides, the cold air caught in your lungs if you went too fast, and I needed to breathe easy. I went up to my crotch in a snowbank and took the occasion to soak my mouth in clean crystal.

Then I saw Moult, about two hundred yards ahead where the bridle path begins, but suddenly he hit the ground, and I heard the .30-.30 speak twice. At first I thought he might be going for me, and I froze, but then I saw he'd fired twice and hit the bear in the throat and the nostrils. I had forgotten about the bear, that fine plywood springboard bear with red pants, cowboy hat, and official badge who rears up, tripped by a laser beam, at all entrances to the Popular Forest; his lips are human and in his clawless, white-gloved, three-fingered hands he holds a sign, mulled with buckshot.

Moulton was up then, cruising at his old lope, frost trailing from his mouth as from the exhaust of a sports car. He'd lost some wind at school, but I still had trouble gaining on him.

It was hard going even on the bridle path. I broke through the snow into drainage ditches twice; Moult's path almost disappeared. The snow was pocked with pools of sludge as if a herd of filthy animals had shaken themselves off there.

I passed a large drift from which an arm and leg protruded. The sun remained decorous in the svelt sky.

I clambered up an embankment, cleared the woods again. Gray links of lake appeared between the trees. The top-heavy forest slanted toward me. Bristly locust and splayed pine, stunted from sun by the larger lumber long gone. I was feeling used up too.

It got steeper and slipperier near the bluffs. I was bent over from the cold and looking for hidden holes. I kept fogging my sight with my own deep breath. Then I heard them. Bells. Not churchlike, but electric. I scrambled up the rocks until I came to a plateau. Beneath the snow you could see the outline of a softball diamond and the stakes of a dozen horseshoe pits. A series of slit trenches were lined with tanbark and broken crockery. Moult's trail crossed the infield and ascended a rock garden. The dwarf evergreens had been uprooted and the imported stones piled in cairns. Up in the treetops on the edge of the bluff nested an enormous egg. I yelled Moult's name into the wind. For a minute I thought I could hear him crashing along above me, but then the bells blotted out everything. They were coming from that big egg, I knew. My legs ached and my feet were soaked. I wanted to butt a tree in desperation. I was losing interest as he lost me. I was tired and confused. I dismissed the egg from my mind. The drone of the bells became absorbed into the natural din of the forest. My heartbeat dropped a level and warm for the first time that day, the perspiration trickling down the lining of my parka, I headed for the lake.

The trees ceased at the bluffs, slate abutments permitting nothing but winter lichen. A simulated birch railing had been erected by the State, and I picked my way along it to the end of a short promontory where there had been a picnic parapet. I pressed my stomach against the railing and leaned over the edge. The lake was frozen solid. It stretched away, angular and ribbed as a gull's wing. At the beach, deeper currents forced up geysers through the jagged ice. They came up inky, turned green at their topmost point, and then fell back invisible upon the ice, amidst the rusted turrets of several coast guard chase boats.

The bluffs were called *Oconomawak Bluffs* after an Indian chief, one of those Indians who leapt into space rather than submit to our forefathers. They were looking for treasure (our forefathers) and when they didn't find it, they destroyed Oconomawak's village and chased him up here, where he jumped, or so the story goes. I don't think, myself, it was a very good place to look for treasure, but whatever, on the parapet there is a bronze plaque commemorating the chase, and bearing the words *Lest We Forget*. I have never understood exactly what it is we are not to forget, but whatever it is, I wish I could. I have an idea, though, of what went through the *Chief's* mind. There had been, from his point of view, a terrible misunderstanding. But I can't even imagine what went through our forefathers' minds as they chased the Chief up there. Whatever did they think when, after breaking breathlessly through the foliage at the summit, they found no trace of an enemy—only a vast inland sea and the treasures of the empire still hypothetical upon the horizon? No wonder their portraits are so sullen and severe.

I sat down to wait for Moult. Somewhere down the bluffs

the egg was blatant. Out of breath on the parapet, I wondered if Moult was running away or searching out, and figured that was probably our forefathers' problem too. We never did get this straight, and now it's too late.

Down in the Weeds, I could hear our most recent forefathers opening cans of tunafish and flushing the oil down their johns. I did not want to be alone, not at all. I just didn't want to be alone with *them*. I wanted their fluorescent light *off* my eyes, my walls. But sitting like a stupe on the bluffs was also profitless. It was merely preferable. And as any foreign person knows, that is not sufficient. I stared at my boots and gazed down at the Weeds. It would serve Moult right if I showed up all a-whimper at their doors and begged them to organize as search party for my poor brother, only to find him warm at home while they were sloshing around with their guilt and guns. As a matter of fact, maybe those people in the Weeds, if not as smart or sensitive as Moult, were braver? They at least were putting up with things, keeping the porch lights on. It was funny. Moulton still felt above them yet hated himself at the same time.

Shit. I had begun to run again.

The bells increased their tempo and resonance. And then I found him about a hundred yards into the trees, gripping a cyclone fence. His arms were stretched out above him, his fingers entangled in the mesh. He was standing one foot upon the other, as if caught in the midst of a leap.

Then I yelled, but Moult didn't move. I screamed falsetto. Not a flinch. I ran crazily toward him waving my arms. But it was like he was in a movie and I was in a booklet. The wind burned in my nose and teeth. Slag heaps of ice, roots and earth had been bulldozed against the fence. The great egg in the treetops revolved imperceptibly but constantly, its booby bells chattering endlessly. Steam escaped from a small hooded funnel. Perhaps in my craze I had lost what Mom and Dad call perspective. I could not even remember being that close to carelessness before. Distant machinery droned evenly, wearily, warily, wolverine. There were shouts, I thought, but I could not see what was said. Moulton's head had dropped back; his face impressed with the crisscross pattern of the fence. The nice sky rolled back above me. I dropped to my knees, and grasping the network of steel in one hand and Moult's calf with the other, followed his gaze.

It rose against the forest like a . . . like a . . . an icicle? A steeple? A totem pole? A fountain? A Louisville slugger? A naked lady from a cake? What can the comparison matter? Ivory, finned, oblique, pert on a khaki crane, rusty, slightly arrested. The bells stopped abruptly, the machinery ceased coaxing. A dull shadow mottled the radar's egg.

It had started out as a secret, then gradually became an abstract idea, if in fact there's any difference. Nobody knew what they really looked like, even through the wars, until they went, for some reason, for a brief time to the moon. I have no idea how old this one was. Older than me, certainly, probably older than Moult, though not quite so old as Mom and Dad. What I remember best is not the silhouette, which we still had to memorize in our civil defense course, but that once you could sign up for a four-year hitch, play a lot of softball and horseshoes, and come up from the underground with a four-year education and a marketable career skill. I wonder what happened to those good old boys.

Moult was still gaping ceremonially. I was getting more and more disappointed with him.

The rocket had now swung out of the silo doors, and it was going *errr errr*

They were automated before I was born and, shortly thereafter, disarmed after never being used. *"Our* holocaust was not collective," as my favorite teacher, Mr. Howe, says.

The government had built amphitheaters around most of them, declaring them national monuments, and if the truth be told, Mom and Dad had courted right here, I think, or maybe it was the one down near the breakwater in the city. Dad said once that watching them was the only fun thing he can remember about that time, although their discussion since has spoilt many a supper.

The radar egg revolved on its magnesium spindles, our fathomer, listening to everything in order to see, but understanding, remembering nothing. Slivers of ice cascaded down the concrete bunker. I don't get mad easy, but I was fed up now. I put both arms around Moult's waist and yanked him from the fence. The steel netting twanged violently against its posts. I felt his powerful thighs contract. He was in what they call his prime. So what. What dutiful enemy could he now brutalize? The Chief had leapt long ago. And with the secret leverage of a diffident child, I soon had him pointed where *I* wanted to go. I steered him from behind and stepped up the pace. He ran naturally once I got him started. We charged up the path and along the slope to the summit. I held fast to his belt so he wouldn't outdistance me again. I ratcheted my elbow against the birch fence to keep us on course. Soon we were back at the parapet, gasping for breath over the edge.

Out in the lake, a convoy of squat tankers, bows aflame with rust, bulled their way through the ice toward the reactor. More supplies. And down the shore, the Private Gun Club was in action. A man in a red jacket flung skeet with a hand trap. Another broke them consistently, dotting the beach below with black and yellow clay. But because of the wind there was no report, only a cartoon puff at the end of the barrel. I gulped wind to kill the nausea, and Moult sucked too—longer, deeper inhalations syncopated with mine. Moulton was smirking.

The wind had become stronger, turning our sweat against us, so we left the parapet and returned to the woods, where we sat down at one of the picnic tables by the defunct horseshoe pits. Moulton cocked the .30-.30 and pushed it butt forward across the table to me. We faced each other, hands on hips, our debate mere clots of vapor which coalesced, then evaporated between us. I refused to take the gun.

Finally, Moulton folded his arms judiciously, elevated his gaze to a point slightly above my forehead, and with great solemnity, put his index finger to his temple, cocked an arched thumb, and fired!

"It's as easy to smile as to scowl," I said, appropos of nothing, and, withdrawing my curled hand from a parka pouch, forced my fingers into a mock pistol.

We played guns without our guns, but not for very long. After a while you reach that point, the long rich arc of paralysis, when the bells stop ringing and you've got to go back to The-Hotel-in-the-Rain. You get tired of asking, explaining, commiserating, making up sense. Quite frankly, I wished my brother dead.

And when something like that happens, so deep, pathetic, and unspoken, pretty soon you just get up and start walking again, not together but merely proximate, nobody leading, nobody following, letting the gaps in the Popular Forest decide the course through a light and swirly snow.

Crossing the creek again, we followed it until it skipped through another culvert at the main highway. The underbrush was coiled, twigs thickened with sheaths of ice. The water there was frozen solid but still stank of tankage. Then we took the cloverleaf into town.

The sign on top of the bank said it was warmer and later than when we started.

We got some broth and bologna out of the vending machine and took our lunch down to the park. In the park there was a tremendous rose garden with sixteen canopied trellises radiating from a cupola. In the summer, it used to be that a helicopter would take you up for five dollars, to get an aerial view of the pattern. There are supposed to be over three thousand different varieties of roses, but they're all red from up there. Each one, though, has its name written in Latin on a tongue depressor stuck in at the proper root. We went to the cupola to sit where there would be less wind. The bare vines twisted up into a turret, like a bombed cathedral, held up by its very cracks. Through a hole in the floorboards, I could make out some rusted machinery. It was just possible we were on an old revolving bandstand.

Moult took the rinds off his bologna. We ate for a while, passing the soy broth back and forth. Through the ashes and snow, a million tongue depressors poked their sepulchral heads. A helicopter hovered over us for a while, then headed for some plumes of smoke on the western horizon.

When we finished lunch, a scruffy sparrow minced into the cupola and toyed with a bologna rind. I peered down each of the archways. The arbors were swathed in plastic bunting, making the garden seem a machine wired for some immense computation. It was depressing, surrounded by all those names and not a single flower.

And that takes me back to my childhood and the laws of things. None of us enjoyed very much being a youngster, I think. That derives from having parents who had nice child-hoods and then a tough row to hoe, so they tend to link us with their childhoods rather than their adult lives, which no doubt are pretty messy, though it's true they try to spare us the details. They gave up things for us, I guess, as no one will ever give them up again. But when a child is celebrated in such terms, all he can piece together later is how cruel he was. I don't think all the loving in the world is going to make any difference now. As Dad says, often and with a strange guttural accent, we're going to have to be very, *very* smart to get along without him, implying that the future will require more than a sense of irony.

I didn't know what to say any more, or even how to stop, look, and listen, so I asked Moult if he wanted to go over to

Rita's and he nodded. And then it was *my* turn to take *his* hand.

Our sister Rita lives with the parents of her husband. They are going to have a baby. I am going to be its uncle. I never visit them if I can help it. I fear for every child added to this world, exceptional or no.

Drifts along the main road were piled high as the mailboxes and packed hard from many plowings. We walked on top of them, six feet above the road; our heads in the leafless trees, occasionally striking a soft spot and going down to the crotch in powdered ice. It was sheer luck that Mrs. Nadler came along just then.

She was waving up at us, looking blue through the tinted windshield of the last Cadillac, but smiling—and, boy, was I glad to see her! If there was anybody left who could straighten Moulton out, it was Irma Nadler.

"And where are you going?" she throbbed, "on the day before Christmas? Do your parents know you're out?" Then she guffawed and her neck disappeared into her shoulders.

Moult, staring down, managed a lofty wave.

"Come," Mrs. Nadler sang out, "I am breaking the law by stopping for a hitchhiker, but I will give my favorite guy a lift."

I clambered down the bank and Moult followed, scowling like a satyr.

As you may have surmised, Mrs. Irma Nadler was our Jew. I don't know whether she considered herself that before she came to live with us, or rather the other way around, since Dr. Nadler had bought the first land here when the monastery began to reduce its holdings, but now she knew, I guess.

Dr. Nadler bought out here when it was still a horseradish farm and sold off piece by piece. He has four acres left, right in the center of us, the only house you can't see from the road. He's left all his trees standing and has neither lawn nor guns.

Irma Nadler was the only person in my life whom I liked more and more.

The last Caddy had pearl-gray leather upholstery folded and stitched in contours like human brains. Explosions of ganglia ran through the polished spaces where the Nadlers sat most often. From those, you could tell that Mrs. Nadler drove when they were together because the death seat was polished by a tiny pointed behind, which sat very near the window and put all its weight on the armrest, like a puppy, and Mrs. Nadler's behind was not small at all and hardly pointed. She wore her hair piled on top of her head like a whetstone, and affected the usual formless dresses and enormous brooches of those who have learned to celebrate their own creased weight.

Moulton got in back, giving me bad-ass looks. I got up in front with Mrs. Nadler. She patted me on the knee and accelerated.

"So where are you goin, sonny? It's on my way."

"Going to see our dear sister," I said, "and you know where *that* is."

"A lot of suffering there . . . terrible suffering . . ."

When Mrs. Nadler said "terrible suffering," it sounded like "table soap-ring," and that somehow authenticated it for me.

"It sure makes Mom and Dad sad," I began.

"They got used to," she snapped. "Now it's for you to."

We drove on in silence for a while. Moult was fidgeting with his gun in the back.

Mrs. Nadler tossed her massive head.

"The world has become very cruel," she said to me in a stage whisper.

It was getting very uncomfortable in the car because Mrs. Nadler had her first-class heater on wide open.

174

"Say," I said, "do you mind if I turn down that heat a little?"

"Sure, sonny," she said, "third lever on the left, down and to the right about an inch and a half."

We went on in silence, getting cooler. I was wondering if I ought to be keeping my hand-warmer and pistol in the same pocket.

Mrs. Nadler swung the heavy car from the road and banged over a curbing into the parking lot of the *Pick'N'Save*. She glided along the sea of stalled and stripped autos for a good five minutes, the engine laboring at low rpm. At last she found a space and fell upon it. As she got out, she half-turned to me, speaking softly.

"I notice you got a gun there, young fella. I'm hoping it's not greasing on the car." Then she slammed the door.

We sat in the cooling Cadillac and watched the mothers on the ramp to the supermarket. Mrs. Nadler was slowly grinding her way up, clinging to the rail, a mauve duck in a shooting gallery. The *Pick'N'Save* had had its windows shot out so often they had filled most of them in with cement block. Which is just as well because flies had hatched in the thermopane and kept crawling up and down the inside the windows. They could never get out to bother anybody, but they still could drive you crazy. And the stench from the offal trucks was unimaginable. It was Christmastime, and the food store shouldn't stink for Christmas! I held my nose and looked up at the *Pick'N'Save* sign. It was a big wiener that touched ends, and right in the curve of the wiener was a man, and from where I was, the wiener went in his mouth and came out of his behind, and this was the least part of this gigantic wiener.

Now the "Jew Canoe," as Dad refers to it, was getting cold. Mrs. N. had been gone almost half an hour. I didn't like the look on Moulton's face. I said we'd better go get her.

We got out, locked the car up, and headed for the ramp.

The *Pick'N'Save* doors were still glass and had pink ribbons across them so that customers would not walk through them before they opened.

Most of the people inside were guards. But there wasn't much left to guard on the day before Christmas. The empty produce counters converged to a single gleaming dot.

Suddenly Mrs. N. appeared before us, charging down an aisle, pretending she was going to run over us with her basket, then swerving at the last moment, she drew to a stop, clutching her breast. She had picked up almost everything that was left, and I recall there was a time when Moulton would have called that *gauche*.

"My God, my . . . what a place! It kills me every time, but I love it. Sonny, do a favor and get an old woman some grapefruit. I passed it but I couldn't stop. Then to poor Rita."

Moult and she stalked one another while I went and got the grapefruit, and we met at the checkout counter. I gave the girl the fruit, but Mrs. Nadler took one look and snatched them away from her.

"Not so fast for just a minute," she snapped. "These are having rinds like cantaloupes. "Where'd you find these, sonny boy?"

"I never bought *citrus* before," I admitted, with a little snarl. The Nadlers always had more money than we did.

"Hoo! Never shopping in his life. A man!"

We left the freckled checker girl mulling over our produce as Mrs. Nadler took the lead again. She negotiated the corridors crabwise, her spectacles propped back on her forehead like racing goggles. When we arrived at the fruit bin, a good thirty feet long, Mrs. N. flung the rejects into a corner, and then started feeling over the side like a man searching for a plug in a soapy tub. She never looked, just felt, bringing out perhaps one of every ten she handled.

"Looks ruthless," she grunted, "but it's only smart."

Soon she had twenty or thirty lined up on the edge of the

bin, ordered by touch, ascending in quality from her to the rear of the store. Then she took my hand firmly in hers.

"Now feel, young man," she commanded, "every one."

We went down the row, my hand on the fruit, Mrs. Nadler's on mine, me squeezing the fruit the same as she squeezed me.

"The thicker the rind, the less of life," she pronounced, "you got to feel juice. When it bounces back a little in your hand, then you know that's health!"

We had reached the climax of the fruit arrangement; they were getting juicier, I could tell that, and at last, we came upon two or three almost perfect ones, firm and buoyant as I imagine lemons used to be in Spain and figs in other countries.

"Make them say 'yes' to you," she said, and swept them into a sack. Then she batted the rest back. "Or they will give you rind every time."

We took up our penultimates and marched back to the counter. The checkerette was awaiting us, sagging sarcastically against the cash register. It was clear she found the whole *choosing* business pointless. I could well imagine what she would whisper to her packing partner as Mrs. Nadler left, and I was ashamed for knowing this so well. It is clear that we are going to have to learn how to be picky like Irma all over again.

When we got back to the car, I saw that Moult had splurged on a big cigar. Already the air smelled vaguely of a stable. While Mrs. N. swatted at the smoke, I put the groceries in the trunk. There were some small bullet holes and some funny-looking candelabras in the back of the last Cadillac.

Then we got in and were off, teetering along the drifted salt-stained roads, Mrs. Nadler pounding out a rhythm, going from brake to accelerater to passing gear to brake as from fruit to fruit. We passed through the town, spewing sludge over the sidewalks, were waved through the barricades, and settled into the auxiliary highway where a convoy of supply trucks flung waves of oil and ice in our eyes.

"I wonder," I said aloud but mostly to myself, "if we should just drop in ... like this ... I mean after such a long time ... without warning ..."

"You mean to say," Mrs. Nadler broke in, "you want to make them think you didn't really want to see them, but it's just an accident you're here?"

"I just mean," I rejoined, "that if we just show up as a matter of curiosity, they might take it as an insult."

"My God! So you can't be *interested* . . . in your own family?"

"Not too much . . . no."

Mrs. Nadler repeated my words to herself, biting them off, "not . . . too . . . much . . ." I shut and rubbed my eyes, the only way I have of resting from the words; if I rub enough the lymph goes bloody and blessedly opaque. But my mouth was running on.

"You got to be careful now about how you care about . . ."

"My God. The whole world is now doctors. I'm wondering sometimes how they make a living off each other."

Mrs. Nadler paused, then flicked her eyes to the rear-view mirror and gunned into passing gear. "You probably know my husband's a doctor, and sonny boy, you sure remind me of him. Every night he comes home from the hospital. 'It's very hard to maintain your objectivity in this profession, Irma,' he says, 'but you got to. You can't get yourself involved or your work suffers,' he says. 'Basically I'm a simple man. A medical man.' That's what he tells me . . ."

"Well, anyway," I insisted, "could you stop sort of up the road from the house? We'll take it from there."

"You're hurting me," she said.

"It's got nothing to do with you," I pleaded.

"Or them," she snorted, braked, accelerated.

The auxiliary highway was badly fissured; fragments of

macadam protruded from the drifts. Enormous icicles grazed our top on turns, and the quaint bridges were choked with slush. A pond was fastened to the edge of a dam, where a silent opaque spout arced into a frozen pool below, like a porcelain pitcher handle. Because of the law against cutting in the Popular Forest, most of the orchards had been savaged back to rootstock.

We took the hills and potholes indifferently; the heater induced sleep. The radio faintly intoned the old-timey frenetic commuters' music.

> *Walk right in, sit right down*
> *Baby let your hair grow on . . .*
> *Everybody's talkin' bout a new way o' walkin'. . .*
> *Do you wanna lose your mine?*

But you couldn't stop Mrs. N.

"I know you want to do the right thing. You're trying to be neutral and that's nice. But maybe you're hurting more than helping. Did you ever think of that?"

We both shrugged.

"Listen. I'm just a fussy old woman who shouldn't bother young people . . ."

Moulton yawned audibly.

"*Listen.* People now want to cure all the time, for what I don't know. It's a terrible thing to say, but I'm so very tired of curing. You know what I mean? Everybody wants to be a professional. And they want everybody else to be professional too, so they won't feel guilty. Professional doctors want professional patients and the other way too. But you get down in with them and they are all rough like nuts. And then you got to be professional yourself. To protect yourself. And you're supposed to say thank you for that. Personally, I just like to grab. But they cure you of that. No promiscuoity here. Plan. Plan. Plan. Plan. Plan!"

When Mrs. Nadler finished, I saw just how ugly and flat

the word *plan* is. Then she adjusted the visor to keep the sun out of her eyes and went on.

"I know about *planning* from my Benjamin, sonny. He is a wonderful man and husband and doctor, but he shows you still. In the old country, before, Benjamin could have done anything. He had a strong and beautiful head. His parents were rich. The burghers hated his family, but he didn't care. He was always very gentle. Then he got to planning, or inclined that way. He made up his mind in South France in the middle of a hot summer. They used to go on bicycling trips, all the students, and that year they went to South France. It was the custom to split up and ride out, each on a different road, and then meet back at the inn that night to tell what they had seen and thought of in the day. One of the days, Benjamin rode out on his road. I don't know if it was a fine day or not, but at any rate, near noon, he passed a high hedge along the roadway. He had that urge to look through, my Benjamin's naturally curious, and so he did. He saw a beautiful walled garden with a pool right in the middle. Soon a lovely young lady comes with a palette of paints and lays them out on a stone table. Then she goes back in the house and comes out with a big canvas and sets it on the easel. Someone is painting waterlilies! And soon, like a dream, comes the fabulous old master, all bent over and fat—what's-his-name! Benjamin said he didn't even mix his paints. They were all ready. He just looked in the pool, dabbed at the palette, daubed at the canvas, looked back at the lilies, putting in the sunlight like nothing at all. Then suddenly, terribly, a cloud came over the sun, and the old man stepped back, shaking his brush at the sky, yelling, *'Merde! Merde!'* "

Mrs. Nadler herself grimaced, shouted, shook her fist. Moulton and I were squirming like kids.

"Benjamin ran back to his bicycle and pedaled fast back to town. Right then, he said, he knew what he wanted to be . . . a doctor! He didn't even wait to tell his friends. He took the first train back to Vienna and started in. Now Benjamin tells me that story when we are courting, he tells it to a Belgian architect coming over on the boat, and he tells it to his classes at the medical college, and all the students think it is very beautiful. And you know, I did not understand it at first, or on the boat, and I do not understand now what it has to do with anything! Except that it is part of a plan, and that men will do anything to have one. So you can get off right here to sneak up and help your family."

Mrs. Nadler slammed on the brakes, and I pitched forward into the dashboard. Moult got out and slammed the door. I said "Thank you" and "Sorry" and "Goodbye" and "Sorry" again, and stumbled out after him. The last Caddy swiveled artlessly away on the ice. I didn't have the faintest idea what she was talking about, much less about Benjamin.

Waterlilies? The Mayor of D.?

She had left us on the edge of an old trash pit, which had come to light in one of the thaws; our heavenly bottles, cans, and jars had been coated, submerged, and regurgitated. Scavengers had already gotten most of the good stuff, but I chanced upon a small block of marbled ice, and through the milky glaze a kindly old aproned lady looked back at me. She was cooking. Her lips were parted, she was saying something, the words frozen in a small balloon near her mouth. "I can't make all the catsup in the world, so I just make the best of it," she was saying testily, and I thought I detected a trace of hysteria in her eyes.

I dropped her to catch up with Moulton. I didn't want him starting anything. Through a break in the trees I could make out an inoperative seesaw, a busted birdbath, and beyond, our destination. It was a nice house, but while its three stories remained the oldest, highest in the perimeter area, its striped awnings now hung tattered and sodden from their frames. Their car was up on blocks, the surrounding snow well lubricated.

We approached the kitchen door; an electric fan spun warmth and odor out to us. There was a tree by the back stoop, its lower limbs severed and patched with tar. Strips of salt pork had been nailed to the tree, and a rare cardinal busily gutted one. I could hear the sow they were fattening, rooting about in the garage.

They always had less money than us.

The door was Dutch, and the mother of my sister's husband opened the top of it before we knocked. A forlorn cadaverous cocker spaniel was squirming in her arms. Her hair was red like Rita's and our Mom's, but not so natural. What you might call a flamingo red. But was she glad to see us! I know, because hers was a very slow smile. If not knowing, willing.

"I'm trying to get through on the phone," she said. "Rita and Shel are in the wreck room . . . how nice to see you. Excuse me just a moment."

She waved us in, dropped the doggie, and hurried away. The spaniel turned to go after her, but his claws did not hold on the linoleum so he spun statically for some time before picking up the trail again. Moulton and I stood in the empty kitchen waiting for some signal. The basement door was closed. It was a new door of cheap green slash pine, and you could still smell the sap. In the next room, small folding tables and chairs were set in a circle around the TV for supper. Over the back of a wing chair I could see the top of the man-of-the-house's head. Smoking. And then I realized I couldn't remember their last name.

Rita and our mother, Rose, are very sly and very brave and, for those two reasons primarily, very lonely. They live in a place which has not yet decided exactly what to do with them, so in the interim the people of the place have learned to say, "Do anything, it is your right." They are not lonely because of being sly and brave, but rather they have to be sly so they can avoid "doing anything," and brave as those who have so many "rights" must be. They don't want to be entitled to everything because they don't want to have to do everything. They, perhaps more than anybody else in the world, would like *one thing* they could do better than anyone else, and have absolutely no rights at all. Both of them are redheads.

When Rita was my age, she was just brave. Once we were walking about in the Popular Forest, and one of those fellows from the city, as is still their habit, was waiting for us. He was sitting on a stump by the bridle path, and as we broke into the sunlight around a turn, he got up and started toward us. When he was about a hundred yards away, he pulled his hat down over his eyes and opened his fly. Then he kept on walking.

I didn't know what to do. I knew he could outrun us, and I didn't want to turn my back on him. But Rita knew. She just walked over to the edge of the bridle path, picked up a stick, and ran straight at him. She ran as fast as she could, holding the stick more like a baton than a weapon, her dress and red braids flying out behind her. The man stopped short when she was fifty yards away, and then as she closed the gap, turned and ran, losing his hat, crashing like a blind bear in the forest.

Later on, she got vicious for a time and finally sly, even reasonable. But of course it is high time to be reasonable. We are frankly obsessed with it. After she graduated from school, she went off to the city for some job. Once in a while I'd get a letter from her saying, "I'm waiting till we fall to bits," or things like that. She used to send Moulton poems. He never showed me any. But I stole one once, though I couldn't understand the words. It went (and goes):

> *Death comes. I have come.*
> *To kill my feathered fears*
> *And when I die*
> *A gift returned unwrapped*
> *Pinwheel in small mist*

Then, at the bottom of the typescript, in longhand: "Putting this in poetry seems to be an excuse for getting down thoughts which are incomplete—but there's a certain freedom to it. I forgot to include the usual grumbling noises. . . ."

And then she got married. Vaguely but not effortlessly, sort of second nature. But what is the nature of second nature? Her husband, Sheldon, isn't telling.

Now the conception of their child took place this way. Rita was the daughter of Rose. Rose was our mother, and Rose was the wife of our Dad. Then Rita married Sheldon, at the time of his graduation, and he had two parents also. Michael and Elizabeth, and Rita was found to be with child. And they went to live with Michael and Elizabeth.

I saw Rita's scrapbook once—sneaked, of course. It was made from lumpy orange art paper and had HIM-NAL written on the cover. It was the story of her HIMS: photograps, trinkets, letters, corsages, ticket stubs glued to the pages. Another attempt to prove certain unallowable correspondencies. On the last page was written, HIM OF HIMS, and this was Sheldon's.

Sheldon was sensitive. He had become acquainted with Zen in nonconceptual ways. When Sheldon sulked and was most silent, Rita was most moved. He always talked as if he was in the midst of a blizzard. He was plainly of two minds about this baby. His father, Michael, had a ferocious grin which would have looked better on him if he were cool and swarthy. Sheldon is also an artist. A flutist. Don't ask me why. What Sheldon liked best was to lay the responsibility for the war on his dad at dinner. I'm not sure of which war, but the last I heard Sheldon's dad had the blood of 250,000 Brazilians on his hands. Since her conception, Rita has rarely been moved, and never by his silence.

I do not believe any sentence which begins, "Since the baby" or "Since the war. . . ."

Sheldon, I almost forgot, was known for his personal discovery that success was rotten. These days, the notion has not a little quaintness. Being right, it appears, is no consolation, even to Sheldon.

Those were all the ideas he had.

I often wonder how we got in this fix. You know, if only someone had just gone up to Christ and said, "Look, you just listen to me for a minute. This cross isn't for you. Take my word for it. What are you trying to prove anyway? You don't need it, and you're not ready for it. Maybe if you had really done something to be ashamed of. But not this time. It's too much for you. You want to make yourself better by suffering? Okay. You want to help these sons-of-bitches? Okay. We all do. But I tell you . . . just remember the other guy who suffers, all the time, and that will be enough. Get some education first. We'll get organized. We'll go underground. We need you. Don't you see that? You can't do this *now*. They won't understand. They'll think you were crazy. And some other guy will take up the ball and we'll never see it again. Look. You don't tie your shoes in a melon patch. Right? If you throw this thing down right now and head for the desert, it'll accomplish much better what you want to do. What we all want to do. We'll get organized and come back. And you'll be even a greater man than if you quit on us now. It's worth a try, don't you think?"

Now, if that man had only come along and done his job, if he could have sold Him, *he'd* be the one to celebrate. And I know this sounds pretentious—all right, sacrilegious, but I wish I could have been there. . . .

Wheelwright, dammit, Wheelwright. That's their name! And I started for the basement, Moult in tow.

Mrs. Wheelwright had changed from her housecoat to a pantsuit. Her hair was braided and coiled on top of her head.

"Already Christmas and you haven't killed the pig?" I said cheerily. I could feel Moult a-hulked up behind me.

Mrs. Wheelwright seemed embarrassed. "There'll be other

Christmases," she said, more mysteriously than nicely. "We're having fried egg sandwiches for dinner," she went on. "You stay now. What's Christmas without children?"

"Thanks anyway. Mom and Dad've got something planned, I imagine."

Mrs. Wheelwright was the best cook around, but I wasn't about to get into anything like dinner with them.

The cocker spun out on the straightaway and crashed into a door jamb. Moulton laughed hugely. Mrs. Wheelwright opened the wreck room door, and some music came up the stairs which bewildered us. I searched out Mrs. Wheelwright's unremarkable eyes and she smiled again, a little faster this time. It makes people suspicious eventually, that slow motion grin.

"Rita got a recorder from Sheldon for Christmas. She's done nothing else for a week."

The music welled up from the basement. It was "Good King Wenceslas." Slow, cerebral, but good for a beginner. Rita was playing a hymn for her Him of Hims. But her nonchalance frightened me. I looked over my shoulder at Moulton. He had stopped cold, cocked his head. He was licking his lips.

The music persisted, and we stood by stupidly. Mrs. Wheelwright looked right through us. The cocker ran a widening circle at our feet. Then "Good King Wenceslas" was finished, and she started scales, up and down, gracefully, without a break. They were together down there. She would be sitting cross-legged, performing, and Sheldon would have his fat head in his hands. The scales expanded an octave, growing shrill at either pole. Mrs. Wheelwright was getting fidgety. Moult was waiting for me. The music didn't stop for a minute. I could not break through that recorder. Whatever it was, escape or warmth, play or protest, I couldn't take it. No one said anything. Across my eyes went the thought, *We got no business here.*

But Moulton was already pushing me down the stairs, and

the door behind us closed to with a rush of compressed air.

Rita and Sheldon were sitting cross-legged on a big pillow, and when Rita saw us she stopped in the middle of a rise and handed the recorder to Sheldon.

"Well, if it isn't Boy Wonder!" She was almost always shitty like that now.

"How's everything with you?" I said.

"What will be, is," Rita said, and got up. I noticed that the child had put a nasty little strain on her boyish hips. She was *very* near due. And her face, if fuller, redder, was still beautiful.

"You can't stay for dinner," she whispered. "We've got barely enough as it is."

"Your mother-in-law already invited us," I replied rather testily.

"Then go eat with them," she flounced. "We don't go upstairs at all. We even have our own entrance now."

The wreck room was the basement of the Wheelwright house, but it was another world. Shel and Rita had decorated it themselves. There was no furniture at all, unless you count the lonely white commode in the corner. For chairs they had pig chop sacks, stuffed with buckwheat hulls; their bed frame, a garage door on cement blocks. From the bed her old cold war menagerie of stuffed animals eyed us warily. The damp of the floor was cured by a matting of newspaper thick as garden mulch, this in turn covered with straw. The walls were papered with Sheldon's old flute scores and Sunday editions. So we faced each other, shuffling around the coal stove, us peers, our poor broke-down family, Rita staring at her tummy, glaring at us. I thanked my stars that I was not that kid to come, and I saw the only reason we were together was that none of us wanted to go upstairs.

Moulton spit on the stove, and it sizzled orange. Rita looked up at him, as she always did, a pure wave of admiration flecked with envy. In the roseate fire of the stove, he was admittedly an incredibly handsome if insufferably quizzical man. Rita took his hand in hers, but spoke to me.

"How's Mom and Dad?

"Now there's a question for you."

Sheldon still sat half-turned away from us. I don't think he knew whether to be confused or angry.

"What'd you get for Christmas?" Rita asked me.

"You know we don't open until Christmas day."

"Well I gotta recorder."

"So I heard. You and Shel can play duets now."

"Sheldon won't play any more. He says he's got as good as he's going to get."

"Can't he get any better?"

"I'm good enough already," Sheldon sulked.

"Rita, you play something then."

"You've heard what I know, honey. I might never be as good as Sheldon."

"You're better than all of us, except Sheldon . . ." I began, but then, above us, through the rafters, Mrs. Wheelwright's steps could be heard.

"I better fix Shel something to eat, Rita said immediately.

She took a greasy pan out from under the bed, set it on the stove and then went to the window sill, returning with two brown eggs. She dropped the eggs into the pan, chopping at the yolks with a fork, searing the white in a trice. Then she broke the mass apart with the fork and, scooping up the glutinous flakes with a hamburger bun, handed it in the general direction of Sheldon, who ate it in three not inconsiderable bites.

Bang! went Sheldon's teeth.

"One to provoke you," Rita sang.

Bang!

"One to surround you."

Bang!

"And one to break your heart!"

188

Rita caught me staring at her.

"I cook too much to be a good cook," she said. "What happened to your face anyway?"

"Oh, fell."

Moulton had gone over and flipped on the TV. I did not think I could take another splotch of news 'n' sports, the grim statistics which we have somehow outlived. Besides, I needed to crap, and I wasn't about to unload on that open commode. "Love your own best," as the President says.

Upstairs again, the door hissed to behind me. I went to ask the Wheelwrights if I could use their john. But they were just about to eat, and I watched them from the hall through louvered doors. It was pretty obvious that the original decor of the wreck room had been moved upstairs to the living room. Everything was so bright and polished it was almost scary. The jaunty divan was red and gold, the floor was black and white, reflecting the family bodies as they walked. It was sort of nautical too, a globe and sailing ship on the bookcase, a ship's wheel and captain's chairs, some fishnet and corks over the bar.

The Wheelwrights were watching the same news 'n' sports as we were downstairs, and Mrs. Wheelwright was making her famous fried egg sandwiches. She was kneeling before the fireplace with her condiments in a small red wagon, while Mr. Wheelwright's blue pipe smoke turned green in the light of the TV, its statistics battering like sleet about his wife at work.

She took a small marrow bone and banged it gently with her little fist, disgorging a gelatinous pellet which liquefied quickly in the pan. Then while still holding the pan above the coals with her left hand, the handle of a cup looped about her right thumb, with her four free fingers she broke an egg into the cup. Then she slid the egg into the pan, where it congealed in an instant as she basted it, without the faintest trace of brown. She covered the pan while she cut two thick slices of dark bread, brushing one with mayonnaise, the other with marrow and paprika, then slipped the egg, its yolk now pink, between them. Finally, she added a sliver of horseradish root, a half moon of pimento, and the sandwich flew like an astonished finch into the chair.

I snuck off, for some reason embarrassed, to their bathroom.

When I got back downstairs, they had already taken the pills and were lying around on the floor together, oohing and ahhing, earlier than usual. Sheldon handed the vial to me, but I refused as I always did, and Rita mumbled, "think you're better than us, kid?"

"No, honest, Rita . . ."

"You were always an insufferable arrogant little snot."

"You ought to stop this stuff at least until you have it," I said.

"I'd get even fatter if I did."

"You'll ruin your goddam tastebuds," I said.

I decided to snuff out the news 'n' sports and put on some old videotapes, some history, or what I call "Pre-Me"; it's hard these days to trust a memory that isn't yours. I didn't care about them taking that stuff, but I just can't hack it. It's worse than TV, being conked out like that, and when I am, all I get is advertisements on my eyes, personalized stuff with my name in computer italics.

Everybody else was now unconscious, and I picked out an old tape about how Tarzan and Jane met. It seems that Jane's parents, due to genteel naiveté and general stuffiness, were killed by the cannibals, and Jane, not yet old enough to fight for the empire or plump enough for eating, is abducted. As a result of being fattened up on native gruel, however, her new charms become apparent, and she is in turn spirited away by, or sold to, it was never quite clear, an Arab chieftain, Who'San, who takes her to his palace where the desert and jungle meet. There Jane is tenderly raised by the ladies of the harem, who just naturally take to her. Then one day, while swimming in a jungle pool, she meets Tarzan. (A crocodile attacks her and he breaks its jaw.)

Who'San knows all about Tarzan. In fact, there is strong evidence that the two control the jungle between them, an unspoken pact. Who'San considers him a rival, though Tarzan couldn't care less. That is why Tarzan is so effective. He couldn't care less. He takes what's offered, and fights only when it's necessary. He couldn't very well just look on while Jane got eaten by a crocodile, for example, and, as Tolstoi pointed out, such things happen rarely. He's never surprised by anything because he never anticipates anything. He's just as loose as a goose and never loses.

At any rate, Who'San sends out a battalion of dervishes to get Tarzan, but naturally Tarzan is warned by his many animal friends, and the dervishes are trampled by a premeditated elephant stampede. Gradually Tarzan comes to realize that Who'San is out to get him and becomes curious about this strange white girl who has upset the jungle balance of terror. His fine-feathered lieutenants report back that Who'San is keeping Jane high in a palace minaret. Tarzan looks up "minaret" and sets off, breasts the swollen river, and swings up onto the palace balustrade where he overpowers the fag sentry, flinging him to the piranha fish. Nevertheless, he has miscalculated and swung onto the terrace below Jane—the Terrace of the Treasure Trove. He wanders among the overflowing caskets, fondling coins and jewelry uncomprehendingly. Suddenly he comes across a locket with cameos of Jane's parents in it, and a light ignites between his eyes. At this moment of racial illumination, however, Who'San confronts him and, misunderstanding Tarzan's motives, draws his scimitar. At that point Janes rushes in, and seeing the locket in the savage's hand, a locket she herself has pondered over and fondled in the past, she too misunderstands Tarzan's motives.

Throwing herself at Who'San's feet, she begs him not to kill Jungle Boy because "Jungle Boy can tell me who I am."

Fade-out, wide angle of Jungle Boy's face, which expresses, in its absence of a single crease or tic. "I don't need this"—the victor driving hence the Spirit of Victory.

I stopped the story there and put on a real oldie, a family series probably, entitled *MacArthur Returns*.

It starts out with this old guy wading ashore to some island, his pants rolled up, and an eagle on his cap that looks just like his face. Then he is driven around the island all alone, sitting in the back of a jeep in his gold braid and executive sunglasses. The natives are all laughing hysterically, jumping up and down, throwing flowers at the jeep, trying to run out to kiss him and getting shoved away by big black soldiers who look like Who'San. Then at the end of the route, in front of the bombed-out capital, a little girl is pushed toward him with a box of soil and the seed of a palm tree in her fist. He leans down, the L of his body at right angles but still at attention, and kisses her a big soldier-firm kiss, and she runs away into the crowd crying for joy.

I flicked that off too—for being even more ridiculous than Tarzan. Jesus, what will they try to pass off on us next?

My peers were stirring now; Rita had rolled beside me. "Play a music, play something nice," she slurs, and I put a stack of records on the changer.

"Ohh," she exclaims, " 'Malaguena.' "

"Close," I said, " 'Clair de Lune.' "

"Ooh," she was going on, "this is ludicrous. . . ." Then she opened her eyes and brightened measurably. "Ludicrouse, lood-i-crush, my word for the week." Then she flopped back, and with her feet and fingers tried to tap along with Debussy.

I lay down in front of the coal stove to take a little nap. Above us I could hear the hesitant but all consuming step of Mrs. Wheelwright, a perfectly compensatory double limp, and I was going to go up there again to see if they were *really*

there; but just before I dropped off, the words began whirring across my eyes:

is this the way it is   stop   *is this the way it is*

I dreamed Rita and I were walking in the Popular Forest
again, in the late summer when everything is brittle, ready to
catch on fire at the slightest word, and the sky is a garish
prairie pink all evening. We walk to where the bridle path
ends with cement posts, wander off into the slough, and return unwillingly, shaking with chills as the sky conforms to
night, knowing we have everything to learn and nothing to
lose.

I woke up later to a funny sound. It was starting to darken,
and Rita was sitting on her haunches brushing her hair with
long, deliberate strokes. She was obviously in a racy mood, a
sort of Spanish Provincial mood.

"Don't brusha now, Reet," I mumbled.

"It makes my face feel lighter," she crept out from under
my logic, her gray eyes glowing from the corona of red hair.

"You know," she went on, "I think you're very insecure in
a way."

I didn't know how to answer that, and just then Rita's fiery
hair fell down over my stomach like a tent.

I couldn't see what she was doing but froze when I felt her
undoing my pants. Rita was always clumsy for a girl, but now
she was so gentle I could just feel a thousand little caterpillars
on my thighs and tummy, her hair swaying back and forth
like the linden trees just before a storm, and her tongue part,
then all, of me. I was wet in my eyes too, all the words were
foggy except for the easy low *errr-er-er-er.*

Then some new spurious words appeared, in capitals.

HIS POOKE FLOTCHED

and then the words began to dance to some exciting non-
sense, words I didn't know the meaning of:

> Beneath on earth pompe pelfe prase they pooke
> Fier pat my hart in sick a flocht...

I felt I had been dropped gently into a warm and shallow sea, and the ripples from my splash were going out and out toward the horizon; my life was going out of me, but I was not afraid at all, and then I thought my back would bust as I screamed for joy.

Moulton and Sheldon were up and groggy like soldiers at reveille, and Rita was still on her knees, swaying, grinning, her face like a flower with petals blown off as I zipped up. I had read about this at an airport newsstand once, and therefore knew what to expect, and how it was perfectly natural.

"Boy," she said, "do your eyes ever go nutty."

I glanced at my trembling watch and gave the sign to Moult to go.

"See," Rita went on nasally, "you're just like the rest of us after all."

I was feeling good but pointless. Sheldon was an artist, Moult an intellectual, Rita was pregnant, I was pooke-stupid, and everybody else was upstairs.

Rita escorted us to the landing, where she kissed me on the cheek and whispered in my ear, "Keep it in your knickers, fella."

I almost slipped on the linoleum as Mrs. Wheelwright came out of the living room with her mouth full. My knees negotiated a separate peace. I got the top half of the door open, and Mrs. Wheelwright reminded me, muffledly, "It's a Dutch door," and I got the bottom half open with my boot. I looked up at her; she was eating another cookie and the crumbs stuck to her lips. We stood silently in the doorway for some time while Moulton got his gun. Her tongue was searching for a crumb.

"Why are you staring at me, child?" Mrs. Wheelwright said.

"I had a very nice time, ma'am, thank you," I caught myself. The dog had stopped floundering and squinted up at me.

"Any time," she said.

I concurred, and we headed down the road to the intersection, intent on catching a lift. Mrs. Wheelwright picked up the dog and stood in the rectangle of half-light long after we left, feeding her dying cocker the remains of her dessert.

"There has not been a fatality for *forty-eight days*," the sign says, fashioned in Olde Englishe except for the number which is handily chalked in. Erect at the intersection for the duration, it has been up to over a hundred, down to zero. When I was little and had more time to think about such things, I wondered whose office it is that believes that 0 is more terrifying than 100; surely the higher the order of accidentless days, the more imminent the catastrophe.

We passed the sign, Moult and I, took our time and temperature from the bank, and, spying no traffic, struck out for home and dinner. It was 5:28 and 23°.

Back in the Popular Forest, we floundered along the bridle path, finding our previous tracks nearly filled in again. Moult's pants were wadded in frozen wrinkles; his white bucks had turned black and were turned up at the toes like a jester's. He walked on the edge of the path where the crust had hardened, gazing at his frozen feet, out into the trees, and back to his feet. You could tell from the way he walked that it was very painful.

Out of cold and boredom I began to speculate on my mute brother, whom, if you didn't know him as I do, you might simply write off as a murderous shit. There was something in his forgetfulness, a "cruel indifference" as the old books say, "a menace to society" according to the new ones. Oh well, all our books are wrong. And I cannot really speak for our experience. We have had no experience to speak of. Or rather, the only experience we've had has been bespoken. "All stories are the same, except for the differences," like Dad says, "20 years growing, 20 years living, 20 years stooping, and 20 dying." It's not exactly that nothing's now symbolic, it's just that everything seems to smell the same. We were born and raised, born and raised in what will be remembered as the time when we could have killed everybody and when everybody, therefore, wanted to kill us. Our species had got up to zero. That, at least, is how I understood the story. We knew what we wanted then—but what we wanted we didn't like much. There were those among us who thought that what we wanted was positively bad for us. But then what we wanted, good or bad, got used up. We lost both our smugness and our spleen, our sloppiness and our severity, even our murderous rectitude. And while saved from the hand of those who hated us, we became the unhappiest people on the face of the earth. As Dad, the loss prevention engineer, is fond of repeating, "Back to the beginning, sport fans," or some such similarly desperate throwaway.

Mom says unequivocally that she grew up in the best of times, a time unlike any other, although when you ask her what kind of car she had, she simply says she can't recall the name but it was the finest one made. "Horsefeathers," replies Dad, "it was a time of blight, of waste."

"Waste was nice," she retorts, "for one hundred years we were a miracle! We are not what we were, no sir."

"If the future is too much on your mind," Dad says, gripping the arms of his chair, "it cannot happen. As for the past, my better half, I for one have no desire to return to the Age of Pets! And anyway," he meanders, seemingly losing the point, "there are no more hurricanes than there ever were; only the reports of them have increased." Then he hums a few bars of "In the Mood."

It is not clear whether we were overpriced or undersold. Or that this was a time unlike any other. But nevertheless, at the crossroads, the sign will soon again be set back to zero.

We stood there, Moult and I, the banal wind spooling erotic snow about us. We passed a dead horse upon which someone had taken some professional-looking whacks.

> Oh, a little less money,
> And a little more murder,
> So we're not the Renaissance . . .

We cleared the forest, startled. The Christmas lights had been turned on! The houses, normally dark and disparate, had reconnoitered in an electrical pageant, and now marched upon us full of jolly fury. The sky was molted green at the rooftops, extinguishing the stars. It was as if the sun had fallen into the ocean. Our day of celebration, full of voluntary energy, to each his own, to each . . . his own?

Strands of light lay everywhere. Hung in winking festoons from the trees, strung through the gristle of hedges; entwined about obsolescent power poles, gas capsules, disinterred septic tanks; framing windows, crowning doorways, shrouding chimneys, garlanding mailboxes, stumps, balconies. Some lay in the winter brush like foxfire, others straddled gutters or dangled from frozen conifers, and others simply lay scattered on the snow where they had been thrown like a broken atom chain.

Windowpanes had been carefully flocked, in special predrifted patterns, but unfortunately real frost had filled these in. And through this ice, plastic wreaths revolved, while on beribboned trees, electric candles bubbled colored waters. Enormous aluminum lollipops and stalks of peppermint were anchored in the snowbanks, and plastic Santas, squatting in their own glow, waved convincingly as parkinglot attendants. Here and there a horseless, driverless sleigh, laden with massive hollow packages, embarked across a yard. Golden doves with pipe cleaners in their claws strained on their wires in the wind. The Millers had a Kodachrome enlargement of the family in their window, framed by birds of peace. The children were as happy as the birds and the birds as cute as the children. The Simmonses had chosen Raphael's "Alba Madonna" for their front porch. The Harrisons had a snowman with a nose which blinked in the night like an airliner. The Nelsons' four papier-mâché lambs huddled for warmth in a spotlight. Elves worked at an assembly line in the Johnsons' patio, grinning devilishly to themselves, while the Coopers' bevy of imported tinsel partridges hooted prerecorded hoots from collapsible pear trees. Baseboard silhouettes of Wise Men and camels stole across the playground toward the Memorial; mother holding child untrembling, the swirling snow filling in their eyesockets.

The PA system was playing the old carols over and over:

Six for the six proud walkers
Five for the symbol at your door
And Four for the gospel makers

There was a stare which Dad used to command when I was very small. A good common Sunday stare which he reserved for the cars loaded with oglers who came down to our end of the road on weekends while he was working in his yard. It made them back all the way out to the main road, groaning in reverse. I wished he had kept his skill fresh or one of us had inherited it.

For the first time, I struck out on my own, leaving the road, and Moulton followed. But he was hurting for sure, and at the first sign of a proper log, I signaled for a rest.

We sat there for a while looking at the snow and the sky. I hadn't realized it, but we had come all the way back through the Popular Forest and were in the unincorporated woods behind the Golf Club, the most direct if difficult route home.

We cleared away some snow and squatted down upon the

frozen sod, a finely quilted grass for future divots. Sand for the traps was heaped among the trees, and above us stretched the powder-blue water tower of Precious Blood Retreat. The order had bought the land when it was still wild onion. Their tower was the highest thing outside the city. When we first moved in, I lay in bed at night and listened to the water running out of the tower and into all the houses. They grew horseradish for years until the ground turned blue. Then they sold the west forty to the state for an airport, they sold the east forty to developers for a golf club, they sold the south forty to the city for a garbage dump, they sold the north forty to Irma Nadler's husband, the doctor, and he sold it to us and 139 others.

Before they sold the south forty, they took out all the rock and sold it to the airport for concrete. Before they sold the west forty, they took off all the sod and sold it to the Golf Club for grass. When they put the garbage where the rock and sod had been, the gulls from the lake moved inland with us. The gulls are clean and quiet birds, but they heckled the clipped-wing swans down at the club swan pond, and one gull flew into the mouth of an executive jet and blew it up. The last thing the Precious Blood did was to import some amphibious Chinese carp, which were reported to thrive on gull eggs and algae but in our Occident seemed to prefer trout and quail. They lummoxed from pond to pond at night now, leaving trails of mucus on the lawns.

The water tower was a real landmark. At Christmastime they put messages on it in lights. This year it said:

CHRIST WANTS MORE

There was some comment about that. It attracted attention because it stretched around the entire tank, and to get the whole message it was necessary to drive an ever-widening circle through the countryside. Otherwise, from a single perspective, you could only get a few letters. From our house, for instance, all you could see was ANTS. Airliners used it for a pylon, and when a pervert took his annual child in the woods, official observers were seen at the tower railing, flashing signals through the night to search parties in the Popular Forest. They'd go right up there as soon as a little girl was late for dinner. Rewards were offered, the state police and National Guard were summoned, the hounds went out, the creek was dragged, and the air was full of helicopters, but it never was any use. The dogs always found the bodies the same way, half buried, decomposed, their underclothes stuffed in their mouths. The newspapers ran a picture of the cop giving a little shoe to a big dog to smell. Sometimes, the body was dismembered, and the police were around for weeks. Tell me, why did they have to find *all* of it, once they knew?

For weeks there is no news but the news of that kid's life— where she went to school, what her father does, tributes from her playmates, the variety of her performance, her fantastic potential, the shame of it all. And after about a week they start coming into the police stations. Hundreds of men. From all over. And *how* they do confess! They describe in the most corroborative detail how they enticed the child, the props of seduction, how and when they disposed of her. The cops trace the men's stories back and find that none of them could have possibly done it. These men had put to memory all that information, all that news, and committed themselves to the child. The actual criminal never confesses. He doesn't need to. He *did* it. They find him with his wife and kids having Sunday dinner and drag him down the stairs. It can make a man furious, crazy, to have nothing, nothing to confess. I see now how Moulton . . . oh well, why speculate? The facts we have are theoretical enough.

At any rate, the Cloister itself was yellow stucco with a red tile roof and a bell-less campanile. We went there several times a year to vote. Our precinct polls were in the foyer of the chapel, the only public place around. My parents always

took me when they voted, a nice touch, though we never discussed the specifics of the referendum. While they were doing
their duty, I stayed in the foyer, and—it always surprised me—
next to the religious pamphlet rack towered a big stuffed
polar bear rearing up on his hind legs. You put a penny on
his grooved tongue, shoved it back through the scissor teeth,
and for a good minute his head swiveled, his eyes rolled, and
from deep inside came a siren roar: *err-err-Err-Err!*

The money was for orphans.

I mention this because something happened while we were
sitting there, all tired out with nothing to do, that nearly
made the day. Moulton and I were in pretty bad shape; we
didn't have too much more to say to each other. Our supply
lines were overextended. So we were just sitting there, heads
between our tails, and I had begun to hear the water dripping
out of the tower again after so many years, at my small sane
age, when three men came barging out of the forest. They
were running crazily, zigzagging, and they all carried huge
sticks with which they beat the ground.

It is one of the facts of the New Living that we don't question what a man is doing as long as we understand what he's
wearing. So when I saw they were attired in surplus air force
parkas, not hooded robes; sweat pants, not pantaloons; football cleats, not *clochepieds;* and their weapons were merely
fiberglas pole-vault poles, I did not prepare to shoot these
wiseguys immediately.

What they were doing was hunting. Their plan, apparently,
was to run the length of the field in *troika,* flushing rabbits
and then busting them with their poles. And sure enough, on
their third sally, one rabbit zigged when he should have
zagged and got clouted by the center hunter. They gathered
around to finish the job, and by that time we were up to
them.

"By God, you got him!" I yelled. "That was terrific!"

The three of them grinned and leaned on their poles. They were stocky, flushed types, and the fur of their hoods was drawn in perfect circles about their faces.

"First one today, too," the center hunter spoke for the others. "Tough going."

"I'll bet. What a fine idea!"

They didn't say anything but just kept grinning. They were probably wondering what we were doing out there, so close to curfew. I was getting a little worried.

"You fellas with Precious Blood?" I broke in.

"For a time," the center one spoke again. "Until the spring, when we take orders."

"Uh, monks?"

"Brothers," they grinned.

"Where to from here?"

They shrugged collectively, shifting their weight on the poles. I wanted to ask them "Orders for what?" but I was afraid Moult might start an argument if it was one of those with vows of silence or celibacy or something; for there was a light in Moulton's eye as he looked down at that fresh-pounded rabbit on the snow—a light not for the killing or even the hunting, but for the lengths they had gone to before they did kill.

"Lemme see one of those poles, will you, pal?"

The center hunter handed me his and I presented it to Moulton. He choked up on it, backed away, and took a few swings. Then he took several vicious swings, grunting and letting the momentum throw him off balance. Then he arched it back over his shoulder and flung it like a javelin. It sailed and bore quivering into a thicket. He plunged in after it, and emerged in a minute with snow clinging to his hair, the pole over his shoulders like a yoke. His face was reddened from either spleen or wind.

The three were examining their cleats.

"You guys must have a pretty good athletic setup," I said. "You ever play anybody in anything?"

They shook their heads.

"Well, for not playing anybody they sure give you a lot of equipment."

Moult bent the pole in the snow, letting it snap back. I was afraid he might do something funny, and I wanted to get out of there.

"Just rabbits?" I pondered. "Why not owls and muskrats too? And there's those damn Chink carp all over the place."

"The rabbits get into the garbage in the winter," the center one replied officiously, "and the vegetables in the spring."

"We can't shoot them," another spoke for the first time. "It's against our laws."

"We can't even eat them," the third said morosely.

I knew Moult was going to ask why they couldn't eat them and it could have been embarrassing, so I interrupted.

"You fellas got a nice chapel up there," I said. "We go there a lot to vote." They smiled mysteriously.

I was trying to figure out how to ask them the story behind the polar bear without getting involved, when I saw Moult screwing the pole into the snow and getting a very troubled expression on his face.

"Well, better be going," I said. "Nice to meet you guys."

We shook hands all around, but just as I thought we were free, Moult did it.

"May I have the rabbit?"

They looked at each other, shuffled their feet, folded and unfolded their arms. The center one made sure we were not being watched, then smiled benignly. "Why not?" And we shook hands again before they ran off, brandishing their poles silently, running in cadence.

When they were out of sight, I handed the bunny over to Moult and he fastened the gift to his belt by the ears. You could tell it perked him up.

203

The rabbit swung in step with Moulton like a scalp. The brush was frozen, and shattered like a glass under foot. At the edge of the field, we climbed the cyclone fence and cut through Mrs. Parker's bird sanctuary to save time. The Parker place had once been the largest and most magnificent around. Mr. Parker had been Dr. Nadler's first customer, as Dr. Nadler had first entreated upon the Church, though they had eschewed one another since. In Parker's case, a successful engineering career had been cut short by his involvement in the Conspiracy. Part of Parker's frontal cortex had been shot away in a raid, and he was allowed to retire under house arrest; he devoted his remaining years to photographing the wild life within his acreage. For this he had been awarded the National Merit medal posthumously.

Since Parker's death, or more precisely since the carp invasion, little birdlife has been seen except for a few grackles and starlings, but the crescent paths which were his testament are still kept up by his sad wife, Stella, whom nobody resents any more for her money. The woods were still webbed with the rusty wires he used to trip his secret cameras, and the Parker foyer was fully decorated with testimony to his skill. Hundreds of startled, extinct animals gazed down from his walls like beautiful movie stars trapped in some profane indulgence—raccoons with fish, deer stripping bark, birds atop rodents, snakes sucking eggs, rabbits with each other.

Suddenly Mrs. Stella Parker appeared ahead of us, turning one of her husband's serpentine bends, leading her black Labrador, Beodyboy.

"Get that rabbit out of sight," I hissed to Moult, "she'll think we've been poaching."

Moult disposed of the corpse in his coat. And we met a moment later, Mrs. Parker brimming with that old-fashioned gentleness which has no object, pleased that we were taking advantage of her privacy. I said all the nice things and introduced Moulton, who refused to shake hands like a stiff foreigner, as he had the rabbit secreted in his armpit. We would have gotten out of it cleanly, in fact, if it hadn't been for Beodyboy. He sauntered up, nosed Moult, and dropped into a solemn point. I don't think Mrs. Parker had ever seen Beodyboy on point before; nothing had been dead and bleeding that close to her. It embarrassed all of us, of course. Particularly when Beodyboy jammed his nose into Moulton's groin. Mrs. Parker apologized and tugged on Beodyboy's collar, but Beodyboy just stood his ground and growled. Moult grinned terribly, and I patted Beodyboy's head as fast as I could. What we should have done, I suppose, was to let Mrs. Parker see what was up, explain things, throw the bunny to Beodyboy, and get home for dinner. But this was no time to start that. It would be easier, in a way, just to stand there, being pointed, until Mrs. Parker left or collapsed from the cold, and we could beat the pee out of Beodyboy and make it for home. For when we move, we leave nothing behind. No scraps, no ribbons in the trees, no graves, no dung. We leave things clean—if not precisely as we found them, still clean— bequeathing a footprint so wide, so equally pressured, that our successors will never comprehend what monster had passed their way.

But as it turned out, we didn't have to. Because Mrs. Parker just picked up a branch and started to whale Beodyboy about the shoulders. Exactly as we would have done, except for different reasons. Beodyboy didn't differentiate and took off for home. It was nice of Mrs. Parker to do that because she loved Beodyboy; he had been Mr. Parker's favorite, after all. It was hard to believe they had been part of the Conspiracy.

We commended her as best we knew how, and then she excused herself, returning around the bend to the enormous house which on this one day a year was permitted to light up the apple sky like an ocean liner. Her plotting was now confused, I suspect, and we were free again, if that's the word.

There are no hills near the lake, so they built one. They dug a hole for the necessary dirt, called what was left a reservoir, and that was all right. But inadvertently they inverted that mountain. That is, they piled first what they dug first so the mountain is built on tiny clods of topsoil while the peak is enormous rectangles of clay and striped granite. So our mountain tends to collapse into itself each year, and is maintained only by the constant ministrations of a corps of steam shovels, dump trucks, and army conscripts. In any case, our hill rose tentatively out of the fields before us, settling like a fallen meteor in its rim of shale. It was on the way and we climbed it for the view and to rest.

In the dark, at the top, things were indistinct. Across the fields, I could make out our house, set in the prairie turf like an ax blade. The forest was darker than the sky; the sky had seeped through the horizon and ran like lymph throughout the electric patches of our Christmas. The water tower was spotlit, its fine message warped as always by parallax. From the hill tonight it read WAN. The monastery's turrets glowed red; the lake, still white and ribbed with frozen currents, angled away like a gull's wing. We squatted down and rested.

It was quite still. The air base had shut down for the holiday; the blunt-nosed orange planes, aerodynamics bulged with radar, were down. The submarines were in their pens. The commuters were home. I was very cold and tired.

In the dark, of the stillness, at the top, I heard water backing up in the tower, the silence too of more solid fuel cached in the Popular Forest, frost-splitting brick paths, drone of precision thermostats, lubric drip of idle engines—waiting only for the coordinates to intersect, ignite . . . in order to retaliate.

Yes, we'll be ready! We'll all be multilingual, able to exist on roots and berries, karate wise, equipped with foreign currency, microfilm, and one dark syringe. And pretty soon we'll have *our* orders, our mission, our goal, and then our team will be toppling or buttressing all governments, perhaps even our own, pretenders denouncing usurpers; probing efficiently, waging the war, carrying on the good fight, scorching the old earth, meeting rising expectations, sharing the wealth, keeping the cord sanitary, massively deterring piecemeal agression, retaliating secretively, selectively, mobilizing means, keeping the peace, maximizing our potential, utilizing our concern, isolate, selfless, stoic, pure white killers. And at Christmastime, we'll come home on furloughs, we'll lay down our foreign currency, our decoder, our secret compartment ring, our warning whistle, our antidote pellet belt, our dark syringe on the hall table; amiable spouse will bring in the soup, and after dinner, if we are very very good, she will turn the crank slowly, and from left to right a landscape will pass in front of the picture window, and she will keep turning until, God, yes, there's that same little tree again with the idiot child feeding squirrels underneath, around for the second time; and we will have corroborated ourselves. . . . We shall live in a true age of art, where our fugitive entertainment will be the sole reality, and within which we shall all become eminently capturable, all. We will have ventilated our passions, exercised our rights, capitalized on our investments, articulated our demands, cut our losses, geared up for the long haul, and nothing shall touch us for a thousand years, nothing.

As the sun slithered from our western flank, I could make out, for the first time in I don't know how long, the silhouette of Mound City on the horizon. The capital of our predecessors, if not precisely our antecedents, the greatest growth industry of the last century, model for this our own portable hill where it was once possible to dig for artifacts at minimum wage. But it was *their* pottery, *their* conch anklets, this cache in a corn field; *their* gourds and weirs, *their* nuts and husks and ducks and mollusks, *their* beads and butchered maidens, found frequently as a foursome, arm in skeletal arm, heads and hands cut off. Their *heads*'d be the last thing *I'd* cut off

—Eh, Heh—those two wonderful words which have alone retained their purity.

Despite the dusk, I could make out the largest and most
symmetrical mound, the lunar observatory, an equinox cen-
tered between two ridges which marked the winter and summer solstices, on the perimeter of the restored stockade. These
great plinths, our first computer, their augury holes filled
with the scraps of that idyllic life, their Stone Age soups; ten-
ton rocks brought a thousand miles downstream, levered in
place by volunteer armies to make a temple, a millennium
before the Britons, two thousand years before the Mayans,
Babylonians, Egyptians . . . their demise as inexplicable as
their origins.

Abandoned well before our blunderwunderplunder, what
had threatened this magnificent community? Another people
infringed upon by their city-state? Oppressed lower classes, a
slave caste? There are, of course, the academic possibilities:

        A. Climactic change
        B. Disease
        C. War
        D. Depletion of natural resources

You would think we could invent a better story than that!
Perhaps, as Dad says, we're back to where we started. Or perhaps it's only the strongest and most whole who refuse to start
over. I recall from an old textbook:

> . . . a society can be defined as Barbarian
> when its literacy and technology become
> opposed forces. . . .

And then I had a vision, an afterimage on my retinas, a ghostly
voice; *"Man,"* it read, *"if man you be in heart, forbear . . .
until you discover what the Surplus is, and where it is . . .*

    "My God!" yelled Moult, "There's someone down there!"

It was his voice more than his discovery which startled me. I peered down into the great white field below us. There was someone there all right, but if it was someone, it looked dead. It was lying right in the center of the field with arms and legs outstretched, an illiterate's signature on the snow; the voter's mark.

We ran down the hill as fast as we could and into the field. At first I thought the perverts were rushing the season, but they would never have left things this way. Maybe cancer. Or thundering apoplexy? We crashed down through the ice as we ran. Moult was getting short of wind, and tears were freezing to his face. Once he tripped and cut his ankle on the edge of his own deep track. He clutched at his wound, but I got him by the back of the neck and hauled him to his feet. Then we were going again, and he soon outdistanced me. We strutted on, knee deep by now, cutting our socks to pieces. A great volume of blood pressed against my eyes—the adrenalin hadn't started yet. I wasn't excited, I was going on pure intent. I had been feeling mean; now maybe we could make a rescue.

It was a kid, all right. About ten, in a purple snowsuit. Moult arrived first but didn't know what to do. I drew up, dropped to my knees to see if he was breathing. Moult fell on the other side of him and began to retch. But the kid was fine. His eyes were wide open, and he was breathing nimbus clouds of frost. Nothing was wrong with him at all, except his nose was running. He looked just like I used to, and Rita's burden would too.

"What ya want, bub?" he said, and not too pleasantly.

"What happened, you fall down?"

"Are you kidding?"

"Does your family know you're out?"

He rolled his eyes indifferently.

"Lost?"

"Nah," he pouted.

I started to grab him under the arms to pick him up—

maybe he'd had a fight and was sulking—but as soon as I touched him he winced and bellowed.

"No! Don't touch me!"

"What? You break something?"

"No, stupe. Can't you see? You'll ruin it! The angel!" I didn't know what he meant and took a deep breath.

"Just get away, will ya? I'll show ya, don't worry."

I backed away a few feet to watch. Moult seemed better, and was eyeing the kid from a safe distance like he was booby-trapped. Very solemnly and deliberately the kid sat up, holding his arms out to the side like one of the old ballet dancers. Then in one motion he sprang to his feet and turned on us proudly. "There!" he said, pointing.

He was right; in the snow was the impression of an angel in full flight.

"A little didactic," Moult muttered to me, "but still an angel." Then he rolled over closer, intrigued. "Hey," he said, "How'd you do that?"

"Easy," the kid said, wiping his nose. "Just lie on your back without moving and sweep your arms up and down like you were flying."

Moult put the rabbit beside him and lay down. But the kid yelled and stamped his feet.

"No. Naah! You gotta do it easy!"

He took Moult's head in his hands and eased him back. He was still too eager, however, and again broke the mold.

"I told ya, buddy. You gotta do it *easy*."

"Try it over here," I said. "There's a good smooth spot."

Moult came over, careful not to scuff the fresh snow, and began again gingerly.

"You can do it on your stomach if you want," he kid continued, "but then you'll get snow up your nose holes."

Moult was flat and I lay down next to him, carefully taking note of our wing space. The kid looked down at us.

"OK," he said, "now . . . fly!"

I waved my arms slowly in a half circle like a signalman. Moulton did the same. At one point our respective arcs intersected and our knuckles brushed.

"Slow, *hey*," warned the kid. "Easy does it."

We were hovering. I took short compact breaths, careful not to arch my back and ruin the outline.

"OK," the kid said again. "That's good. OK! OK!" Moult and I looked to him.

"OK, now's the harder part. Gotta get up. But no hands, see? Or you'll bust it sure."

Then he held my feet. I sat up slowly. My groin burned from the running. But after some effort I was up. And Moult was too. With the kid's help. We rolled forward on our haunches, up and away from the impressions.

"Not bad at all," the kid said, "pretty good."

They were, too. One medium gruff angel and a large indifferent one on either side of the kid's smaller perfect one. Ours seems to career more, like helicopters. But they were good, considering.

"Say," Moult said. "Say now, that's all right."

The kid wiped his nose. "OK."

"Moult," I whispered, "Moulton, we *got* to *go*." He nodded, for the first time in a long time actually awed.

"And you," I said to the kid, "you better get home. Your mother's probably going crazy wondering where you are."

The idea seemed to strike him as a fact, but he lay down again.

"Sometimes," he said, "I make 'em with just one wing. Then they look sadder, or like somebody carrying a fan or a horn or a big ax."

"Yes, that is what they would look like," said Moult, caching our bunny carcass within his parka again.

"We got to get going," I said. "So long, kid."

"Yeah, bub," he said. "I'd wave to ya, but I'd break it."

We crossed the field at a trot. We didn't look back or talk.

We had thought him dead from a distance, but all he was doing was starting his own business.

The snow was heavier now, spooling webs in the crotches of trees, ringing the blackened, burned-out stumps. At the Popular Forest boundary, Cowboy Bear sprang up, thanking us for once again being considerate. Since the morning, somebody had drawn a large tumor on the lap of his red jeans. At the highway, two plainclothesmen in a pastel ranch-wagon were looking bored, and we gave them a wide berth.

Then, as we crossed the last of the brush, the lawns opened up, the Christmas lights regilded the road, and over the PA warning system they were still playing the old incomprehensible carols.

> *Two, two, the lily white boys*
> *Dressed all in green O . . .*
>
> *One is one and all alone*
> *And evermore shall be so.*

Ah, dinner, my eyes read, dinnertime.

It was well past curfew, so I stepped up the pace, and quickly outdistanced Moult. Through the kitchen window I could see Mom chopping something up. She looked pissed.

Maybe she had been arguing. But in the blue capsule of light she looked like a veteran navigator figuring a mission that was by now second nature, though still potentially death dealing. The nature of second nature, denatured.

I went in by the back door and took off my boots in the hall.

"So," Mom said without looking up," the hunter is finally home."

"And," I said in my most officious voice, "we gotta rabbit!" As I held it up for her, she put up her hands and she screamed.

"Wherever did you get that?" she moaned.

"Monks."

"What?"

"The guys at Precious Blood."

"Jesus Christ! Fred!"

"What's going on up there?" my father yelled up from the basement.

"Your *son* just brought a dead *rabbit* into the *house* . . ."

"Well, get it outside. . . ." A thoughtful pause from the cellar . . . "and be sure the garbage lid's on tight. We don't want anybody getting tularemia."

"It was a free gift," I pleaded.

"Well, you can just take it right back to whoever gave it to you." She was hacking at the turnips and potatoes as if they were snakes.

"Let's eat it, Ma!"

"Oh? And who's going to clean it? And who's going to cook it? And who's going to degrease the pot?"

"Moulton's favorite is hassenpfeffer."

"Oh no, sonny boy. Not on Christmas Eve. We're not going through that Moulton routine again."

"But mom . . ."

"You've got one nice sister, John, and that should be enough for you."

I forced a grin.

"Your Dad and I are tired of Christmas," she said, more to herself than me. "We don't expect you to understand."

I saw it wasn't any use, so I got my boots back on and went out to the garage. Across my eyes was running *and wash up good before we eat.* She didn't even have to say it. I dropped our rabbit into the garbage and slammed the lid down as hard as I could.

A strong wind had come up from the plains. We would have to dig all morning to free ourselves. Dad had already been shoveling a path. He was never much good at receiving free gifts. Dad's problem is that, to keep from anger, he is fey.

213

And I'm getting pretty fey myself. The best defense is a good feyness.

No doubt I will be accused of precocious cynicism, willful and quite unbelievable for a boy my age, of carrying on when I should have been respectful, played it straight, grimfaced and doomed. Thinks too much, ya say, acts funny but no fun, ya say, self-centered fibber, bad attitude, you little smartass, no kid of mine would get away with that, ya say—well, let us celebrate the in-de-term-in-ate. I'll stand on that. With neither pride nor hope or class, perhaps, but what we call *will*— not because there's any such thing—but because that's the final word we use with *others,* when we know their griefs to be inconsolable, their tasks, insurmountable. I can see it in *your* eyes . . .

At least I won't spend the rest of *my* life yelling, "Give it back, give it back!" I grew up wanting to say something that would break your heart. Now I'll settle for a little speech that will break out of character. It's getting tougher all the time to match the names to the faces. . . . Hell, that's what Moult was all about. Unlikely, unlikable, but neither uninteresting nor unusable.

I actually wasn't all that depressed. It's just very still, that's all. Static. All encompassing static. We live at the end of the road, and Dad has promised to build us a turnabout so you won't have to back out any more—a teardrop, he calls it. Which will be handy when he gets round to fixing the car. It's still, it's dark, but the dark, frankly, has never bothered me. We make too much of the dark; we suffer only from our lack of shadow there, and if we can make up the mauve wolves and purple bears who eat us in our dreams, then we can also cast our mind's thick shadow on the blackness, and remember when we sit up screaming that *we're* the only animals who watch our visions, whirring versions of ourselves, being devoured. Those animals who eat us in our sleep are there to wake us, our best pets.

The stillness, however, is not as easily dispensed with.

My jaw was hurting something terrible, my ankles were raw, but I got out the flashlight and followed my tracks back toward the field. At the end of the drive I had to duck down into a culvert as the Beautification Police went by; their violet searchlights were quickly extinguished by the storm.

In the field I found the angels easily and recounted the three of them. It was snowing harder. In another hour they would be obliterated. My own best witness, of course, had left the scene. And Moulton was playing guessing games again crouched and hiding from me somewhere. I didn't call for him. He wouldn't be back. What the hell. If Mom and Dad can't even go along with the Moulton bit, they're in pretty bad shape. Whose story would they believe?

For him I won't apologize.

You remember from the Good Book there's really only two ways that we come to learn things, I mean when no prophets are handy and the air isn't exactly ringing with ghostly voices. One way is through "a dream," and the other is a "visit from an angel." Sometimes the angel visits *in* the dream, but more often than not you have either a dream *or* a visit from an angel. That is why there has been so much argument about religion. Remember, for example, what happened when Herod sent the Wise Men out and they tried to give *their* presents away? They didn't know if they were witnessing a birth or a death. *And being warned in a dream not to return to Herod, they departed to their country by another way.* That is very different, for example, than Gabriel appearing before your mother, say, or the various voices from above or below, sometimes even from within—voices from rocks, winds, bushes, *et al.* Now the difference, see, is that if the message comes to you in a dream, you're asleep, right? So you can't do much about it. And when you're awake, and a big invisible voice suddenly comes out of the third balcony, you can't do much about that either. It's only when you're both awake *and* the angel comes that you can ask a meaningful question like "How shall I know this?" That was a long time ago, and now we have neither angel nor hidden voice, dream nor temple; only words and will—and a few rocks and bushes, of course. This is how we live now. No difference between sleep, dream, and waking, no difference between bodiless voices, voiceless bodies, their various homes.

I know that Rita would put me down for trusting my eyes and not my feelings. Believe me, if you can, I would believe in my puerility and perishability if I could; but Rita, if I don't know what's happened to us, how am I supposed to *feel* about it? We have lost our Second Nature, that's for sure, and the lesson seems clear enough: No more Surplus!

For the moment, I felt a trifle trite, immobile. If I hadn't known better, I might have thought I was suddenly much afraid of dying. I glanced up at the blazing red towers of Precious Blood. No doubt the monks would take me in, train me for some worthy mission. But I will be no ordinary orphan. If I die, I will die like an insect, balanced, upright in amber, with no excuses and perhaps even no resentments, a "prophet" being merely a man who knows he will die without having cured the people he loves.

But I would not die yet; because, simply, it was time for dinner. It's only that sort of thing which cannot be put off indefinitely. And I'd need a better explanation for Mom and Dad this time—perhaps one they will regret?

I knew then that I could no longer rely on the tape or my play brother to see me through; it wasn't necessary to forget the words of others, only to stop repeating them merely. I didn't know how exactly this would work out, but I resolved to put both out of mind. Somehow I would have to learn to get along somewhere between fantasy and the facts, respectful and suspicious.

This was the second new thing to happen to me today. I

couldn't tell you if this was a good or a bad time. If you need that sort of thing, look to the roof of your local bank.

Back at the house, I tightened up the garbage lids before going in. Then I screwed up my face, dropped my voice, said my name over and over until it was just a sound, held my balls in both hands, and opened my eyes as wide as I could.

The tape was gone!
I *felt*, Rita, like one of those pioneer trappers in the old videotapes—in a cave overnight, say—when my new and more tractable Indian guide turns to me and screams the forest is *too* quiet! We are sitting before our fire. We have carried too many carcasses with us for too many days. We have eaten all there is. . . .

All the books left to us were about going *into* the forest—you know, those jaunty forays by the young-in-heart, passaging their rites, having, in spite of their deadly earnestness, some surprising adventures, which somehow added up to more than that disguised and venal quest for the treasure of themselves. All well and good. But now we know that in the middle of the forest, in the heart of the garden, on the bottom of the ocean, at the very center of the planet, there is only the intriguing wreckage of a machine that no longer works.

My guide is humming softly—wordless rhythms, bands of light. We discuss coming *out* of the forest one day soon, hides tanned and contoured about our shoulders wearing necklaces of teeth and claws over our hearts which will inspire marvelous rumors which will become barefaced outrageous stories which will make some sense of our most recent and most incredible survival

DEMCO